Such a Girl

SUCH A GIRL

a Novel

KAREN SIPLIN

ATRIA BOOKS

New York London Toronto Sydney

ATRIA BOOKS
1230 Avenue of the Americas
New York, NY 10020

ISBN: 0-7434-7554-2

First Atria Books hardcover edition March 2004

ATRIA BOOKS is a trademark of Simon & Schuster, Inc.

Manufactured in the United States of America

for my family

for Harris

follow me, the wise man said
but he walked behind

L E O N A R D   C O H E N

encourage her to establish better

relationships with people

He's standing across the street, waiting for the light to change, but I know it's him even before he starts walking in my direction. I think: *I'm not ready for this.* Because my least favorite thing in the morning, besides waking up, is meeting people I know unexpectedly.

And it's been nine years.

There are certain meetings in a person's life that should be one hundred percent significant. They should define a moment, answer a burning question, or resolve something. Right now is a good example. I should have something to say to this man, something fairly significant. After all, we were once inseparable and *in love.*

But I don't. Have anything to say, that is.

I just have this memory of him. We're standing in front of the boathouse in Northhampton. His head is shaved. He's wearing a beaded necklace and a ton of friendship bracelets on both wrists. His skateboard is tucked under his arm, and his eyes—light brown, big, intent—are watching my every move.

Jack.

Just last week someone was talking about him. It seems every week someone's mentioning his name. Because Jack owns Sullivan Brewery in New England; Jack just bought a five-bedroom house on four acres of land.

I decide I'd rather not run into him.

I lower my head and take a drag from my cigarette, confident he'll pass by without noticing me. But instead of walking past me, he walks toward the hotel's entrance, which is adjacent to the employee entrance, where I'm standing. He stops, comes back, says my name. I look up and try to do my best impression of being shocked to see someone.

"Wow." I flick my cigarette past him and smile. "Sullivan."

I call him by his last name, the same way most of my ex-boyfriends call me "Stark" oh-so-casually when we run into each other somewhere. It's a defense mechanism. It always makes me feel bad, like I'm not even worthy of a first name. I don't know why I do it to Jack. I don't want him to feel that way.

"How long has it been, Ken?" he asks.

He calls me "Ken," short for Kendall, the way he used to. He makes it seem like nothing's changed.

"Years, I guess."

"Nine, I think," he says softly.

We stare at each other awkwardly. He takes in my unkempt hair, ill-fitting cargo pants and white-socked feet stuffed into old Birkenstocks. Graciously, he remains expressionless and looks directly in my eyes.

"You look great," he says. He was always good at lying.

"Same to you."

I'm not lying. He's actually more handsome than I thought he would turn out to be. His glasses are small, round and rimless; he used to wear contacts. His hair has grown. His body, which has always been long, agile and thin like the body of a swimmer, is hidden underneath clothes straight out of an L.L. Bean catalog. He looks rugged and stronger and changed.

"I'm surprised to see you." His tone is still soft, neither friendly nor mean.

"Been a while." I nod, keeping my tone light. "You live in Maine, right?"

"Maine."

"Nice," I say. "And you still brew beer."

"Yeah." He tilts his head to the side. He wants to tell me everything I already know, but I guess he doesn't want to brag because all he says is, "I still brew beer."

"And you're in New York."

He nods, still staring at me. I try to read the expression on his face. And then there's the slight shake of his head that I remember—like he's trying to banish some thought from his brain—and the expression is gone. He points to the hotel. "I'm staying here."

"Oh?" My voice almost gets caught in my throat. "*This* hotel?"

"Yeah." He avoids my eyes.

"Business?"

"Yeah," he says. "You live around here?"

"No." There's a silence. I try to catch his eye again, but he's doing a good job of diverting his gaze. "I live in Brooklyn. With Gary."

"Right." As though he's just remembering. "I think I heard that."

"I work here," I say. "At the hotel."

"Oh." Another silence. This one is longer. He glances at me but quickly looks away again. "That's a coincidence."

"Sure is," I say. I replay the last fifty conversations I had with Gary and Nick this week—we were all in college together—but a mention of Jack actually coming to New York today doesn't come to mind. "Have you talked to Gary and Nick? Do they know you're in town?"

"No," Jack says distantly. "I checked in late last night."

"Nick mentioned he ran into you last August," I say casually, as though Nick hasn't mentioned it a hundred times. As though Nick doesn't talk about how excellent Jack's life is every time they exchange an e-mail. "He said you might be in New York, but he wasn't sure when. I think he had the impression it would be sooner."

"Family emergency," Jack says. "I'll call him."

"I'm sure he'll be happy to hear from you. He said he's been e-mailing you a lot."

Jack smiles, then he looks at the hotel entrance as though he's ready to dart away.

"Well," I say, giving him an out.

He swallows hard. "It's good to see you." I hear the involuntary emotion in this simple statement. "I mean that."

I hug him suddenly, and I feel his body stiffen. When I let go he steps back.

"You smell like smoke," he says disdainfully, and then he adds, "I quit."

"Congrats" is all I can think of to say. And for a second, I'm distracted by the way he's looking at me. Like he's trying to remember what he ever saw in this girl standing before him.

I try to imagine what he sees.

When he knew me, my hair was always neat and polished in a pageboy haircut. Now it's messy, the front bits standing up in the air. My eyes have always been too close together though, and my eyebrows have always been too thick. But maybe he notices that I still lift weights and run when the mood hits me.

Strange, I think, that I care.

"Maybe I'll see you around," he says casually, moving away.

"Maybe," I say.

"Dinner?" The casual front disappears, and he moves closer. "In a couple of days?"

I don't know about dinner. There's no way in hell I want to spend several hours with my ex, rehashing the past and how poorly I treated him. I tell him life is hectic, especially this week. He doesn't believe me—weird how I can tell that he doesn't—but it's been too long between disagreements to suddenly have another one.

He watches me as I escape inside the employee entrance. I glance back, and I realize he looks disappointed.

It's a look I remember.

The last time I saw him—nine years ago—I was twenty-two, a senior at the University of Massachusetts at Amherst. We'd been dating for over two years. And as I take the elevator down to C2, I think how unexpected it is to have this current image of him—this Adult Jack Image—in my brain.

Not that the odds of seeing Jack on a Manhattan sidewalk have ever been slim. Since Nick ran into him last year and they exchanged numbers and e-mails, Jack's been threatening to visit. And the hotel is a very popular New York destination.

It's just that I hadn't planned to see him today. Or any other day ever again.

And New York is a big fucking city.

That's not to say I've never run into some ex-boyfriend or ex-friend in front of the hotel's employee entrance. Usually, though, the people I run into aren't guests. They're fans waiting outside the hotel for a glimpse of an actor or singer who is a guest. Clutching a movie poster tightly, waiting hopefully for the appearance of Denzel Washington or Brad Pitt. I'm never sure if they're more embarrassed when they see me, or if I'm more embarrassed for them.

It's times like this when I wonder if people are right when they say the world is a big place.

The operator next to me offers to buy coffee. Her name is Maria, and we never speak to each other, not even to say hello. But our supervisor, Kirk, hasn't come in yet, and the morning operators are desperate to go outside. Even if that means buying coffee for coworkers they don't like.

"Coffee makes me tense," I tell her.

Maria stares at me dully.

"Don't get me wrong," I continue, "I can't live without it. But it definitely robs me of . . . something. I only drink one cup a day."

Maria raises an eyebrow. "So that means no."

I nod and turn back to my switchboard. "Thanks, anyway," I say.

Maria stands up and does that thing with her eyebrow again. This time it's meant to mean *no problem,* I guess.

I always feel like I indulge myself too much when I talk to people in the office. An ounce of kindness from any of them and I'm spilling my guts. It's pathetic.

I put my headset on and call my apartment. The phone rings three times, which means Gary, my roommate and best friend, isn't home, and we have no messages. So, I call Gary at work, but the line's engaged.

I have an urge to call Amy and tell her about Jack. Amy was also in college with us. Another one of my closest friends. But she's on yet another sojourn to Los Angeles, looking for work in Hollywood. She'd probably just say something unkind and disappointing about him anyway—she and Jack didn't get along—so it's best that she isn't in town. Instead, I type Jack's name into my computer.

He has a room on the seventeenth floor.

Nice room.

High floor.

We're not meant to check a guest's history. Only Guest History is allowed to do that. But we all do it anyway because some of the stuff Guest History puts into a guest's history is simply amazing: writes bad checks; drinks too much in bar after midnight; masturbates in sauna; having affair with costar, do NOT give wife key.

Jack's guest history profile is blank. It's his first visit.

I sit back in my chair and go over our conversation. I try to recapture a memory that's only ten minutes old. But it's all lost: the way he looked at me, the tone of his voice. What isn't lost are the things I've tried hard not to remember over the years, these things that are all of a sudden rushing back. Like the way we kissed for hours and hours in his bedroom. Like the way he treated me like a real girl. Like the look on his face, which I've imagined a hundred times, when he woke up that morning and found me gone.

"Are we working?" Kirk's looking over my shoulder. I hadn't heard him come in. "Seven calls waiting!"

Maria sits down and curses under her breath. I watch Kirk take off his jacket and put his briefcase under his desk. Like he really needs a briefcase.

"Good morning Kendall," he says when he notices me watching him.

Kirk's from the West Coast, gay, thirty-eightish. In the two years—it feels longer—that I've worked here, I've grown tired and sick of the sound of his voice. Every day he complains about how angry, rude and aggressive New Yorkers are. I try to point out to him and all of the other nonnative New Yorkers in the office that the problem with New York is not New Yorkers.

It's the out-of-towners who move here and inflict out-of-town aggression. Most of the native New Yorkers I know never get anything we really want.

Kirk sits down, types his password into his switchboard and starts taking calls. I try to ignore his voice, but I can't. I can't even stop staring at him. I hate when he answers phones. He watches his monitor, making sure we're answering calls consistently and not lingering on one particular call too long. He's like a really annoying high school teacher.

I don't hate my job, though. If I had a choice, I would quit. But how many average people have a choice when it comes to work? Gary says we aren't average, but he works overtime every chance he gets, so I know he knows that isn't true.

I'm a PBX operator. Hotel Operator for short. You don't get much more average than that. Or marginal. Some people have called my job, and me, marginal. Telephone operators are even on the lowest rung of the hotel caste system, believe it or not. Lower than Housekeeping.

I work with several other marginal people, nineteen to be exact, mostly women. There are six consoles in this stuffy, windowless office, and for every shift there's five or six of us, phones plugged into our ears like mini Walkmans, answering call after call after boring call. I stay because the pay's okay and there isn't much to it.

I don't like to be challenged in my work.

"Six calls holding," Kirk announces.

Actually, the phone calls are the one unexpected perk about the job. Some of my coworkers say, hands down, the best perk is the free cafeteria, but I don't agree. It's definitely the calls.

Most people don't think it's an awful thing that my coworkers and I listen to hotel guests' personal, private calls. They want information. Because the phone calls we listen to are better than daytime television, and it's the best office gossip an office worker can get.

I try not to make telling people everything I hear a habit. Not only because I could lose my job, but spreading information about guests is a betrayal to everyone I work with. It's like telling the office manager that a coworker is smoking in the bathroom instead of using it. It only messes things up for everyone.

Once, a housekeeper sold some information to a tabloid and was fired. Selling information is pretty stupid. For one thing, a tabloid couldn't possibly pay enough to guarantee never having to work here again. And, really, there's not much you can get away with. Every call is documented in the computer, and every room that's cleaned is recorded in a housekeeping log.

Besides, the information we "obtain" is just to help us get through the day.

For a minute, I think about what it would be like to listen to the next phone call that comes in for Jack. I have a strict policy about listening to calls that come in for people I know: I don't. Not that anyone I've known has ever stayed here before.

Whenever a coworker calls in and asks for another coworker, or a guest, I never listen to the call. Some of the operators do, which is how I know the head of Housekeeping is sleeping with the assistant general manager, and the chef concierge sells marijuana to the entire kitchen staff, as well as a few loyal hotel guests. But that's not my thing. At least I know I can come into work and look all of my coworkers in the eye.

"Fifteen calls holding," Kirk says.

The minute I turn on my switchboard the name Judith Swenson flashes onto my screen. Judith Swenson is the CEO of a toy company in San Francisco who likes "heads to roll" if things don't go her way. I can't handle Judith this early in the morning because the first call usually sets precedence for the rest of the day. I still have seven hours and fifty minutes left. I pass the call.

"Uh, who just passed a call to me?" Trina, another operator, asks loudly.

"Seventeen calls!" Kirk sounds frustrated and frantic. He looks directly at me. "Did you pass that call?"

"Shit. I did it by accident," I admit.

"Keep it clean, keep it clean," Kirk scolds. Kirk is always scolding me. Apparently, I have the foulest mouth in the office. "And do not pass calls."

Working at the hotel used to be overwhelming. All of these hugely successful people with enough money to buy an island can really get on an operator's last nerve. Every request is a privilege, but guests treat them like life-or-death situations.

Do Not Disturb. Call Screening. Wake-up Call. Voice Mail. Room Change. Name Change. It never ends. And God forbid an operator makes a mistake. Some guests have gone as far as trying to get us fired.

Working at the hotel used to be infuriating. Especially when a celebrity or—for chrissakes—a *designer* becomes unhinged because a call is put through and a Do Not Disturb is broken. Some guy who makes ten thousand dollars before he even sits down for breakfast wants to take away some operator's ten-dollar-an-hour job because she broke his DND and put that call through from his mother. (She was crying!)

And then my anger wore off. Now I mostly feel numb.

"Is this a personal call?" I hear Kirk say into his phone.

Involuntarily, I lean back in my chair to witness his conversation.

"We don't allow personal calls in this office," he continues, looking at me. "She just started her shift. I suggest you call her at home."

"What if it's an emergency," I shout, suddenly anxious to speak to someone from the outside, someone I can tell the story of meeting Jack to. Kirk rolls his eyes and disconnects the call. An operator on the other side of the room snickers.

"Ten calls!" Kirk announces, then looks at me again. "Why aren't you wearing your uniform?"

I sigh.

Kirk and I go through something close to this nearly every day. I think he gets a perverse thrill out of harassing me. I can actually tell when he's gotten laid the night before because he'll walk into the office and not even look in my direction. I'll say something that, on any other day, would really get him going, and he'll just smile or nod or dismiss me with a wave of his hand.

Despite his threats to write me up, I rarely wear my uniform. It's a form of protest. I hope it'll catch on one day and the other operators will stop wearing them as well. Then management might agree to make wearing the uniforms optional.

"Put on your uniform," Kirk commands.

"We're in a basement," I remind him. "I'm not wearing a uniform because wearing a uniform in a basement doesn't make sense."

"I second that," Wanda shouts.

Kirk, always ready to prove he's in charge, stands up and walks over to my console. He once told me if hotel operators didn't have a union, I'd probably be the one to start it. I took it as a compliment.

"This is not a basement," Kirk tells me. "This is Level C2."

"Yes, sir." I salute him with a conciliatory smile.

"Either change or clock out," he demands, ignoring my smile.

"But no one can see me."

"*I* can see you," he says.

There's a standoff for a couple of minutes. We stare at each other, not backing down. After a while, his bottom lip starts to quiver and there's a hint of a blush seeping through his light brown skin. This strikes me and I feel for him.

I think about the time all of the Puerto Rican women in the office banded together and told Human Resources Kirk was a racist and favored the black telephone operators. A heinous lie. As someone who is on the other end of his wrath five days a week, I can vouch that isn't true. Then there was the time he docked an hour off of Wanda's pay because she was fifteen minutes late from lunch. She threatened to beat the hell out of him after work. Visibly shaken, Kirk went home early with a headache.

For some reason, I don't want to be the person who sends Kirk home with a headache today. I think it has something to do with Jack, his close proximity, and the fact that I'm imagining his eyes on me, waiting to see what I'm going to do.

I take off my headset. "Okay. I'll change."

"Change at break," he commands.

He retreats back to his desk and checks the monitor. "Fifteen calls holding," he says. He almost catches me stick my tongue out at him.

When there's a lull, Kirk starts to straighten his desk. All eyes focus on him. Waiting. Waiting for him to get up and leave. After an hour or so, he goes out, and there's a collective sigh of relief. I call Sage.

"I'm taking my break in thirty minutes," I say.

He's busy checking someone in. He grunts and asks the guest for identification.

"Thirty minutes," I say again and hang up.

Sage is waiting for me in the locker room when I arrive. He's straddling the bench in front of my locker, a joint in one hand and a can of Lysol in the other. I straddle the bench as well, refusing the joint when he offers it to me.

"She dumped him this morning," he says.

"Oh?"

"She came down around nine and asked if she could have a room change," he continues. "But she didn't want to pay for his room as well, so we said no. Not unless he checked out or gave us a credit card. That was out of the question because she didn't want to tell him she was leaving the room. So she flipped out on my manager and said she was going to The Mark."

I nod.

Sage works at Front Desk. We used to date until he dropped me for the wife I didn't know he had. And while he's trying to get that part of his life together—to divorce or not to divorce—we still see each other.

I know it isn't right, having sex with a man who will never be able to commit to me, but I actually don't want a commitment. When I'm with him, I enjoy myself. That's really all that matters. It wouldn't happen if I didn't get anything out of it.

"So he left about thirty minutes ago," Sage says. "Said he'd be back. He'd get the studio to cover a new room. Do you know who I'm talking about?"

"Yes," I say. "The Texan and his girlfriend."

Right now, I'm following the unfolding drama between a twentysomething television studio executive and her aging lover; a married businessman with HIV and a penchant for male prostitutes; and the Texan.

The Texan is a young actor I'm madly in love with in a fan sort of way. He's been in a couple of independent films and is about to be in *Quest for Peace,* an epic Hollywood flick about the life of Alfred Nobel. The operators announce his name when it flashes on their switchboard. If Kirk isn't around, we switch seats so I can take the Texan's calls. I do the same for them when, say, Antonio Banderas comes up on my screen.

Sage is also following the travails of the Texan and his manager/lover. He depends on me for all the really juicy gossip he can't get at Front Desk. He thinks the Texan's life is better than every story line on *The Young and the Restless.*

I don't watch *The Young and the Restless,* but I have to agree. The Texan's life is definitely soap-opera worthy.

Sage and I originally became friends when we realized we were always turning up at the same clubs. We pretended not to notice each other until we met at Messy Tilda's in Jersey City. Messy Tilda's and Jersey City were hot scenes for a couple of weeks, and all of the celebrities staying at the hotel flocked there. Sage came over to me and asked what my deal was.

At the time, I was just getting used to the world of hotel operator eavesdropping and all the crazy things my fellow operators did when they got a juicy bit of information. Mainly we would hightail it over to the bar, club or restaurant our favorite celebrities were hightailing it over to. We'd call the club, claim to be from Concierge and have them put our names on the guest list. Then we would prowl.

Unlike my fellow operators, I've only slept with one hotel guest. He was young, single and not exactly famous. He'd had a small role in a major film with a major actress. I'd heard his call to a friend in California. Apparently, he'd had a crush on the actress the entire time they'd been filming, and he'd admitted his feelings to her during the wrap party. She'd rejected him in front of the key grip.

That night, he'd said he just wanted to go out and find some cute chick to have meaningless, mind-blowing sex with. Someone he'd never have to see again. Someone who wouldn't get attached to him. He'd sounded like a bit of an egomaniac, but to be honest, most of them do. And I'd had a rough day. Little did he know, the cute chick who sent him drinks and flirted with him, the cute chick he was having meaningless, mind-blowing sex with in his very expensive hotel room was operator number five.

Anyway, the night Sage asked me what my deal was, I was lurking, looking for a television actor I was in lust with who was meeting a friend at Messy Tilda's. I was also rethinking my whole life as a hotel operator who eavesdrops. Not the eavesdropping-on-celebrities bit. Just the showing-up-at-the-same-club-and-sleeping-with-them bit.

I was on my way to being drunk, and Sage didn't have any trouble convincing me to admit how I'd ended up there. In return, he admitted that he got all of his information from a friend at Concierge. He would spend the entire night flirting with celebrities; it boosted his ego when some of them were actually receptive. And then he would use hotel guests' car service identification numbers to get free rides home in town cars.

It was all very thrilling to him. Like me, he wasn't big on sleeping with hotel guests, though he admitted that he did if he was feeling especially lonely.

We have a lot in common, Sage and I. We find comfort in the strangers whose calls we listen to, whose lives we infiltrate. It's like being addicted to a soap opera in a way. Tuning in every day to get the next dramatic installment of a life we know we'll never have to live. Sharing a closeness with another human being without having to be close to them. Knowing their full stories without them knowing we know them.

"What's up?" he says now in Spanish. "Why do you look like that?"

"Like what?" I ask, though I know I must look like I've seen a ghost or, more logically, like I've seen someone I haven't seen in a long time. I think about telling him I saw Jack this morning. But Sage doesn't know about Jack. And I don't want to explain the past. I hear about Jack; I try not to talk about him.

"*Mi corazón,*" Sage says. "Where are you?"

I touch his knee. I can't tell him where I am right now and he nods, like he understands. He tells me that my touch means more to him than any words. He understands that sometimes there are no words.

We're quiet. He smokes. I draw invisible designs on the bench between us. After a long moment, he switches back to English. "She tipped me fifty bucks and told me to call her at The Mark."

I smile at the bench. "Who?"

"The Texan's girlfriend."

"You keep the fifty?" I ask.

"Damn straight."

Sage isn't exactly good-looking, but he has sex appeal. Hotel guests—male and female—constantly offer to pay him for "dates." Underneath his uniform everyone can tell he has a great body. His sexuality comes from the way he moves: a slight gangster-boy-hop with more sensuality than intimidation. But it's the way his shaved head makes him look slightly dangerous, and the way his legs are spread wide, and the way his hand dangles at his crotch, that get me.

"You want me to?" he asks.

"What?"

"Call her."

"I don't care," I say.

It's the way he rolls his eyes heavenward, nods at me and says, "Come closer. I want to kiss you," in Spanish when he can't make me jealous.

I stay where I am and stare at him steadily. I don't feel like being kissed by him right now.

"Seriously," he says. "What's up?"

"Seriously," I say. "Nothing."

"I'm sorry I couldn't let you stay last night," he says. Sage lives on the Lower East Side. Alone. At least until his wife allows him to move back into her house in Queens. "My mother-in-law wanted to have dinner. You're mad about that?"

"No. Really. I'm not mad." I smile, and his face relaxes.

"You should move out," he tells me. "Get your own place."

"I like living with Gary."

"But . . ." He doesn't finish.

"What?"

He shrugs, stares down at the bench. "I don't like you living with other guys."

This is the part I hate.

"He's gay," I remind him. "Not to mention, my best friend.

And it's not like he watches me shower . . . and . . ." *and aren't you married?*

"You make enough money," Sage says. "You can give him a couple of weeks to find a new roommate . . ."

"I really can't afford anything else." *And it makes me cringe when straight guys get all insecure about their girlfriends and gay men. I'm not even your girlfriend, which makes this worse.*

"Yes, you can," he says.

I think about the eleven thousand dollars I owe various credit card companies and how little I have to show for what I spent. An important course they forgot to teach in college was how to avoid debt. And I'd like to live on my own someday. Not because I want to nip Sage's sick fantasies or nightmares of Gary and me having sex in the bud. But because I'm thirty-one and ready. Sage doesn't realize how long it took me to get to a place where I could even afford to split rent with a friend.

"What are you doing later?" Sage wants to know.

"Why?"

"Let's go for a drink."

"I can't," I say.

He scoots closer to me. "Why not?"

"Just can't."

For a split second, he looks concerned. "Date?"

I shake my head.

"Then what?"

"I have to take care of something," I say.

"Oh." He looks rejected.

I feel guilty. But daily updates about my life weren't in the cards from the beginning. I don't ask him about his life outside of our world together, and he doesn't offer any information.

He scoots backward, putting more space between us than there was before. He watches me. He says, "That's my shirt."

I unbutton the shirt and throw it at him playfully.

He continues, "Aren't those my pants?"

I stand up, take them off and throw them at him. I stand in my underwear, grinning, watching him smoke.

The door opens. Sage sprays the Lysol. I'm leaning against my locker when a group of women from Housekeeping breeze in.

"Hey," we all say in unison.

One of them wags a finger at Sage and says, "Sage, get the fuck out of here."

Sage blows her a kiss and she giggles.

Front Desk is one of the most highly regarded departments in the hotel. It's a notch above Concierge; a notch below Sales. Everyone respects you if you work at Front Desk, Concierge or in Sales. Sage is one of the only Front Desk agents who socializes outside of his department. I'm not unaware of the looks we get from people when we take lunch or leave the hotel together. I like to say we're in an intercaste relationship.

I open my locker and stare inside. "Sage."

"Yeah?" He pinches out the joint, sprays some more Lysol. When I don't say anything for a while, he stops playing with his can of disinfectant and looks at me. "Yeah?"

"Nothing," I say. "I'll call you later."

When he leaves, I take my uniform from the locker: a black, Quakerish skirt, off-white blouse and black vest. I sit on the bench again and sigh. One of the women, the one who recognized Sage earlier, winks at me on her way out.

"Hey, Kendall. How you feeling?"

I tell her I feel pretty good, and then I get dressed.

*   *   *

Leaving the hotel for the evening, I feel a mixture of anxiety and relief. The doorman, Ramon, is the only person standing outside. We wave at each other, and I tell him to have a nice evening.

"You do the same, sweetie," Ramon says.

As I walk to the train I think embarrassment and disappointment have replaced my anxiety and relief. Disappointment because Jack wasn't outside waiting for me. Embarrassment because some part of me thought he might be.

There's a dog at the front door of my apartment when I come up the stairs. It's baring its teeth at me. I've never seen this dog before and I'm not wild about enormous Rottweilers without leashes. My first thought is that it looks dangerous and can't possibly belong to anyone in the building. Because pets aren't allowed.

The thing to do at times like this is lie on the floor and play dead, I think. Or maybe that's the thing to do to prevent a bear attack. I can't remember.

The dog's growl is fierce, and I haven't done anything. I haven't even moved. What's wrong with this picture? Don't they write tragic news stories about this? Too bad there aren't any witnesses. If the dog attacks, someone might say I provoked it.

A door upstairs opens, and a woman's voice bellows, "Scruffy! Where are you?"

The dog's ears perk up, but he doesn't take his eyes off me, and he doesn't stop growling. It's pretty cool how he can growl and glare and perk up at the sound of his owner's voice, as well as scare the living hell out of me, all at once.

The door above slams.

"There you are," a woman's voice says, followed by the sound of her patting her thighs. "Come here, baby. Come here."

The dog trots up the stairs and I move tentatively to my door.

"Hello," the woman says from the top of the stairs. I look up. She has long black hair that hangs limp and wet past her broad shoulders. She's an unrefined version of Mimi Rogers.

I smile up at her. "How's it going?"

She smiles too but doesn't answer my question. The dog growls again. The key in my lock shakes a little.

I say, "Dogs aren't allowed here."

"Excuse me?" The voice is suddenly chilly.

"I think . . . well, actually, I'm pretty sure dogs aren't allowed in the building." Normally I wouldn't give a shit about people breaking trivial rules in this building, but I'm not wild about other people's animals. And the last thing I need, or want, is to come home every day to that unleashed growling beast roaming the halls.

"Scruffy's not my dog." The voice is clipped, yet authoritative. I look up again to see that the woman's face has transformed into a hard shell as she rubs the dog's back and makes coo-cooing noises at him like he deserves to be rewarded for scaring me.

"Good," I mumble.

"He's visiting. Dogs are allowed to visit." She scrutinizes me. Dark eyes daring me to contradict her.

"Okay," I say. "That's probably true."

"It is true," she says. Then, "Are you subletting?"

It's my turn to say, "Excuse me?"

"You don't own," she states coldly. "You weren't at the meeting."

"No," I say slowly. "We don't own. We weren't at the meeting."

I think that's a smile—tiny, yet triumphant—making an appearance on her face. "Nice to meet you," she says. She straightens and walks back to her apartment. The dog lumbers after her obediently.

Inside, Gary's chopping vegetables. He's a welcome sight. These days, he's rarely around. He spends most of his time at his boyfriend Nick's house fifteen blocks away. He raises an eyebrow at me, half smiles. An indication that he's heard my conversation with the stranger in the hallway.

"What the hell was that?" I say.

"Ah. So you've met The Bitch Upstairs," he says evenly.

"Upstairs as in right above us, upstairs?"

He nods, eyebrow raised again.

I sigh, put my bag on the floor.

"And she has a kid." He points up, and that's when I hear it. The sound of a child running across wood floors.

"You're kidding," I groan.

Over a year of living under an empty apartment has ended. I wait for Gary to tell me it's a joke.

"At least you missed the *moving-in* part," he says. "It didn't take long, but I couldn't get any work done for at least four hours. I spent most of the day writing at Starbucks."

"Damn. That hurts."

He nods, confirming. "I can't get rid of this caffeine headache."

"Drink decaf."

"Right." He nods.

Gary's thirty-one years old, a waiter pursuing a writing career. He's currently working on a screenplay.

"She's called Betty Blacksmith," he adds with a smirk.

"Now you're kidding."

"Nope." He punctuates that with a loud chop into a stalk of celery, which brings my attention back to the fact that he's actually chopping celery. Gary never cooks. Yet now he's chopping vegetables to the beat of the stomping girl upstairs: *Doompdoomp doompdoomp . . . doomp . . . doomp . . . doomp.*

"Gary," I say.

"Wait a minute." Gary brandishes the knife in the air. If Betty were actually in the apartment, she might be in serious trouble. "According to the guy on six, she's owned that apartment the entire time it's been empty."

"Odd."

"The bitch is odd," Gary spits. "And I thought she looked familiar. The guy on six says she's been to every board meeting."

"I've never seen her," I say.

"You know the guy down the hall? Jeff?"

I shake my head. "Doesn't ring a bell."

"The old president," Gary continues. "Well, he just sold his place and illegally handed the presidency over to Betty."

"Presidency of what?"

"The co-op board."

I stare at him. "I didn't even know we had a co-op board."

He rolls his eyes. "Well, now you do. And she's the president of it."

"How did that happen?"

"Fuck if I know. I just know there's something rotten in Denmark."

"You're no Macbeth," I say with a smile.

"Good, because I was going for Hamlet." He starts to chop the vegetables again, incensed. I watch. If Gary's chopping veggies, not sitting in front of his computer working on his script, something big must be about to happen.

KAREN SIPLIN

"Gary," I say.

"How do people get away with it?" Gary asks. "Jeff nearly took my head off when you moved in because we didn't ask the board for permission. But he can just transfer power to some woman without a meeting? Without a vote?"

I try to feel the rage that Gary feels about this injustice, but I can't. "Let's knock on her door and demand a vote," I say lightly.

"I understand there are very few owners in the building now that Jeff's gone. But he could have transferred the presidency over to that woman on two. Yeah, she's always soused, but what the fuck? And we can't vote, sweetie." The *sweetie* comes out like a sneer. "We're plebeians who don't own. We don't have a voice."

I shrug and point to the vegetables on the counter.

"Are we having company?" I ask.

"Oh," he says casually. "Guess who's stopping by to say hello?"

"Who?"

"An old friend," he says.

"Does Nick know?" I grin. There was a time, not long ago, when Nick actually asked me to spy on Gary because he thought Gary was cheating on him. I didn't do it. But it was one of the only times I've ever seen Nick out of control. He called me at least seven times a day to find out where Gary was, and if Gary had spent the entire night at home. It turned out Gary was working on a novel, not a lover.

"Nick's bringing him."

Gary watches me as I try to think of an old friend who would stop by to say hello. I toss out a few names of people Gary and Nick used to hang out with before they started dating.

"Your friend," Gary says. "Not ours."

He comes to mind the minute Gary says this. But I can't believe it would be him. I hadn't imagined I'd see him again so soon. Twice in one day? A record for seeing old boyfriends, I think.

"Jack?"

A mixture of surprise and disappointment clouds Gary's face.

"Sorry I ruined your fun," I say. "I bumped into him this morning. He didn't say anything about stopping by, though. In fact, he didn't even know where I live."

"Where'd you bump into him?"

I sit at the kitchen table and stare at Gary intently. "You didn't know?" I ask. "You swear?"

"Don't insult me," Gary says, insulted. "You know I would have told you if I knew she was going to be in New York."

A hint of a smile from me. After all these years, there's still the cat in Gary when it comes to Jack. Referring to Jack as a *her* has always been his Thing.

"She called Nick this afternoon to say she's in the city," Gary continues. "Then she offered to meet us in Brooklyn. Nick, of course, wants to show her the house and trade house buying stories, or whatever."

"And how did that translate to us being here?"

Gary rolls his eyes dramatically. "You know this is because of you. She would never come to Brooklyn to see some house."

"You think?"

"Let's see." Gary puts a finger to his lip and strikes a coy pose, as though he's thinking. "She asked if you would be at Nick's. I told Nick to say you have things to do at home. She said fine, they would stop here first to see the apartment. Little vixen. She thinks she's subtle."

I stare at the table, disturbed.

"Where'd you see him?" Gary asks.

"He's staying at the hotel," I say, looking at him again.

Gary's left eyebrow rises. "*Your hotel*?"

"My hotel."

Gary opens his mouth. He's about to say something but changes his mind.

"What?" I say.

"Just a strange coincidence." He shrugs, thinking. "It must have been . . ."

"Strange." I nod. "It was. Very."

Gary shakes his head, then shudders at the image of me running into Jack at the hotel. He's never been wild about Jack. In fact, none of my friends were. Because Jack was not good boyfriend material. In college, he was dark, angsty and dangerous. Not the kind of guy a girl like me should be with. I was all sun and light and goodness. B-Plus Girl. Girl in long Indian skirts and sandals, flowers in her hair, anklets and silver rings. Smiles and positive energy. Jack's darkness, angst and danger were a turnoff to my friends.

When Nick and Jack bumped into each other in Boston last summer, they had drinks and caught up. According to Nick, Jack was different. *In a good place.* Meaning Jack owned a business, had a house, looked good and spent money freely. He was finally someone worth knowing.

I knew that Nick's desire to keep in touch with Jack—even though they'd never liked each other—was fueled by his need to show Jack up a little bit. Nick used to call him sexy-dangerous-cool guy in a condescending manner, but I could always tell there was a little envy involved. Who doesn't want to be sexy, dangerous and cool in college? Who doesn't want to lie back on the grassy campus and stare up at the sky while everyone else is in class? Who doesn't want to have eyes that silence people with a single, intense glance?

I also suspected—privately and with some trepidation—that Jack kept in touch with Nick to find out some things about me. I didn't suspect it because I have a huge ego, or because I think Jack still has feelings for me. In my wildest dreams, I would never imagine that. I just knew.

Now I stand up and head for the bathroom, slightly bothered by my own thoughts. Why does he want to be here? In the same room with me. With my friends.

"I hate company," I say. "Can we call him at the hotel and ask him not to come over? I was hoping for a quiet evening."

"Weren't you just complaining that Amy is the only person who visits?" Gary calls after me.

The truth is, when I moved in I thought I'd see more of Gary and our friends. I imagined we'd have dinner parties every Saturday night and brunch every Sunday, and people like Amy and Nick, even Sage, would stop by at all hours just to hang out or say hi. Of course, the way to go about things is to actually invite people over if you want company. No one stops by just because you've willed them to.

It happens in college; friends show up with beer and chips and ideas of studying. But it doesn't happen afterward—when you're on the edge of adulthood—unless you sell drugs, or you're Nick. Nick always has company. Just like in college. Every time I visit or call, some friend is laughing in the background, or another friend has just left. Gary tells me not to envy it. He wishes he could pull Nick's phone cord out of the wall and have one night with him alone. He wishes Nick would come to our place and just watch television.

"I guess it's a good thing Nick is coming over," I say from the bathroom. "Even if Jack's the reason for it. Now that I think of it, we should force him to have dinner here more often."

I hear Gary sigh. "My boyfriend likes his eight-hundred-thousand-dollar brownstone more than our eight-hundred-dollar-a-month rental, and who would blame him?"

"Me," I say as I close the door.

When I come out of the bathroom, Gary hangs up the phone. "They'll be here in fifteen minutes," he informs me.

I feel a knot start to develop in my stomach. Gary watches me as he dumps a bag of Fritos on a plate.

"You think he eats chips?" Gary asks.

I shrug. "How would I know anything about Jack's eating habits after all these years?"

"You used to be so anal about your diet. It was very annoying."

"I'm not anal anymore." I grab a handful of chips. Then I meet Gary's gaze. We watch each other, not saying what we really want to say.

After a minute, Gary shakes his head. "This is wrong."

"It's not a big deal."

"I didn't say it was," Gary clarifies. "I said it was wrong. What are we supposed to talk about after so many years? Not that I'm under any illusions that he wants to talk to me."

The buzzer rings and I look at Gary sharply. "I thought you said fifteen minutes."

Nick walks in with a bottle of wine. I'm sitting on the counter near the sink, eating Fritos nervously.

"New neighbors?" he asks, handing the wine to me, then sweeping Gary up in a big hug and kiss. Gary laughs, kissing back. And I smile at them.

They're cute together, Gary and Nick. Nick with his huge bowl of curly black hair that he refuses to cut or shape or do anything with. Gary with his smooth dark skin, round, shaved head and neatly trimmed sideburns.

"Yeah." I sound disgruntled.

Nick nods. "Disheveled. Long black hair?"

"Annoying," Gary adds.

"Really?" Nick looks sympathetic.

"She has a kid," Gary explains.

"A kid that runs a lot," I say.

"Have you complained?" Nick asks seriously, looking at Gary.

"As long as she's in school I can write during the day."

"He spent the day at Starbucks," I tattle.

Nick gives Gary a chastising look. "I thought Starbucks coffee gives you headaches."

"Honey, one took up residence after my first coffee and hasn't left yet," Gary says. "I think it likes it here."

"Then why?" Nick does his almost-whiny voice, which always verges on irritating me enormously. "Why don't you use the guestroom?"

Gary says nothing. He doesn't like to use Nick's house when Nick isn't in it. He likes to keep things separate, in case things get iffy. Nick doesn't understand iffy, but I do. What if all of the wonderful things that belong to Nick begin to feel like they belong to Gary as well? What if, one day, they have that terrific argument and Nick reminds him what isn't his? You don't come back from reminders like that. They're ugly and traitorous. Gary is protecting Nick as much as he's protecting himself.

"Where's Jack?" I ask, all about the casual delivery.

"Jack's parking the car."

"How does she look?" Gary asks.

Nick looks at me. "How does Jack look? He told me about running into you this morning."

Gary lets go of Nick and they stare up at me, waiting for a verdict.

"He looks different," I say, still handling the art of the casual delivery expertly. "Like an L.L. Bean New England guy. Very weird. Very rugged."

Nick sucks his teeth, grabbing a cucumber slice from a plate and sticking it in his mouth. "He looks good. Damn good."

Gary rolls his eyes. "She never looked *damn good*," Gary says. "And do we know why she's really here?"

"He's meeting with beer distributors," Nick explains. "Someone's interested in distributing Sullivan Brew in the Tri-State area. Could be very lucrative."

Gary and I share a look. In unison we say, "To gloat."

We all laugh.

And then he walks in. Jack. He's changed his clothes since this morning. He's all dapper and macho in Armani-like clothing. This is so different from the Jack we knew. So trendy and corporate.

Gary looks him over subtly, then shakes his hand awkwardly.

"How's the hotel?" Gary asks.

"Wonderful," Jack says. "It's like a home away from home. Actually, better."

Gary and Nick nod, fascinated. I eat another chip.

"Ken." Jack looks at me. Nick and Gary look at me as well. Expectantly. I jump down from the counter, and we shake hands.

"What's with the thumb ring?" I ask, turning his hand over in my own. He hadn't been wearing it earlier.

"You remember it," he says, meeting my eyes.

"Of course." I gave it to him. "Why are you wearing it?"

"I always wear it."

My eyes say *I know you're lying*. His eyes dare me to confront it. Instead, I drop his hand, move away from him, and ignore the tingling feeling burning the lining of my stomach.

"Nice to see you again," I say, unintentionally rubbing the hand that held his against my hip.

"Yeah." He looks at Gary and Nick, who are concentrating a little too intently on placing the vegetable and chip platters on the table.

"Twice in one day," I say. "Who would have guessed?"

Jack flashes me a cocky grin. I'm not sure why this bothers me. My face burns.

"All these years and you still can't get enough of me," I continue.

The grin remains, but his face darkens. For a split second, I think I shouldn't have said that. I flip through the memories stored away in my brain. Had I said something like this before?

"What is it about you that brings out the evil in me?" I ask.

Jack tilts his head, shrugs. "Maybe you still love me?"

I smile, but there's no smiliness in it. He's hit the right chord, I think. I say, "Who says I ever did?"

"Now, now, girls," Gary says in a voice he reserves for the nights he's out with his gay friends. Nick comes over and tugs at Jack's leather jacket before Jack can respond to any of us. Jack relinquishes the jacket.

"Make yourself at home," Nick tells him. Jack looks away from me finally, his eyes following Nick and his jacket into Gary's bedroom. "I'll throw your coat on Gary's bed. Kendall can get you a drink."

"Yeah." I nearly jump at the sound of my own voice. I open

the cabinet near the sink and show him our various bottles of spirits. There isn't much to go on. We usually drink at Nick's. "What are you drinking?"

Jack glances at me. His eyes settle on the cabinet.

There have been plenty of men in my life. Most of them, I try to forget. When I run into one, it's like a jolt, an unpleasant reminder of my mistakes. I remember the things we used to say: I miss you, I want to see you, I'm still angry, I love you, I hate you. And when we see each other—days, months, years after we've ended—it's like we never said any of those things at all. It's like we're strangers who have never seen each other naked.

It's kind of like that with Jack this very second. When he glances at me, I can't believe all the things I've shared with him.

"What are you drinking?" I ask again.

He looks at me now, eyes dull and lifeless. "Got any Johnnie Walker Blue?"

"Blue?" I ask. "I've only heard of Black and Red."

"Yeah." As though he knew I wouldn't have a clue. "It's the good stuff. Aged about twenty years."

"And it's over a hundred and fifty bucks," Gary adds testily. "Why don't you open the wine he brought?"

My eyes narrow, and I slam the cabinet shut. I look at the bottle of wine on the counter as though the words *Cabernet Sauvignon Reserve, Robert Mondavi Winery* mean something to me.

"Also an expensive treat," Nick informs us as he comes out of Gary's bedroom. "Thank you, Jack. I've been dying to try that."

"Why didn't you just bring your beer?" I try for a bored tone.

"Do you not like wine anymore?" Jack asks.

"Love wine," I assure him heartily. "But beer. You know. Beer's your business." I catch the severe hint of sarcasm in my tone. A far cry from bored.

Jack tilts his head slightly, like he's trying to figure something out about me. Then he kind of smiles. "I never knew you to pass up an expensive glass of wine you didn't have to pay for," he says. "So I brought a bottle. I thought you'd appreciate the gesture."

From the corner of my eye I see Gary open his mouth to defend me.

"This why you came?" I cut Gary off. "Work out some issues with me?"

Jack's taken aback, then embarrassed. He shakes his head, humbled a bit. "Not at all."

"Good." I screw the wine opener into the cork and pull it up. "Not that I believe you."

This gets a smile from him. Sincere. Sexy. I look away. Not a good idea to notice Jack's smile is still sexy.

"Really, don't open it now," he insists. "Save it for a special occasion. It's perfect with . . ."

I open it. I pour and hand out the glasses. Nick holds up his glass, as though he's going to make a toast, so Gary and I do the same and wait.

"Nice color," Nick comments to Jack but doesn't toast to anything.

Gary and I lower our glasses, slightly humiliated. Sometimes Gary wonders what he sees in Nick. I wonder, too.

The wine is dry and I hate it. We all comment how delicious it is. Then we drink in silence. For a while, we pretend to be comfortable like this.

Jack starts to look around. "How long have you lived here?" he asks Gary.

"Five years. Kendall's been here a little over a year."

"Ever think of buying something?"

Gary glares at the back of Jack's head as though he wants to kick it. He hates the *why are you still renting at your age* conversation. Jack turns to look at him.

"No," Gary says.

Jack nods. "It's a huge responsibility. I can't picture you owning a house. When you're ready."

CONDESCENDING BASTARD is written in CAPS across Gary's face. Nick, feeling the air in the room constrict, reaches out and hopes rubbing his boyfriend's back will placate him.

Jack turns his attention to me. "Where'd you live before this?"

I frown. I'm not sure if I want to answer. It seems like an odd and intensely personal question.

"This was my first move," I admit. I've never been that person who cares what people think.

"Since college?" he asks.

I nod, biting the inside of my mouth. Still, it takes a lot to admit it. To him.

"You lived with? . . ." he stops.

"My parents, yes."

"Really?" There's genuine surprise in his voice.

"Yes."

There's a long, awkward silence.

"How's the house?" Nick asks finally.

Slowly, Jack looks from me to Nick. "Lonely. You should visit for Christmas."

"We've been discussing a ski trip for Christmas," Gary tells Jack.

"You can ski in Maine," Jack says smoothly. "And there's this cabin in Bangor I go to. I like to ski there. Actually, I prefer snowboarding these days."

"Snowboarding?" I say, unable to pass up another opportunity to tease him. "Never took you for a snowboarder, Jack. A little reckless at your age, don't you think? I thought you would have grown out of that."

Nick flashes me a look, but Jack grins.

"I'll always be a little reckless," he says. "I thought that was what you liked about me."

"True," I say without hesitation. "I was also twenty."

"I was planning to make something," Gary interrupts. "But maybe we should just call it an evening?"

I smile, liking that idea. Teasing an old boyfriend is fun. For about ten minutes. Now I'm ready for him to leave.

"I'd actually like to take you out." Jack looks to Nick, then Gary, then me. "We can catch up on the past nine years."

Impromptu catching up on the past nine years. Not my thing. Besides, I can't afford dinner, and I wouldn't let Jack cover my tab if I were starving. Nick says he knows the perfect place to "catch up" in, which means it's a restaurant I wouldn't be able to afford even if I had a little extra cash to spend. Nick never takes other people's financial situations into account.

I drop the big bomb of untruth that I have a date at ten and won't be able to go with them. The three men stare at me in silence, as though the idea of Kendall Stark on a date is inconceivable.

"Someone from work," I add insecurely.

Gary's eyebrows shoot up. He knows I'm sleeping with a married guy from the hotel. He knows we don't "date."

Upstairs, our new neighbors' door slams, and the intrusive *doomp doomp doomp*ing I was starting to get used to not hearing starts up again. Nick ducks, as though a plane has flown too near his head.

"What's all that racket?" he asks.

I stare at him. While I'm aware that our new neighbors are a tad noisy, I'm mostly wondering when Nick started sounding like he's eighty—*racket?*—and I'm wondering why Jack is still staring at me so intently.

He doesn't seem to hear the noise. He says, "Next time, then?"

"Absolutely." I flash a big, fake smile that even makes me cringe. "How long are you staying?"

"I'm not sure yet," he tells me. "I have twenty-one days booked at the hotel, with the option for another week."

Meaning the hotel won't book his room until he makes a definite decision he doesn't want to stay. What the hell?

"Three weeks in New York?" Gary squeaks. Better him than me. "Why so long?"

"Yeah." I try to sound jovial, rather than unnerved. "You can gloat in less than a day. Actually, you've already done that. You can go back to Maine now."

This pisses him off. The ferocity in his face lights a torch in me.

"How long have you been carrying that chip?" he asks tensely, looking me over. "I thought I noticed one shoulder was higher than the other."

"Fuck you, Jack," I say casually.

"Kids," Nick scolds, sounding a lot like Gary. "I thought we were past this."

Jack lowers his eyes, then looks at Gary. There's still anger in his face, but I can tell he's trying to push it back and put a cap on it. I almost smile at the fact that I've made him so angry. It feels good in a way. I can still reach him. All of a sudden, I can't take my eyes off him.

"I'm here on business," Jack tells Gary seriously. "I may have a distributor for my beer here. An opportunity of a lifetime. And I'm looking for a place."

The *looking for a place* comment throws me off. What, exactly, does that mean?

"I sold my condo in Boston," he answers the question on our faces. Well, on Gary's and Nick's faces. He won't look at me. "I've always wanted a place in New York."

"I thought you live in Maine," I say.

He looks down. Better to look at the floor than at me.

"He lives in Boston five months out of the year," Nick answers for him. "But I guess that will change once you find a place in New York."

Jack nods, smiling at Nick.

"Well," Gary says tightly. "If you came here to shock us, you certainly did."

"I didn't come here to shock you," Jack says coldly.

"So," Nick says after a moment. "Are we going?"

I walk them to the door, try to catch Jack's eye again, but he's good at avoiding looking at me.

Gary hesitates, then thinks better of trying to say something witty about Jack behind his back. A good idea, since Jack's back is less than a foot away. Instead, Gary says he's going to stay at Nick's tonight and he'll call me tomorrow.

I close the door, lean my head against it.

Jack's moving to New York City.

Seems appropriate, I guess. He always liked it here.

For a minute, I think I know why he came here tonight. To throw his great life in my face. At the same time, I know that isn't his style. And I can't imagine I rate that high on his people-to-show-off-to list.

Yet here I go thinking about what we had and what we didn't have. Here I go wondering if we'd still have it if I hadn't left him. Here I go asking myself, stupidly, whether I should make an effort to see him again.

He was not the first boy I loved. I loved Isaac from *Love Boat*, Billy Idol and my biology teacher in tenth grade.

Boys I didn't have a shot with.

He was the first tangible boy, a quasi-loner who loitered in front of the library and smoked illegal "cigarettes." He had four friends, of whom he appeared to be the leader. The two girls were toothpick-skinny and a little odd. The white girl had a limp and encircled her eyes with thick black chalk so they were sunken and hauntingly dull; her hair was gelled into razor sharp points, covering most of her face. The other girl wore her hair in a massive, curly Afro entwined with pink ribbon. Her lips were painted deep purple, and her eyes were never without her trademark blue-tinted shades.

The boys mainly wore ripped jeans, leather jackets and black combat boots. Their bodies covered in tattoos. Jack's tattoo was on the back of his neck. Black ink against brown skin. It was an intricate design of interlocking triangles and circles. Later he explained—in that typical angst-filled-college-boy-way he had perfected—that it was supposed to be the mechanisms working inside his head, that he'd been drunk when he'd had it done and that it was fake.

The first time I spoke to him was at a party in Puffton Village. Jack was in the den with a girl, a blond girl I'd seen waiting for him after class. He was leaning against a wall, looking bored and tense, looking at his cigarette. His leather jacket was sprawled out on the floor next to them. The girl was hissing at him, angry, crying in fits. He glanced at me and nodded.

"Hey," he said and I thought he kind of smiled. Jack had never smiled at me before, even though we'd had three classes together. I took the smile as a sign that maybe he wanted to know me better.

We'd been to a lot of the same parties. He was always leaning against some wall or refrigerator being silent and cool. I'd caught him watching me a couple of times, and I was sure he'd noticed me watching him back.

There was also the swim meet I'd won. He'd been there, watching me again. There was the time we had Physical Anthropology together. Our professor suggested Jack call me and set up a study session. Jack seemed alarmed when I said I would love to meet him for lunch before our next exam. I wrote my number on the back of his hand and noticed he was trembling. He never called, but I knew he wanted to.

In the den I watched the girl say something else to him, something I couldn't understand. Then she stormed away and I looked at him. Jack was the guy who walked into class late, eyes red from lack of sleep, always a day's growth of beard. His clothes were always tattered and dirty from some impromptu Frisbee or soccer game on the field. He drove his father's shit-brown Beetle and skateboarded through the halls. I was attracted to him.

"Aren't you supposed to go after her?" I asked.

He didn't say anything as he took a drag from his cigarette. Just stared. I noticed his jaw tense, then relax again.

"Is that what I'm supposed to do?" he said after a minute.

I shrugged. "It helps when you decide you can't live without her."

He laughed.

"Can I touch it?" I asked.

He swallowed hard, his eyes moving down my face to my lips, to my breasts, and back to my eyes again. "Touch what?" he said, sounding bored.

I moved closer and touched the tattoo on his neck, only glancing at it briefly. I smiled at the slight part between his lips.

"Pretty," I said.

His face darkened. He pulled away from me and took another drag from his cigarette.

"What'd I say?" I asked, confused.

He looked at me. "What do you want from me?"

"Nothing," I said softly. "Maybe. Friendship."

He narrowed his eyes as if he was suspicious. I waited for him to say something else.

"Ken, right?" he finally said.

"Kendall," I corrected.

He smiled. Perfect. Genuine. Sexy. And then he asked if I was enjoying my stay at UMass. I thought it was a funny way to put it.

"Ask me next year," I told him.

"Why next year?"

"If I'm not here, you'll know I didn't enjoy it."

After that, he would say, "It's Ken," every time he saw me.

Thwack!

My eyes pop open in the middle of the night. I think I was dreaming about Jack, but the dream is completely obliterated by this *thwack*ing. I cover my head with my pillow, and the sound is muffled only slightly.

Moving in.

Furniture is being moved across the floor above my bedroom. The *moving-in* will be over once they've moved in, I think as I drift back to sleep.

I'm up again at five. More *moving-in,* and it has me up and wrecked and smoking cigarettes in the bathroom. I sit on the cold, hard floor and wait it out. The bathroom is the only place I can't hear them.

Then I'm up again. This time the culprit is a sharp pain ripping through my jaw. It's just me dozing, my head hitting the rim of the toilet. I stick my head out of the bathroom and realize the noise has stopped.

I throw all my cigarette butts out in the garbage and go back to sleep.

Two hours later, the telephone rings.

"How was your date?" Gary asks.

I yawn and stretch and sit up in bed. I can hear him smoking a cigarette, and I imagine he's leaning against the cash register in Sam's looking as casual as all hell, staring out the window at all of the people who are free.

"Breakfast shift?" I say.

"I hate breakfast. Everyone's so mean on their way to work."

"Everyone's just mean," I say. "I couldn't afford dinner."

"I figured that. You didn't have to lie. I would have loaned you the cash."

"Didn't want to go. Not really."

After a moment he says, "It wasn't too bad."

"No," I agree. "It wasn't."

"He looks good. I liked him better with contacts."

I have this flash of a memory. It's the very first time Gary and Nick are meeting Jack. They ask him about his major, and when he says he's thinking about changing majors again they ask how many times he's changed it already. And Jack's slouched back in his chair, eyeing my friends, looking slightly amused, not answering.

"You never liked him," I say.

A long pause on the other end. And then, "I meant he *looked better* without glasses."

I hear a customer ask for a large decaf with extra skim milk and four sugars. When Gary returns to the phone he says, "You're not curious about dinner?"

"No."

I am curious about dinner. I don't want to admit it.

"Okay," Gary says, but the silence is heavy between us and I know he won't let it go at that. He rings up another coffee. "She asked about you."

"Can you not . . . can you not call him *she?*"

"Okay, *he*. Him. His."

"Thank you."

"*His* very bad attempt at getting info out of me failed. He tried to be all nonchalant about it, and at first I pretended I couldn't tell he was interested. Then I told him to ask you whatever he needed to ask you. And then I told him, on second thought, not to ask you anything. To leave you alone. I'm looking out for you, darling. He'll never bother you again."

Maybe it's the lack of sleep or, subconsciously, the dream. Whatever it is, Gary's comment rubs me the wrong way. "Don't look out for me," I say.

He's silent.

I continue, "Don't speak for me. Don't give me advice. Don't tell me what to do. Don't tell me what you think I should do. Don't have a talk with Nick and Amy and decide what you all think I should do. Don't rule me."

Silence, still.

"Okay?" I say.

"Sweetie, relax," Gary advises, miffed. "I was not trying to tell you what to do. So take it down a notch."

I nod, even though I know he can't see me. "Gary," I say. "I'm sorry. I didn't mean to snap."

"No problem, baby," Gary says lightly. "You didn't hurt me. I think this man has got you all tied up in knots."

"Not really."

"Seriously," he says.

"I've hardly considered him since he left last night."

"I believe you," he says in a tone that makes it clear he doesn't. "He said you look different. Too thin. Tired. He said it in a way that made it clear he hasn't forgiven you."

"Really." I try to sound casual.

"Not in a bad way, though. Maybe like he'd give you a shot at friendship."

I think about that. Friendship. And I wonder if it would make more sense to just avoid him. "It doesn't matter," I say.

"No," Gary agrees, softening. "It doesn't."

We're quiet.

"Ken . . . ," he says.

"What?"

"You ever . . . you ever regret leaving him?"

"Nah," I say.

"Good girl. You shouldn't."

"Just once, maybe," I revise.

Gary hesitates. "Okay. Once isn't so bad."

"No. Not so bad."

"He didn't brag as much as I expected him to."

"Maybe he's saving it," I say.

"For you?"

"Yeah."

Gary sucks his teeth. "Believe it or not, that's exactly what I was thinking."

I chuckle.

"What if you run into him?" Gary asks. "Like on the elevator."

"I don't get out of the office much," I say.

"What if . . . would you get into trouble if you went to his room? Could you hang out with him after work, I mean? Like if we all stopped by one night?"

"Why in the hell would we do that?"

"He invited us."

"I wouldn't get into trouble because I wouldn't go."

"Yeah," Gary says quietly. "That would be weird. Hanging out in his hotel room. Considering . . ."

"Considering?"

"Considering he was once no-direction guy and now he's Mr. Direction with a purpose. Even though it's beer."

So, you're dating no-direction guy? Amy asked after that first lunch with him.

"Leave it to Jack to make money making beer," Gary continues now. "Bitch."

I smile at the phone.

Someone calls out Gary's name in the background, and he says he has to go.

"Gary," I say before he hangs up. "Don't talk about me too much the next time you're with him. Okay? Don't tell him what I've been up to."

"Okay," Gary promises before he hangs up.

"The hotel is a mini universe . . ."

Go to hell.

". . . and our guests will realize they like this universe better than the real one . . ."

Screw you.

". . . as long as you get your job right. You are the first person they talk to when they contact this universe. You are their introduction into our world. You are the reason why they return, and the reason why their friends and family give us a chance . . ."

"Kirk," Wanda interrupts my supervisor's long-winded tirade, "I have Security on the line for you. That psycho bitch in room 502 pulled all of the phone cords out of the sockets and cut them up. She won't let anyone into the room."

I grin at Kirk, and his face clouds with anger and frustration.

"Keep it clean," Kirk warns Wanda, then he points at me before he leaves the office. "I'm not finished with you."

The entire morning I've been passing all calls that come from the courtesy phones in the hotel restaurant, bar and lobby. All calls that don't have an identifying name attached to them. I don't think Jack is sitting in the hotel lobby dialing our office just so he can hear me say, "Hotel operator Kendall. How may I direct your call?"

Still, I don't want him to hear me say it.

Kirk's angry because I've been avoiding my duty as the perfect hotel operator, willing to accept all calls that display themselves on my console. I've told him there's a drunk guy in the bar who keeps calling me, and Kirk has told me all hotel guests deserve my attention.

Whatever.

I take the next call. It's a woman. For Jack. I nearly fall off my chair. I haven't had a call for Jack since he got here. I sit with the call for a second. Then I type in his room number. My finger hovers over the release button.

"Hello," Jack says.

The caller on the other end hangs up.

"Hello?" Jack repeats. "I can hear you breathing."

I realize he's hearing me breathing because I forgot to move my headset to mute. I disconnect the call. Immediately after, I get a call from operator number six.

"That guy checked in again today," Wanda says.

"Which guy?"

"The Texan. He checked out yesterday. He's back."

"You take any of his calls?" I ask.

She hesitates. I check the switchboard. Ten calls holding.

"I'll call you back," she says.

There's a sudden barrage of phone calls and Wanda doesn't have a chance to call me back. Ten minutes later, Trina walks over to the dry-erase board and adds some new instructions.

"The guest in room 1700 is requesting that all calls be screened until further notice," Trina announces.

I stare at Jack's name on the board.

"I got the Texan," Wanda shouts from the other side of the room.

We run past each other and switch seats.

"Hotel operator Kendall," I say breathlessly.

"Good afternoon, hotel operator Kendall." The Texan's voice oozes sexuality.

"Good afternoon, Mr. Smith."

"Well," he drawls. "You pronounce my name real well."

I'm about to say something inappropriately flirtatious when Kirk walks through the office and frowns at me.

"How may I direct your call, sir?" I say demurely.

"Let me have room 4802."

"Certainly, sir."

Kirk walks out again. I connect the Texan to room 4802, and this time I remember to switch my headset to mute. I watch the door cautiously to make sure Kirk doesn't come back in while I listen to the call.

The conversation isn't incredibly interesting; it isn't worth being fired for. But I stay on, listening to the guest in room 4802 stroke the Texan's ego, telling him how hot he's going to be once *Quest for Peace* is released. The last time I listened to a phone call between the Texan and a costar, it was the same bullshit. I get bored and disconnect the call.

"Is he *the one?*" Wanda asks as we switch seats again.

"There is no *one* for Kendall," Rodney, the only male operator in the department, says mischievously.

"How would you know?" I say, pinching Rodney's arm.

He shrieks and slaps at my hand.

"Seriously," I say. "Do me a favor?"

"Depends," Rodney says.

"Would you? . . ." I lower my voice. "This is between us."

He nods.

"Would you listen to the calls for 1700?"

Rodney types the room number into his computer, reads "Jack Sullivan." He looks up at me. "Who the hell is that?"

I shush him. "I think it's an alias for a soap actor I like."

Rodney grins. "You follow soaps? Which ones?"

"Which ones do you watch?"

"ABC," he says.

"I watch CBS," I lie.

"Why can't you listen?"

"I am," I say quickly. "But Kirk's been watching me and I haven't been able to listen properly when he's in the room."

Rodney nods slowly, giving me an odd look. I'm not about to tell him I know Jack, and I can't bring myself to listen to his calls personally. Somehow, it's not as terrible if someone else listens for me, and as long as that someone thinks he's listening to a television actor, it's not really a betrayal. To be sure he'll do it, I add, "I think he's gay."

An eyebrow shoots up. "Really?" Interest.

I nod, wink.

Rodney writes the room number down on a Post-it and puts it on his monitor. I sit at my cubicle just as Kirk comes back into the office.

Kirk says, "Weren't you sitting on the other side of the room a minute ago?"

"Uh, yeah," I say. "I couldn't figure out this conference call thing, so Wanda took the call for me."

Kirk looks at Wanda, then back at me. He says, "Well, don't you think it's time you learn how to do the 'conference call thing'?"

I nod, and Kirk settles down at his desk.

The next name to come up on my monitor is *Sullivan, Jack.*
I recoil as though I've been bitten.

"What?" Kirk's staring at me.

I stare back. "Nothing."

We stare at each other a little longer.

"Then take a call," Kirk says.

I look at my switchboard. I'd love for this call to go away, to miraculously pass itself to another operator. But this won't happen. His name will continue to flash on my monitor until he hangs up or I pass the call. And I can't pass the call while Kirk's sitting here watching me. Not after this morning's lecture.

"Five calls," Kirk announces at me.

I take the call.

"Hotel operator Trina," I say quietly.

There's a slight hesitation. "Ken?"

I don't say anything. I'm thinking, *Shit.*

"Hello?" he says.

"Yeah. Jack?"

"You're going by Trina these days?" he asks.

"Um, yeah. Sometimes."

He chuckles. "When you get a guest you don't want to talk to. I'm hurt. Does my name come up on a screen or something?"

"No," I say, even though I'm sure he's well versed in the inside operations of a fancy hotel.

"I was hoping I'd get you," he says. "I just called a minute ago and requested—"

"Call-screening until further notice," I finish for him, glancing at Kirk. Kirk's whispering into his headset.

"Yeah." I hear a hint of a smile in his voice. "You know?"

"I have to know," I say.

"How does that work? You write it down?"

"We have a huge dry-erase board on the wall," I explain. "We check it every time a call comes in."

"Sounds like a lot of work."

"You'd think so."

He says, "I've been getting a lot of hang ups."

"Sorry," I say, reverting to Hotel Operator Kendall. "We can put a DND on your phone until you check out, if you like."

"A Do Not Disturb?" he says, reverting to Hotel Guest Jack. "No. I'm expecting some business calls."

"Right. Of course."

"Actually, I was wondering if I could take you to dinner . . ."

My eyes wander to the monitor. *Seven calls holding.*

". . . tonight. How late are you working?"

"Pretty late," I say abruptly.

"We can meet for a drink."

"I need to get up early," I say.

"How early?"

"Very early."

"Why are you fighting me on this?" he asks.

"I'm not . . ." I start to lie, and then I change my mind. "I don't want to spend an evening trading barbs with you."

He sighs. "Let's start over. We can meet for a drink and it can be like we're meeting for the first time. No yesterdays."

Why would I want to have a drink with you? I think. And why are you being so persistent?

"I wasn't lying when I said I have to work late and get up early," I tell him. "I didn't sleep well last night."

"Neither did I," he says significantly.

"I have new neighbors," I clarify. "They were moving in late."

"Okay." He sounds disappointed. "I'm meeting Nick and Gary this weekend. In Brooklyn. Maybe we can hook up then."

Again the *why* comes to mind.

"You know what? I have to go," I say. "The phones are crazy." I disconnect the call just as Kirk looks at the monitor.

"Thirteen calls!" he screams.

I take my break with Sage. We walk to a secluded block on Second Avenue, where he lights a joint. He tells me about a businessman who checked in with a hooker.

"Two minutes before I go for my break this guy's wife shows. I tell her that she can't go up because she isn't registered. Then I call him, but he doesn't answer. And I know he's up there with this whore, so I'm thinking he's probably having the best sex of his life. I'm thinking this while I'm staring at his wife, smiling at her. And she's giving me these meek smiles. So I tell her to go to the bar and have a drink, courtesy of Front Desk. But you know I'm going to bill this motherfucker for it. I leave him a message saying he has a guest and she's waiting for him in the bar. He calls back five seconds later to say he'll be down in fifteen minutes. So, I call the bar and tell them to send her the best seventeen-dollar chocolate martini she has ever had. And a fucking lobster roll."

I laugh. "Good for you."

"When I left, I waved at her with a big smile on my face. Poor woman."

Most of the time I'm impressed by how blasé Front Desk agents are about incidents like this. When Kirk has a day off, our office is like lunch hour at an OTB. Operators screaming out updates about who's shagging who in their hotel rooms, laughing giddily at all the exciting news. Front Desk agents are trained not to bat an eye when a man's wife or girlfriend walks into the lobby unexpectedly while he's in his room with a paid escort. It's just another day at the races for them.

The thing that gets me about situations like that is just how long the wives are willing to wait before they get permission to go to their husbands' rooms. And they always wait, smiling pathetically at Sage, accepting seventeen-dollar chocolate martinis and thirty-five-dollar lobster rolls just before they start to cry.

I find it all very depressing. Because some part of me is still a romantic.

"If you get a chance," Sage says, "check out his calls. I want to know what happens."

I'm tempted to ask him about Jack. I'm sure Jack and Sage have met, though Sage is usually too busy to take a good look at any guest who isn't a celebrity. I want to know what kind of guest Jack is. Does he tip well? Does he tip at all? Does he order room service in the middle of the night? Does he get angry at Housekeeping if they forget turndown service? Does he request extra complimentary candy?

Sage would probably know.

"You want to hang out this weekend?" he says before I can work up the nerve to ask him about Jack. He passes the joint to me. "I'll come out to Brooklyn."

When Sage comes to Brooklyn during the week, we lie in bed and watch television. He's a television junkie. He can get me hooked on any nonsense I would never watch if I weren't with him. Whenever I try to watch the same show without him, it just doesn't seem the same. And while I wouldn't mind losing myself in television this weekend, my mind conjures up this image of Nick dropping by the apartment with Jack again.

"I'd like to meet your friends," he says when I don't answer.

"Why?"

"Because I've never met any of them."

"And why would you want to?" I ask.

He shrugs. "I guess I thought it'd be nice to meet the other people you like."

"It might be nicer to stay at the hotel this weekend."

Sage smiles distractedly, then rubs a hand over his head a few times. Sometimes he can finagle a room. It's pretty tough, because the hotel is usually full. Reservations and Front Desk managers try to keep empty rooms a secret so they can take turns impressing their friends.

After a minute he says, "Gonna be tough. But I'll see what I can do."

When I come back from break, Rodney calls me over to his cubicle. "I don't think 1700 is your soap actor," he tells me. "He keeps getting business calls. Not entertainment-related calls."

"Okay," I say. "Thanks."

"And he might be gay. I'm not sure yet."

I smile. "Really?"

"Well, he's not accepting calls from a girl. She wouldn't give me her name."

"You told him?"

"No. She hung up when I asked who was calling. Maybe he's in the closet?"

"Maybe."

"You want me to keep listening?"

It feels kind of trashy, spying on Jack after so many years. But.

"Would you?" I say. "I'll keep my ears open as well."

The apartment is quiet when I come home. I stand in the middle of my bedroom, undress in the dark and silence, and drop my clothes on the floor. I put on my pajamas, lie in bed and stare up at the ceiling. I push away all thoughts of Jack in

New York, in the hotel, and the mystery woman trying to reach him.

Instead, I think about what Sage said.

He wants to meet my friends. All of a sudden, he wants to meet my friends. It negates the entire purpose of a torrid affair. Not that what we have is torrid. Or an affair, really.

And it's not that I don't want Sage to know Gary and Nick and Amy. I just want to keep them separate. Because there's some part of me that knows Gary, Nick and Amy will have an opinion about him. The way they had an opinion about Jack. The way they treated Jack like he was *less than* and eventually convinced me that he was.

Maybe if Jack weren't here, it wouldn't matter so much. I wouldn't have this fear that I'm still weak, still corrigible. I wouldn't have this fear that what my friends think of my choices would still make a difference.

But Jack is here. And I'm remembering things I don't want to remember. Feeling things I haven't felt in a long time. Worrying that he still thinks I'm disloyal for going against my true feelings about him and breaking it off because my friends said I should.

Does he still hate me? If he does, why is he here and why does he keep hounding me? That's all I keep wondering when I know I'm not supposed to be wondering about him at all.

On Thursday, the guest in room 1700 requests a Do Not Disturb until further notice. On Friday, the DND remains, and we do not hear a peep from him. No one in the office cares, including me.

And then.

I find myself making up calls to learn whether or not anyone in the office knows something new. I say, "I have this call for 1700. Anyone hear from him? Does he still want the DND?"

"Isn't that what it says on the board," Maria points out.

"Who's in 1700?" Wanda asks.

"Nobody special," Trina tells her.

No help.

And then.

I call Gary at work.

"Anyone hear from Jack?" I ask.

"I think Nick spoke to him. Why?"

I stutter. "He has this DND on his phone. Do Not Disturb. And it's almost like he doesn't exist. Just curious . . ."

"Nick said he's meeting with distributors this week," Gary informs me. "And in that very Jack way that hasn't changed, he's in a zone. We probably won't hear from him for a few more days."

I remember Jack's zone. It was the world he entered when he set a goal he wanted to reach. No one was allowed in. In college, it was All. About. The. Rowing. As much of a slacker as he was, when it came to rowing he was intensely motivated, and very impressive.

He was a sweep rower, which I thought was more difficult than sculling and wondered, vaguely, why he bothered. He and his partner would wake up at five in the morning and make it down to the boathouse in Northhampton by five-thirty. They liked to race and would drive as far as Colorado to compete in an eight-minute Standard. I was horrified that Jack would miss a week of classes for a Standard Race. What was the point? And he would laugh when I questioned him about it. He'd say, "Life's short, Ken. Take advantage of it. Why are you just sitting here?"

God, I hated when he used to say that.

Anyway, zone times meant Jack was unavailable. He wouldn't answer his phone, and he would never return calls.

"Worried?" Gary asks now.

"No," I say. "Just . . . curious."

"Right," Gary says. "Curious."

"Okay, we can change the subject now."

"Fine." Gary laughs. "How are our neighbors?"

Not the subject I would have picked, but Gary hasn't been home since Tuesday night. Ironically, the apartment has been peaceful and quiet.

"Gone," I say. "Maybe they were a figment of our imagination."

"Someone is definitely punishing me," Gary moans. "Nick's neighbors are adding a garage. I've been writing to the sound of power drills and hammering. I wasn't sure if that was worse than a hyperactive kid and furniture being dragged across the floor in the middle of the night."

"That's a shame. The apartment's been empty."

"Weird. I wonder what's up with them."

"They're not the only people I wonder about," I say.

"Why don't you call him?" Gary asks.

"Who?"

"Jack. If you're worried."

"Not worried. Concerned."

"Same thing," Gary says.

"Not really."

"Let's not play semantics. Why don't you just call his room and make sure he's okay."

"DND. Can't break it."

"It's *us*," Gary insists. "It's *Jack*. What's he gonna do? Get you fired?"

"You never know," I say. "Why don't you try his cell phone?"

"I don't have his cell phone number. And I'm not the one who's worried, sweetheart."

"Concerned."

"You know what? Whatever. I have to go."

Operators are supposed to alert Security if a guest hasn't removed a DND after three days. In my experience, a three-day DND means the guest is dead, drunk, drugged or has skipped out on the bill. If I call Security now, even though it's only been two days, someone will go up and knock on Jack's door. If he's okay, and cranky, and demands to know who contacted Security, it could bite me in the ass. I don't want Jack to know I'm keeping an eye out for him. Not now. Not yet.

The thing is, you never know what a guest is thinking, or what a guest is into. I've heard some seriously demented shit on these phones. I'm not concerned that Jack has had strange packages delivered to his room that contain liquid nitrogen or ammonium nitrate. I'm not concerned that he's had strange visitors who may have murdered him in the middle of the night. Like one or two other guests I've encountered, he may have simply forgotten he requested the DND on Thursday.

But Jack isn't one-or-two-guests-I've-encountered. He's Jack. He was once my boyfriend. He's someone I really cared about. And that's why I'm so concerned.

My college adviser used to say that if she could have ten years ago back, she'd live her life differently. How ironic is it that nearly ten years later, as I find myself on the seventeenth floor of the hotel I work in, I agree? I don't even have to know what I know now. I just know I'd handle a lot of things differently.

For one thing, I wouldn't have had that last fight with Jack. Or, more specifically, I wouldn't have said some of the things I said. Because they were cruel and untrue and wrong.

And standing him up? Also wrong.

Standing Jack up was supposed to have been my way of saying I wanted to end it. Us. But he would call, and I would eventually meet him. And we would kiss. Hard. Passionate. Desperate. And there would be another week of us and the fighting and the head shaking from my friends. Even Amy— moments after Jack bought her a sandwich from the cafeteria because she was always broke—would remind me he was a bad choice for a boyfriend.

And I listened.

That's what got him in the end. That I always listened.

"You can think what you want about me," he'd say. "You can have this holier-than-thou attitude about me when you're with your friends. But if you pass a car accident, you're going to look."

And I'd smile at his analogy, which seemed like all kinds of crazy at the time. I never looked at car accidents when I passed them.

"When are you going to stop fucking with me?" he asked that last night we were together.

A month after I left him, Jack sent me a very brief letter.

Ken, I hope one day you'll realize how important you are. Not only to me. First step: Stop listening to the rest of the world and start listening to yourself. Love always, Jack

The other thing I would do if I could have ten years ago back is not take advice. Advice isn't something a person should accept lightly.

The red privacy light next to the doorknob is glowing brightly. I stare at it for a minute, comparing it to a car accident. Is it crazy to think you may still be in love with someone you broke it off with nine years ago?

I'd like to think I've changed. That I have new interests and attractions. That a guy from my past can't walk into my life again and make me wonder if I ever stopped loving him. But I'm about to knock on his hotel room door and break a DND, which proves that I have changed. I am different.

Because I used to be a goody-goody. I followed every rule, even the stupid ones, and cringed when someone I knew broke one. I break rules now, rules that *should* be broken, like the wrongness of the uniforms in my office, and this. This ridiculous caste system that makes me feel like I can't knock on my friend's door because he's a guest and I'm a hotel worker.

But.

The not breaking a DND rule makes sense to me. What's the

point of a DND if someone just knocks on your door after you've requested one? This is the rule that shouldn't be broken. But here's Jack being the reason I break it. Here's Jack being the reason I'm in this position I still don't like to be in. Flushed, excited, not IN CONTROL. These feelings. He shouldn't be able to make me feel this attracted to him and repelled by him at the same time. Not after all these years.

I knock. Once. Loud and aggressive.

I wait thirty seconds before I do it again, risking an outraged Jack calling Front Desk to say someone is knocking on his door who isn't supposed to.

Then I hear him laugh and say, "Right . . . right . . . of course . . . I'm looking forward to meeting you as well."

He hangs up the phone but doesn't come to the door. I think better of pressing my ear against it to hear what he's doing. I start to walk away. And then the door opens.

I stop, close my eyes, flush terribly.

When I turn around, Jack's leaning against the hallway wall, watching me. His face is expressionless, so I can't work out if he's enraged or amused or apathetic.

"I thought this thing, this red light thingy, meant *don't bug me*," he says finally. Not a hint of a smile or anything. "That's what they told me at Front Desk."

"It does," I say, leaning against the wall like him, keeping my distance.

"Then. Why bug me?" He moves forward, closing the distance. I think about stepping back. One step back would put a comfortable space between us.

"You've had a DND for two days," I point out.

"Yes." Slow. Drawn out. Slight nod of the head. "For a reason."

I suddenly feel apologetic. "I'm making sure everything's okay."

Now there's the cocky grin I both love and hate. "I didn't know hotel operators made house calls."

"This isn't your house," I remind him. "It's a hotel. A guest with a two-day DND is a pain in the ass. I know you. So I wanted to let you in on that."

He shakes his head, laughs a little. "Women."

"What about women?"

"I call. You hang up on me. Now you break my DND. Can you say fickle?" He moves closer, as though there's any room to spare.

"Oh, please." I roll my eyes. "I came to check up on you. To make sure you're not dead."

His tongue darts out of his mouth briefly with a different grin. This one kind of wicked. And this is the feeling I hate. The feeling I had whenever I was around him.

Panic.

I know I should pull back, possibly walk away. Anyone can show up and catch us now. Guests, Housekeeping, Room Service, Security. I don't know how I'd explain being here to Kirk.

"Did you get permission?" he asks as though he knows what I'm thinking.

"I don't need permission to check on you."

"I meant from your friends," he clarifies. "They'd have a conniption if they knew. You coming up to my room to check on me."

"My friends don't dictate what I do."

He cocks a brow. "Why don't I believe that?"

"Because you're lost in the past?"

"No." He touches my cheek lightly, surprising me. Despite my instant urge to jump, I remain still. "People like you don't change so easily."

"Not about change," I say, feeling an annoyance build. "I grew out of it."

"Grew out of what?" he asks huskily.

"Grew out of whatever you're accusing me of being."

He laughs. "You don't grow out of being . . . too convincible."

I pull back a little. "I'd call that a radical interpretation of the text."

"If not too convincible?"

When someone presented a case, I listened and weighed my options. My friends presented their case about Jack every day. Not directly. But with subtle jabs and comments. The truth is, I *was* pretty convincible. But I was also scared. Of my feelings. I feared how strongly I felt about Jack. I don't blame Gary, Nick or Amy for the problems their issues with Jack eventually stirred up between us. I'm past all that nonsense. The bitterness. The anger. The regret. I can't blame them for the choice I made. I know I made it. And now, even though I'm not sure how honest I should be with Jack, I decide to be as honest as I can. He deserves it.

"I was scared," I admit.

His fingers stop caressing my face. "I've been waiting years to hear you say that."

I swallow hard. "Have you?"

"No. Not really." He moves away, distracted by the sound of a cell phone ringing in his room. I remember that he can be cruel. "You want to come in while I answer that?"

I've just done the whole honesty thing with you.

I shake my head. "No. I'm on break."

He opens his door. "Come in. For a second."

This is wrong. I know it's wrong. I'm on a fifteen-minute break and I'm on a guest floor without permission. Kirk would not be happy if he found me here. And Katie is probably downstairs, calling attention to the fact that I'm late and she's hungry, and I can't begin to work out what excuse I'm going to make up. And didn't he just insult me?

"Ken. Come on. I have to answer it."

I step inside. I didn't realize 1700 is a Deluxe Suite. The room is bigger than my apartment. Jack must be spending more to be here than I make in a month.

"Nice digs."

Jack smiles as he goes for the cell phone lying on his bed. I move into the living room area to give him privacy.

His briefcase sits open atop the desk near the balcony. I stare at it, tempted to look inside. But I hear him finish the call abruptly, so I stare out of the floor-to-ceiling windows instead. Nice view of the city.

"You want a drink?" he asks, coming from behind the huge armoire that separates the bedroom area from the living room area.

"Sure. I'll just go back to work intoxicated," I say, as though I don't get high when I take my breaks with Sage.

Jack opens the mini bar, pulls out a trial-size bottle of Chivas, and pours the alcohol into a glass. I didn't think anyone actually drank the alcohol from the rip-off that is the hotel mini bar. I stop myself from asking how much that just cost him.

He drinks, watches me.

"What are you thinking?" he asks.

"I'm thinking, Gee, this guy sure does drink a lot of everything that isn't beer."

He grins. "I can't drink someone else's beer anymore."

"Why not?"

"I don't enjoy it." He shrugs. "It's like being an aspiring film-maker and going to see a shitty blockbuster movie with your friends. You waste your time wondering why your movie isn't being offered at every bar in the country, or sitting in some five-star hotel's mini bar."

Off the look on my face he adds, "I'm not saying my beers aren't shit. I happen to think they aren't, but I drink something like this"—he opens the mini bar and points out the generic beers on offer—"and I start obsessing over what makes *that* beer the beer of choice. Didn't the world get the hint of cardamom I added to the Solstice? You know?"

"No. But you can't go by me. I don't like cardamom."

He laughs, gives me a playful sneer.

"Obviously someone important likes it," I say seriously. "Because you're here."

He's quiet for a long time. I look at him, feel flustered that he's still watching me closely.

"So are you," he says softly.

That feeling of panic makes an appearance again. I look out of his window, completely aware that he's advancing on me.

"Speaking of being here. I should get back to work." I slide away from him and head for the door.

"Still excellent at the quick exit," he calls after me, a hint of bitterness in his voice.

And my temper flares that easily. I open the door, planning to slam it very hard after I walk out, but I end up slamming it and staying inside.

"One of us works here," I remind him hotly. "And she wasted her entire break checking up on you. Without a thank you."

He sets his glass on an end table, and our eyes lock. My throat constricts. My temper subsides, and I regret not slamming the door while I was on the other side.

"Your entire break?" he asks.

My eyes move to the alarm clock next to his bed, then back to his face. "And then some."

I don't move as he comes in for what I think is going to be a kiss. I'm wrong. He doesn't try to kiss me. His lips tickle my ear when he speaks. He says, "What if I offer to make it up to you?"

I take a slow, careful breath and realize I'm trembling.

"You can call Kirk and tell him you needed help with a phone or something." My voice cracks a little and I want to kick myself.

"Or something?" He brushes his lips against my ear. My body reacts immediately. I feel betrayed by it. I can hear him grin. "Who's Kirk?"

I'm rocketed back to reality upon hearing Kirk's name come out of Jack's mouth.

"My boss," I answer, one hand on the door, opening it, heading out. "Sorry to run out on you, Jack."

Kirk doesn't look up from his desk when I rush into the office. I slow down and try to look innocent. Katie isn't at her cubicle.

"Mr. Sullivan called and explained what happened," Kirk announces as I take my seat.

I stare at him, flabbergasted. "Huh?"

"He was very apologetic." Kirk is watching me now, pointedly.

"Er . . ."

"Because you made it known you were on your break," Kirk continues. "Which you should never do again."

"He asked," I mutter.

"You can add the extra fifteen minutes to your lunch on Monday."

In the cubicle next to mine, Rodney starts to hum.

"FYI," Kirk goes on as he packs his briefcase and puts on his blazer. "Mr. Sullivan has requested his DND be removed and would prefer all calls to be screened until further notice."

Jack's name is scrawled on the board next to three celebrities'.

"Is he the guy you were looking for?" Rodney leans over once Kirk is gone.

It takes me a minute to figure out what the hell he's talking about. Right. The soap opera actor. "No."

"Hmpf." Rodney shakes his head. "He had you up in that room for aeons."

As I take the stairs two at a time I smell cat. I stop for a second, sniff. Cats aren't allowed in the building, but I'm pretty sure that smell is a cat smell. It's definitely not human.

I meet my new neighbor on the second-floor landing. She looks disheveled. Her long black hair is stringy and wet. She holds a glass of orange juice in one hand and a sloppy briefcase, overflowing with papers, in the other.

"Oh," she says.

"How's it going?" I ask.

"How's what going?"

The question catches me off guard for a second. "Uh . . . the moving?"

"Fine," she answers curtly.

"Because I heard you," I say. "Moving in. Yeah. The other night. Maybe it was morning."

She just stares.

"Okay," I say. "Well. If you need any help . . ."

"I'm Betty Blacksmith. President of the co-op board. I own the duplex above you."

I nod. "Welcome."

"You are?"

"Kendall."

She doesn't blink.

"Stark," I add. "Four. D." Why am I babbling?

She scrutinizes me with those cold, dark eyes. I almost shiver.

"Okay," I say. "See you."

She doesn't move. I feel her eyes on my back as I head up the stairs. When I reach the fourth floor, the urine smell is stronger, assaulting my nose as I stop at the sight of an orange-and-white cat lounging in front of my door. It rises to its feet and lets out a piercing yowl.

"Is that you I smell?" I ask it.

It stares at me. The stare is familiar.

"Betty," I call out, but the sound of the building's front door slamming shut alerts me she's gone. I turn back to the cat. "Did you just piss in front of my door?"

The cat stretches.

"You know," I say, "you aren't supposed to be here. We have a rule about cats and dogs."

The cat doesn't care. I guess the new president of the co-op board is above the rules. I bend down and look at the name on its tag. *Hercules*. Belongs to Blacksmith and Robinson. The cat slaps at me. Its sharp claws graze the back of my hand, nearly drawing blood. I pull back, yelp, stick my tongue out at the evil creature as I stand.

When I open my door, Hercules makes a dash for an entrance. I close it on him. I do not love cats. But I have this feeling I'm about to be tortured by one.

Despite being totally against working weekends, I come in for the Saturday afternoon shift at Kirk's request. Kirk has called me at home before, but I've never picked up. I'm usually sleeping, not to mention late for work. Hence, the phone calls in the first place. This morning, I was awake, banging on my bedroom ceiling with a broom.

The neighbors were restless.

I come in to work because it doesn't hurt to get on Kirk's good side once in a while, and I'm curious if Jack will make an appearance on my monitor. It's almost been twenty-four hours since I ran off on him.

After three hours of total boredom—weekends at the hotel are less than eventful, which is why I avoid them—I haven't heard from Jack, and he hasn't received any outside phone calls. I wait for Nadja to finish her personal call, and then I call him. The phone rings four times before going to voice mail.

"Parker Firestein has entered the building," Trina announces, then gets up to write it on the board.

Damn. I type his name into my monitor. Parker Firestein. Early check-in. Air-conditioning in every room on HI. Windows open. Frozen Water. Chilled Strawberries.

A faux pas on my part is guaranteed whenever Parker Firestein enters the building. I am the reason Trina stomps up to the board and writes, in loud block letters: PARKER FIRESTEIN—ROOM 4600—WILL BE STAYING WITH US FOR 3 DAYS!!! PRONOUNCE HIS NAME MISTER FIRE—STINE. PLEASE. HE HAS A VERY BAD TEMPER.

I tend to call him Mister Fire*steen* when he stays here.

Of course, as soon as Trina goes back to her seat I hear, "Hell! I am not dealing with him now. I have my period."

She passes the call to me. Bitch.

I answer the call cheerily, "Good afternoon Mister Firestee . . . iiine."

Complete silence.

"Sir. I'm very sorry." And I sound it. Very sorry.

"You might as well call me anything," he says in a voice so tight I'm almost relieved. I'm not the first person to mispronounce his name today. "Anyway. There are much more devastating things going on in the world than the mispronunciation of my name."

It would be wrong of me to mention I'm happy he's cognizant of that fact.

"The troubles in Afghanistan, Iraq, India, Pakistan . . ." he checks off lightly. "North Korea, Jersey . . ."

Jersey? "Sir. Mister Firestein. How may I help you?"

"DND." All business. "Starting now. UFN."

WTF?

"UFN, Mister Firestein?"

He chuckles. "Until. Further. Notice. Store that in the compartment of your brain you store very important information."

"Certainly sir," I seethe.

Later, there's a massage debacle. Who would believe in today's world, with the troubles in Afghanistan, Iraq, India, Pakistan, North Korea and Jersey, there could really be a massage debacle?

Mrs. Firestein calls three hours after Mr. Firestein's arrival. I check the board to confirm the original DND request has not been amended. It hasn't. Mrs. Firestein, a little confused, repeats, very slowly, just in case I'm a complete idiot, that she is Mr. Firestein's wife of twenty years.

I reiterate, very slowly, in complete control, that I cannot break a DND without permission. I brace myself for a tirade. But Mrs. Firestein simply thanks me and hangs up.

Twenty minutes later, Jake, the weekend Front Desk Manager, comes into the office and asks who took the Fire*steen* call. The son of a bitch will get us all horsewhipped if he continues to pronounce that name incorrectly.

"Mrs. Fire*stine?*" I say. "And that would be me."

"Mr. Fire*steen* wants to talk to you," Jake informs me ominously. "Be very nice."

I give Jake a questioning look that says, *Please elaborate.* He ignores me, types something into Kirk's console, then passes the call. I flash him a new look that says, *You and me. Outside after this.*

"Hotel operator Kendall."

"Hi Kendall." Sugary sweet Parker Firestein. "Did you tell my wife I had a DND on my phone a little while ago?"

"Yes, sir."

"May I ask why?"

"Didn't you request one?"

Never answer a guest's question with a question. It's considered presumptuous.

"You tell me," he says. The sugar is gone.

"Well, sir." I look at the board for backup. "You requested a DND UFN when you checked in."

"Is that so?"

"Well, when you entered your room. I assume. I took the call. I informed the office of your request immediately after you made it. When Mrs. Firestein called—"

"Fire-*STINE*."

"Yes, sorry, sir. When Mrs. Fire*stine* called I checked the board. There had been no change."

He's quiet, clearly trying to work out an angle to make this my fault, not his. I've been here before.

"I was having a massage," he tells me.

"Wonderful sir. I hope you enjoyed it."

"Yes, very much." He sounds pleased that I've inquired. "Isn't it a given that, if Mrs. Firestein calls, she should automatically be put through to my room?"

I take a deep, inaudible breath. I can see Jake making hand motions at me, but I ignore him. I must have some reputation in this hotel.

"I'm very sorry, Mr. Firestein. Unfortunately, sir, I am not authorized to break a DND for anyone. If you specify, during your request, or anytime afterward, that there is a specific person, or persons, you would like to accept calls from, I'm able to make those exceptions. Otherwise, I cannot."

"She's my *wife*."

"I understand, sir."

Parker Firestein laughs for a full minute. It would be rude to hang up on him. I am required to listen. So I shoot daggers at Jake, who is nodding his head maniacally (apparently, I've said all the right things), while I wait for the laughter to stop.

"Is there anything else I can do for you, sir?" I ask as soon as the laughter ceases.

"Why don't you let everyone know that in the future, when Mr. Firestein requests a DND, *Mrs.* Firestein's calls can be put through." His voice is ice. "I'll be sure to bring this up with Hans. Your General Manager."

He slams the phone down.

"Thank you, sir," I say out of habit.

I turn back to Jake and tell him—just as icily as Parker Firestein told me—all the new information Guest History can add to the man's guest history. Jake, clueless as all get-out, winks at me and takes off.

My day ends soon after. I walk out of the office—nineteen calls holding—and vow never to work another weekend again.

In Brooklyn I walk in the direction of Nick's house instead of my apartment. Sometimes I do this without thinking.

My first months in Park Slope found me starving for affection and company, especially at night. I wasn't used to being alone. In college, I'd always had roommates. And then I moved back in with my parents. Living on my own was no longer the exciting concept it had been when I was seventeen. It was disconcerting.

When Gary's roommate left New York to get married, I jumped at the chance to live with him. Living with one of my best friends from college seemed like a natural and safe progression from living with my parents. But living with Gary is kind of like living alone. He's rarely around.

In the beginning, when my parents asked how things were going, I wanted to be able to say everything was terrific, that moving out and becoming completely independent wasn't as tragic as I had pegged it would be. But the apartment was always cold. And the fire escape right outside of my window gave me the creeps.

"I keep telling myself that in a few months I'm going to be okay," I admitted to my parents one evening. "If I keep leaving myself notes, I'll eventually remember to buy milk and toilet paper in the evenings. I'll ask Gary to patch the windows in the winter. And maybe I'll get those iron bars for my bedroom."

My parents said, "You can come back as often as you like. You know that."

Not what I needed to hear.

The fact is no bed I've ever slept in has been as comfortable as my bed at my parents' house. No room has felt as warm or safe. Nick's bed, the canopy in the guestroom, comes in a very close second. Which is why, for a while, I could be found there.

On very cold nights, or nights when work took more out of me than I could stand, I was guaranteed to find Gary and Nick and their friends nestled comfortably in front of Nick's fireplace, drinking brandy after a meal. I would walk in, and a chorus of "Hey Ken, grab a plate of something and join us," would rise up from everyone.

Being part of Nick's world, so different from the one he inhabited in college, yet so very much the same, became a Thing for me for a while. It was familiar, which is what I wanted. And it was new, which was attractive.

I couldn't have the big, expensive stuff that Nick's New World of Having Things consisted of, but I was fascinated. And I liked it. Despite Gary's nonchalance about all the things his boyfriend could afford, I knew he was fascinated too. Briefly, I understood the allure of him, and people like him. But like most things, it gets tired after a while.

Still, I find myself heading toward his house after my particularly nasty afternoon at work. It's that familiar comfort I'm seeking out.

Nick's brownstone is indistinguishable from the other brownstones on his block. He calls it a "work-in-progress" because he isn't sure what he wants to do with it. He would like to be different. Painting it purple or blue would tickle the hell out of all of us. At the same time, he has doubts about being a radical. He doesn't want to lose the clout he has gained with the block association. Breaking the unspoken rule about uniformity might just do that.

I like the tree in front of the house, a sagging maple. He'd had a statue here at first. Some sort of Michelangelo type thing, which hadn't gone down well with the homeowners who had kids. An erect dick is not what the tykes should be waving good morning to on their way to school every day.

Now there's the tree, which I like. I would have preferred Nick's keeping the statue though. Just so someone in this world of haughty homeowners with children wouldn't cave in to peer pressure.

The front door is open. This doesn't surprise me. All of the places Nick has lived have always had the same vibe over the years. *Come in. We're open.*

I hear laughter when I walk inside.

He's here.

Why didn't I think he would be? He hasn't been in his room all day. The most logical place for him to be would be here. And that's the thing. This is the least logical place for Jack to be. Because he didn't like Nick in college. And Nick didn't like him. Does having money change things so drastically? If not, why is he here?

I stop in the hall, a little anxious.

Jack and I were together for a year and a half. Sometimes, it felt longer. At first our relationship had been all about the sex, and that had been fine with me. Sex with Jack was gorgeous and reckless and risky. But after three months, Jack became something more to me and I became something more to him. We craved a deeper intimacy.

Amy complained that the world around me disappeared when Jack entered a room. No one else—nothing else—mattered. She was right. Jack was all there was. I hated and loved that feeling at the same time. And I couldn't get a handle on it.

It's funny how some things don't change as much as they should. That same feeling hits me when I enter the kitchen. Like it's just Jack and me in this world, and nothing else matters.

He's leaning against the sink, a beer in his hand. He stops laughing the second he sees me. I wave awkwardly and his smile fades.

He says, "I'm going back outside," and Nick turns to look at me.

I watch Jack open the screen door and slip through it. I wonder if he's angry with me about something. Then I scold myself for wondering such a stupid thing.

"I thought you were working tonight," Nick says, kissing the air as we touch cheeks.

"I did."

"Beer?" he asks.

I take the bottle from his hand. It's sleek and narrow. I stare at the dark blue label wrapped around the bottle's dark brown body. The silver block lettering reads SULLIVAN BREW. BELGIAN WHITE. HAVE A TOTAL LIFE.

It gives me a start. *Have a total life.* That's something Jack used to tell me all the time. He was rebellious and idealistic and he believed having a total life was the one pure thing in the world. He'd say, "You're just going to sit there and play by the rules? Be young, Ken. Don't waste this. What's old age going to be like with you?"

"Sure," I say now, handing the bottle back to Nick as he rummages through his refrigerator.

"We have Belgian White, Stout and India Pale Ale. We also have Winter Solstice." Nick sticks his head back out to grin at me. "Jack says to save it for a special occasion, but—"

"Pale Ale's good," I tell him.

Jack, Gary and Amy are lounging in the backyard on the deck Nick and Gary built last summer. I had expected the house to be brimming with Nick's work-friends. Not seeing them here makes me sigh with relief.

Nick's work-friends are amiable and curious. But it's their amiability and curiosity that makes being around them so exhausting. It's their feeble, yet sincere, attempts to not sound condescending—*Do you still work at that . . . hotel, is it? And what do you do again?*—and the guards I have to put up to deflect judgment—*I answer phones and yes, I'm still loving it*—that make being around them so tiring.

A breeze drifts through the screen doors and I think it feels good right here, in this spot. Maybe I shouldn't go out there. I'll just watch them from Nick's kitchen and be safe. But Amy sees me and waves me over enthusiastically. Jack turns around and watches me join them.

"Hi, sweetie," Gary says as I kiss him on the cheek. He looks content, or he's just very good at hiding his anxiety. No reason to be anxious around Jack anymore. They've had their first couple of meetings. Maybe one or two nasty comments still hang between them, but they are experts at pretending the other doesn't exist.

Amy, I realize, is on her cell phone, twisting some of her long red hair around her finger and drinking her usual brown candy over ice. This is her way of avoiding Jack. Ignoring him completely. She motions for me to share the lawn chair with her without looking up. I won't ask about the trip to Los Angeles. If it had been successful, she'd still be there.

She looks away from the cell phone, covers the mouthpiece with her hand, leans into me conspiratorially and whispers, "*Jack,*" like I haven't discerned he's sitting two feet away from us.

"Thanks for pointing that out," I say tightly.

She nods, winks at me, and returns to her call.

"So." I turn to Jack and Gary. Both men are watching me.

"So," Gary mimics, glancing at Jack.

Jack's eyes remain steadily on me. I flush. Gary notices, smiles, settles into the chaise longue as though he's preparing to watch good television.

"You like the beer?" Gary asks.

I look at the bottle in my hand and realize I've been drinking it without properly tasting it. "Very much."

"The Pale Ale," Jack says. "That's a popular one."

We hold each other's gaze for a moment. My eyes drop to take in the name on the blue gas station jacket he's wearing.

Sully. His grandfather.

I look away quickly when I remember Sully passed away four months ago. As soon as he received Jack's e-mail, Nick told me Sully had succumbed to liver cancer. I liked Sully. He and Jack were close. After I left Jack, I never saw Sully again.

I meant to send a card.

"Jack's decided to move to Park Slope," Gary changes the subject in an airy tone of voice. "He's been filling us in on all the gory details of buying a house in the neighborhood."

"Anything we should know?" I ask, playing along.

"All I can say is we'd *better keep the rental.*" I can hear Gary's attempt to hold back his sarcasm and annoyance. Jack was probably bragging before I got here, and Nick was probably trying to outbrag him. Another one of my pet peeves when we're with Nick and his work-friends: the pissing contests.

"Any advice for a guy moving into your 'hood?" Jack asks me.

"Yeah, don't wear sandals," Gary advises. "There's shit every-where."

Jack laughs.

"He's not kidding," I warn. "All about the gentrification, but can't clean up after their dogs. Do you have a dog?"

Jack shakes his head.

"Adore kids," Nick adds, coming out with another bottle of Sullivan Brew for Gary. Gary sits up again and takes it, then makes room for Nick to share the chaise. "Like the shit, they're everywhere."

Jack frowns. "And that's not good?"

"Depends if they live above or below you," Gary tells him, giving me a knowing wink.

"You don't like kids then?" Jack asks.

"Not the kids," Nick says. "Not exactly. It's more the parents. The way they talk to the kids like they're short adults. So the kids act like adults and think they know everything."

Jack nods.

"Don't be honest," I say. "No matter how down-to-earth and confident a person appears to be in this neighborhood, he isn't down-to-earth and confident enough to handle the truth."

"You think that's exclusive to Park Slope?" Jack asks.

"No." I shrug. "Just thought I'd toss it in. A little life wisdom for you."

"You were always good with the life wisdoms," he says.

"You think?"

He grins. "Not really. But you always had something to add."

I don't hear the sarcasm in his comment, but I sense it was meant to be sarcastic. Before I can say anything, a *ding* in the kitchen sends Nick to his feet.

"Soup's on," he says and heads inside.

*   *   *

Cell phone safely in her purse, Amy stares at Jack openly as he eats dinner. He chews slowly, all too aware of her eyes on him. When he looks up, mouth poised to ask what she's looking at, Amy smiles.

"Jack's here," she says so pleasantly he can't find fault with it.

He stares at her, a smile threatening to appear on his face. "I am."

Where did I get the idea that Jack and Amy don't like each other? He stares at her curiously now, and she stares back. Right. I remember. The last time they were together he called her a bitch because she'd stopped giving me his messages. She slapped him. *Hard.*

This is better.

She says, "This beer thing. Beer's your life?"

"I wouldn't say beer's my life," he answers casually, then looks at Nick. "Dinner's great, by the way."

Nick beams, motions for Jack to help himself to more food.

"It's what I do." Jack turns back to Amy. "Different from life. I hope."

"Not so different," Amy tells him.

He doesn't say anything.

For a while, we eat in silence. Jack's presence makes us thoughtful. Usually we're a jovial crew; talking at once, not listening to anything being said because we know we're not saying anything terribly important.

Tonight we don't want to say trivial things in front of Jack. We're trying to be the idea some people have of adults in their early thirties: thoughtful, topical, silent when there's nothing of significance to be said.

By the way we're glancing at him in between bites of food, I know we're also wondering the same things.

What does he want? Why is he here?

He's an intruder.

By the way my friends glance at me right after they glance at Jack, I know they're thinking it's my fault he's here.

When I catch him watching me I can see there are also questions in his eyes. I have answers for him.

They're still my friends despite everything we've been through. Misunderstandings, disagreements, petty arguments and the occasional lack of anything worthwhile to say. I love Gary and Amy more than I used to; I love Nick less. They're still the three people I feel the most comfortable with. We're equals. We have different values, goals and dreams. We differ when it comes to politics. But we don't judge it, and that's very rare. I've yet to meet anyone since I graduated college I would want to get to know as well as Gary, Amy and Nick. And no, I never think about you, I don't regret getting out of bed that morning and walking away.

These are my answers.

"Whatever happened to the aspiring author?" Jack asks.

We all stare at him. He's no longer looking at me, but at Gary.

"Who are you talking to?" Gary asks. A legitimate question, even though Jack is looking directly at him. We were all writers in college.

"You." Jack's gaze is intense. "Amy. Kendall."

Gary holds Jack's gaze, purses his lips. "I write scripts now."

"Right." Jack nods. "How much do you get paid for that?"

"I don't," Gary answers.

Jack tilts his head, uncomprehending.

"I haven't sold one yet," Gary clarifies.

"Oh," Jack says, and a silence falls over the table.

"We don't ask how much you get paid," I say after a minute.

Jack stares at his plate. He shrugs. "Ask."

"How much—"

"I will sell one," Gary cuts me off and leaves it at that.

"What about you, Ken?" Jack turns to me. "Still writing?"

"No."

"Why not?"

"The same reason Nick doesn't write anymore. Work."

"But this gig at the hotel," he says. "It's not a career."

"Well, no," I answer slowly. "It's work. . . . Why?"

"I just remember how goal-oriented you were. All of you, actually. *Where am I going to be in ten years?*"

"What, people shouldn't hold themselves to different views later in life?" Amy inquires. "I think we had the wrong outlook back then. Being all goal-oriented and whatnot."

Jack frowns. "Really?"

Amy shrugs, indifferent. "Yeah. I think so. I mean . . . what matters is being happy. Not the way you come to it."

"Okay." Jack nods. "I'd agree with that. Are you happy?"

The day I asked Jack to meet my best friends he sat up in bed and said, "Why?"

He knew Gary, Amy and Nick. He'd seen them with me before we started dating. He'd never wanted to meet them formally, but after being his official girlfriend for three weeks, I felt it was time. Because it was the thing to do as an official couple. Meet the Best Friends.

Jack was interested in me because, next to my friends, I was the girl who held back. He said he'd never met someone who held back as much as me. He knew I had a crazy streak. Anyone who rolled her own cigarettes in the cafeteria and called the likes of Amy, Gary and Nick her best friends had to have a crazy streak.

"You're good," he said. "At so many things. But you don't see past the being good at it part."

I watch him now, wonder if he remembers saying that.

"Where do you get off questioning whether people are happy or not," I say, suddenly angry with him. "Beer guy."

Jack looks at me like I've just done a bit of projectile vomiting. "What does that mean, *beer guy*?"

"It means you make beer," I say evenly. "You didn't find a cure for AIDS. Don't people make the choices they make, and that's it? The choices they make."

Jack chuckles. "I think you're reading into something that was never said."

"You've been implying, *all night*, that we're losers."

He doesn't deny it, just stares at me for a minute, baffled. It almost makes me uneasy. My friends are silent, watching. Jack holds up his hands, ending his part of the conversation. Since when does he let me get the last word in?

"You think Nick or anybody would be kissing your ass if you owned the rinky-dink equivalent of Schlitz, struggling to meet your revenue every year?" I push.

"Hey," Nick protests. "I don't kiss ass."

"Now, now," Gary mediates. "Let's not get personal."

I look at Gary. I can tell he loves this.

God, we're so immature.

Jack, on the other hand, is the picture of maturity. He takes his glasses off and squeezes the bridge of his nose. The look on his face is neutral, guarded.

"No," he says. "What's your point?"

I don't answer. Not because I don't have one. I just haven't worked it out yet. After a minute, he chuckles.

"What?" Amy asks him.

"Just something . . ." He puts his glasses back on and looks at Amy, then Gary, then Nick. "Something Nelson Mandela said. There's nothing . . . there's nothing like returning to a place that remains unchanged to find the ways in which you yourself have altered."

We're silent for a while. We're thinking about the context in which the statement was made, not how it refers to us.

Then "Fuck *you*," I say.

And there's this flash of a smile from him. So quick I'm sure I made it up in my head.

"I haven't got a clue what's gotten into you, Ken," he says quietly. "But, how about we change the subject?"

"Great idea," Nick says, glaring at me.

"What's Maine like?" Amy asks out of the blue. Like Nick, she doesn't like arguments. And while I'm sure Jack's disparaging comments, and his new holier-than-thou attitude, haven't gone over her head, she's choosing to ignore them.

It surprises Jack. He's never known this part of Amy. He stares at her for a long time, confounded. Jack takes a swig from his beer, throwing his head back so we all have a glimpse of his beautiful long neck. We wait.

Maybe Nick is relieved the arguing is over. Maybe Gary's sorry it didn't end with Jack storming out of the house. I think Amy's just truly curious about the answer to her question.

And I'm noticing him. Not in an *oh, that's Jack, an old boyfriend* kind of way either. It's more like an *after he touched me he'd lick his fingers and it both thrilled and disgusted me* kind of way.

Jack clears his throat. "It's the most romantic place I know," he says.

His words, and the way he's said them, sober us all up. He's had the last word in the end, after all. We sit back in our chairs and stare at the dirty plates on the table. He has the house and the business. He has the romance.

Lucky bastard.

"I think I'm going to call it a night," I say. "I have a headache and I need to sleep it off."

"Go upstairs," Nick commands. "Take an Advil and lie down. I have yummy dessert. It'll make everything sweet again."

I stare at Nick, wondering when he started sounding like he's twelve. *Yummy?* Then I shake my head. "Sleep. In my own bed. Is the bathroom down here still wacky?"

Nick nods. "Use the one in my bedroom."

"I can call a car for you," Jack says, calling a truce in his own way.

"What's fifteen blocks?" I say.

"Fifteen blocks with a headache," he counters. "Let me call the car."

"Thanks. No." I push my chair back and stand up.

Our eyes meet briefly, not long enough for anyone to notice.

People choose their friends by income. It becomes blatantly obvious when you get older and still have a job, not a career. I'm sure all of Jack's friends make six figures or more, like Nick. The closest I've ever come to six in relation to my salary is the number six after the three and five on my paycheck each week. Before taxes.

I try to be comfortable around people like Jack and Nick's work-friends, but I suspect I'm too honest and they're too judgmental for true comfort to actually exist. When you're honest with people about the kind of money you make, they mostly pretend not to care. They treat you like they dig your honesty, but really, they've crossed you off their mental list of people they want to get to know better, people they want to be seen with at a party. That's what most things come down to these days, even though most people would die before they'd admit it: who you want to be seen with at a party.

And Jack is here to gloat, yeah. To let us know the guy we looked down on, the guy I dumped because the group of people downstairs thought I should, has turned out better than the rest of us. And it's obvious he won't be inviting us to any housewarming parties or Christmases in Maine.

I come out of the bathroom and Jack is sitting on Nick's bed.

I stop in the doorway. We don't say anything for a minute.

"What if we change the theme of the evening?" he asks with a smile.

I shake my head. "No."

"Why not?"

"Because I knew this would happen if we spent more than twenty minutes together," I say.

"What?"

"*This.* You being awful to my friends."

He laughs. "I was awful?"

"What did we do to you?" I ask. "Better question, what did they do? I know what I did."

"Oh?" He looks amused.

"I hurt you."

He scoffs. "Not about you."

"Listen," I say, moving away from the bathroom and standing directly in front of him. "I know you're here to show off. Maybe not to me, but definitely to all of us. The Group. The Plural. The Contained Unit, as you used to call us."

"I did?"

"Even though I know we don't mean that much to you anymore, I know it feels good to be you in front of us"—he stands up, and I falter—"right now . . ."

"You know this?"

". . . The unpaid script writer, the delusional film director and the hotel operator . . ."

"You think Amy's delusional?" he asks.

"No . . . I . . ."

One of his fingers latches onto one of mine. He smiles, acknowledging that I've lost my voice for a second. Then he presses against me gently.

I continue, "Gary writes scripts he isn't ready to sell and what's wrong with that?"

"Did I say there was anything wrong with it?" His hand reaches up and cups my face. Against my will, I close my eyes and savor the contact.

"In your Jack way you did," I whisper.

He laughs softly.

"We all . . . we all have a right to do what we want," I tell him.

"It's not them . . . ," he starts.

I open my eyes just as his fingers slide delicately over my lips. I want to tell him to stop. I do. There were days like this when we'd fight in front of our friends, then sneak away and kiss in someone's bedroom. It always felt wrong, but really good. And I know it *shouldn't* feel the same way it did when we were young. But it does.

"It's you," he continues.

"You just said it wasn't me."

"You're still here, I mean. You haven't flourished. Why did you do nothing when you spent so much of our time together telling me I had to do something else?"

I don't respond. Can't. After a minute, Jack pulls back to look at me. I choose not to hide anything. I allow my conflicted emotions to dance plainly across my face for his judgment. And he looks fascinated. His mouth opens slightly, his eyes betray his own confusion. For a moment all of our walls are gone, and we're laid bare, open, vulnerable.

I lean in and kiss his lips gently. I can't help myself. He closes his eyes. His hands slide around my waist, find their way under my shirt and inch up my back. Our kiss is slow and delicate at first, like we're afraid something will break and turn sour, like we know it's wrong to be here doing this.

And then the kiss becomes more insistent, almost greedy.

I'm breathless when we part for air. I say, "Life was very easy."

"Okay," he mumbles into my neck as he unclasps my bra.

"I'm not saying—," I begin, but he grinds himself slowly against my thigh, and I choke on my words. "You've got me being real honest here, so pay attention."

"I am . . ." He works his way to my chest. His fingers find my breasts and tease my nipples. I try to get the next bit of conversation out before I can't speak at all anymore.

I say, "I'm not . . . saying life needs to be hard in order to . . . want to be something better. I'm saying I know . . . I'm very well aware that if it hadn't been so easy I might be doing other things. I'm saying I don't think there's anything wrong with working at a hotel."

"I didn't mean to imply that there is," he says.

"Well, you did."

Jack becomes very still, stops kissing me. He lowers his eyes and watches my fingers play at the edge of his pants.

"What if . . . ," he begins, then stops.

He moves away from me and sits on Nick's bed again. I straddle him and start to nip at his face gently, lovingly, like a newly purchased, eager puppy. I haven't felt this silly in a long time and I'm enjoying it, despite the fact that he suddenly seems far away.

"What if . . ." He tries to speak, but I continue to nip at his lips. "Ken." He pulls back, but I move with him, licking his teeth. I feel him respond to me. He knows I feel it and he relents. He smiles into our kiss. I think I feel the low rumble of a laugh in his chest. And then, just like that, he stops smiling. "Ken, baby," he says, firmly placing his hands on my chest and pushing me back. "You need to stop."

"Why?"

He moves his hands to my hips and lifts me off his lap. I land on the bed next to him with a thud. He stands up.

"What?" I ask, alarmed.

"What if you worked in a shitty hotel?"

"What?"

"You heard me."

My giddiness fades and is replaced by fierce annoyance. "What the fuck, Jack? What the hell are you smoking?"

He won't look at me. "You can't tell me, can you?"

"What are you . . . ," I start, then hesitate. "Why are you playing games with me?"

He looks at me sharply.

I continue, "You're the one who came here and got me all hot and bothered in three minutes. I mean . . . I mean a thunderclap struck in the distance and you're here. Feeling me up and shit. What the hell is that about? Why are you looking at me that way?"

"Please. Would you get out?" he says evenly.

"Um. No." I look around our surroundings. "This isn't your hotel room."

He looks stunned.

"Forgot for a minute?" I say.

Still, stunned. Not used to people refusing his requests, calling him on his bullshit.

"A couple of days at a hot-to-trot hotel and you're all Mr. Celebrity," I continue. "I don't kowtow to celebrities; I'm certainly not going to kowtow to you."

He walks out. I hear the sound of his footsteps on the stairs, and then I hear him join the others.

"He really doesn't like us, right?" Amy says when the car service arrives and we pile into the backseat. "Could you tell? The way he didn't want to stand next to you when Nick took the picture? And then, he did that whole adjustment with me in the middle so Gary would be on my left and he wouldn't have to stand next to either one of us."

I nod, not really wanting to talk about Nick's stupid Polaroid camera and the twenty-minute hell he put us through just to take a few pictures. To my surprise, though, Jack asked to keep two of them.

"He looked good," she says.

"How was Los Angeles?" Anything not to talk about Jack.

Amy snorts. "I spent the whole time online in the hotel room. I'm lucky AOL accepts the Sears card, otherwise I'd be screwed out of my e-mail accounts."

"You're paying for AOL with a Sears credit card?"

"Uh-huh. I spent all the money from my last job on the plane ticket out there." She shakes her head solemnly. "I wasn't prepared for the purgatory that we call job hunting."

I rub her thigh reassuringly.

"We have dinner with a guy like Jack, our age and all, and the differences are monumental."

I pull a twenty-dollar bill out of my bag and hand it to her. Money is not off-limits with us. It isn't unusual for Amy or Gary to give me some cash when they know I really need it. I do the same for them. Ironically, we avoid borrowing money from Nick because he has it.

"That's like the blind leading the blind," she says. "I know you need it right now."

"Just take it," I insist. "Pay for the cab with it."

She hugs me and kisses me, tells me I'm such a good friend. She doesn't say what we both know. That her parents are thinking about charging her rent. They've already stopped allowing her to eat the food in their fridge.

The car stops in front of my building less than five minutes later.

Before I get out of the car, she grabs my wrist and pulls me back in. She says, "I know you don't like to talk about Jack."

I shake my head. "Amy—"

"He doesn't deserve us, you know? Our friendship. We're still too good for him."

"Let's not talk about that," I tell her. "It doesn't matter. He got what he wanted out of this visit. We won't be seeing much of him."

Amy looks relieved. "Thank God. I was afraid you were going to be all into him again, which is not a good idea."

We kiss cheeks. She instructs the car to wait until I'm safe inside the building.

The guest in room 3601 is having telephone troubles. I take the call. In the hotel lobby I wait for the elevator, wearing the ill-fitting blue smock operators are required to wear when we fix phones. I'm also carrying a shopping bag with two new telephones and new phone cords. I feel technical and ridiculous amongst the glamorous people.

When I took the job, I didn't know being a telephone technician was part of the package. I thought hotel operators had little to no contact with guests, and that's why I applied for it. I would have applied for a job with Verizon if I'd known I would have to fix phones and meet people; the pay and benefits are better.

It turns out every time I get a phone repair call the guests are always in the room, rabid with anger because they're expecting an important call. My bedside manner isn't endearing, so I've trained myself to say only ten words whenever a guest abuses me verbally.

"I'm very sorry, sir," I say. "I'll report that to my manager."

I'm lucky to get out of most rooms alive, but I do manage to leave feeling menial and insignificant.

As I wait for the elevator, I watch Sage behind the front desk. He avoids looking at me and concentrates on checking guests in. Soon, a crowd is surrounding me, quiet and menacing. They're all big men with dark hair, wearing dark suits. They stand with their legs spread and their hands in front of them.

Bodyguards.

I nod appropriately and keep my smiles to a minimum. I realize the short man standing next to me is an actor I grew up watching and now despise because of an argument we had a few days ago on the phone. He erased all of his voice mail messages by accident and blamed me because I couldn't make them exist again.

When the elevator arrives I attempt to follow the group in, but a big swarthy guy sticks his arm out in front of me rudely and demands I take the next one. My first instinct is to tell him to go fuck himself. I was here first, and don't I look like a lady? But I spot Kirk coming out of the front office. He stops next to Sage and watches me.

I step back, bow slightly at the swarthy guy and tell everyone in the elevator to enjoy the rest of the day.

When I look at Kirk again, he smiles and rolls his eyes sympathetically. It's good that he's seen me shunned from the elevator. It gives me some extra time before I have to get back to the office.

Luckily, the guest in room 3601 is out. Quickly, I unhook the phones in the bedroom and bathroom. I exchange the old phones with the new phones I've just programmed. I check them, make sure they work, make sure every speed-dial button speed-dials to the right place. When Sage picks up at Front Desk, he asks what floor I'm on. He says he'll meet me in the stairwell in ten seconds. I get out of there.

A woman from Housekeeping is stealing a minute with a cigarette in the stairwell. I sit on the steps next to her in silence.

"You smoke?" the housekeeper asks in a thick Eastern European accent.

"Nah. Just hanging," I say. "Enjoy."

The housekeeper smiles, puts the cigarette out on the wall and looks at me again. "I have to clean here later."

I shrug, don't care, and the housekeeper leaves.

The elevator rings, and a couple of seconds later Sage comes into the stairwell. He sits on the step behind me.

"That thing I said last week," he begins. "About meeting your friends? I didn't mean it."

"Okay."

He starts to massage my shoulders. "I saw your boy today," he says.

"The Texan?"

"I think he's going to Instinct tonight. Want me to get us on the guest list?"

Instinct is the latest celebrity hangout the hotel is pushing. Concierge agents are always on some club or restaurant guest list. That's why Concierge is the best gig in the hotel. Free food at the hottest restaurants; free dancing at the hottest discos. It's the best way for a nobody to feel like a somebody for an evening.

Some of the kids at Concierge are like celebrities themselves, though. If they don't like a place, they don't recommend it to the hotel's celebrity clients. If they do, the place is put on the map. Sage has a couple of friends at Concierge. One phone call and we can be somebody for an evening.

"I'm not dressed for it," I say dully.

Sage stops massaging my shoulders and moves down one step to sit next to me. "We can go next week," he says. "The

Texan got the studio to hook him up for three months. He's in transition, apparently. Moving to New York. Imagine a studio paying for you to live in this hotel for three months because you're moving?"

"I hope the movie does well for his sake."

Sage says, "Okay, let's get back to basics."

"What do you mean?"

"I mean, something's up. You don't have to tell me what it is, but I know it's here."

I raise my eyebrows, but I don't confirm it. What am I going to say? That something . . . someone has come back into my life and I can't stop thinking about him? I don't foresee Sage getting all outraged and violent about it, but I do foresee jealousy, and that makes me not want to tell him. I don't even want to admit to myself how strange I felt when I walked into the office this morning and Jack's request for a DND until further notice was scrawled across the board.

"I know I've been quiet."

"For lack of a better word, quiet's okay," he says.

"On one hand I'm really good," I begin. "Happy. Satisfied. And then someone does something that leaves me wondering if I should be wanting more. I'm . . . I'm content, but I don't know if I should be."

"Whoa," Sage says. "That just came from left field. What's up?"

"Don't you ever feel like that?"

"Like I want more?" he asks. "Sure. Or something else. Sometimes it just feels right with Paula. The way we are now. And then I have those moments, when someone says something that rings true to me, and I know we can't give up. We can't leave it unfinished."

"That's different," I say. "You can't compare my stupid musings to your marriage."

"Your musings aren't stupid."

"But you have a kid to think about," I insist. "Not a biological kid, but still. A kid."

Sage stares at me for a long time, and then he smiles. "Yeah, but."

I understand that, I think. I appreciate it. *Yeah, but.*

"Let's start having fun again," Sage says. "Let's start doing the things we used to do when we first met."

"That would leave me feeling unsatisfied," I say.

"Not that." He rolls his eyes, knowing exactly what I'm referring to. We used to joke that when we got tired of each other, we would double-date the guests. "Just having fun. Flirting. Dancing. Scoring free drinks."

"Okay," I say noncommittally.

"When do you want to go? Next Monday? Monday's a hot night for this new place everyone's checking out. The Texan's having company next week. He's taking some of his West Coast friends there."

"Okay." I touch Sage's face. "Maybe I'll invite Amy."

"Your friend Amy?"

I nod.

"I'd like to meet her." He smiles and tilts his head so he can kiss my hand. This is the part I like. When we kiss and make up.

"I can get you into a guest room this evening," he says. "If you still want it. We can only stay a couple of hours, though."

"Yes, please," I say, hiding my disappointment that we can't stay an entire night.

"Good. I'll meet you at seven."

When I return from my telephone errand, Katie rips off her headset and throws it down on her desk.

"Who is the *cunt* in 1700?" she roars.

Wanda shushes her, afraid the guests on the other lines will hear her. I stare at her, dumbfounded. I've never heard a man referred to as a cunt before.

"Tell me she's the Second Coming of Christ," Katie continues, unhampered by Wanda's concern. "*Please*. She has to be the Second Coming to think she can speak to me like that."

"*Girl*," Rodney chastises, shaking his head. "You better keep your voice down."

Katie is the only operator who routinely unnerves me. This tiny East Indian girl has a fierce mouth and a tendency to threaten people with violence. Right now, she stands away from her console, hands up, as though it's holding a gun on her. She looks like she's ready to kill something.

This doesn't stop me from addressing her.

"You mean the guy in 1700?" I ask. "That, um, Jack Sullivan guy?"

"*Fucking bitch cunt cunt cunt*," Katie singsongs loudly.

"Katie," I say impatiently. "I just asked you a question."

A couple of weeks after she was hired, Katie and I had our first and only argument. I asked her to lower her voice while I was on a call. I think I had a chance to say two words in my defense when Katie warned, "If you keep talking, Stark, I will rip your fucking heart out through your throat and stomp on it."

The room went silent, and everyone waited for my reaction.

I had no evidence that Katie had either the strength or inclination to rip my heart out through my throat, but the visual bothered me and I didn't know what to say. I was actually speechless. In the cubicle next to me, Rodney started to laugh. That helped. I started to laugh as well.

These days Katie brings me cookies from the cafeteria if she happens to be on break when the hotel chef is feeling generous, and she claims I'm the only operator she likes. I don't believe her. Everyone in this office has stabbed someone in the back. I'm sure Katie is no different.

Now Katie narrows her eyes at me and emits a growl. The growling that always gets everyone. "No. Not the guy. The bitch staying with him. The bitch who requested the DND, may she burn in Hell. Why do I keep getting her?"

Wanda and I share a look just as the Front Desk manager breezes through the office. He smiles at us pleasantly. Katie and I take our seats.

"Are you going to tell us what happened?" Rodney asks, but Katie is already on the phone. A personal call. I can hear her whispering fiercely at her boyfriend, something she does whenever she has an issue.

I stare at my monitor, unable to move. Then I type Jack's name into my console to check that he's still registered here. He is. If there's a woman in the room with him, Front Desk hasn't logged her information yet. I take a deep breath.

"Katie," I call over my cubicle, even though she's still on her personal call. "If you get another call from them, pass it to me."

Fifteen minutes later, Katie asks me to input her wake-up calls so she can catch her bus. She's rushing.

I take the page of wake-up calls from her and tell her to have a nice evening.

"The bitch in 1700 is going to have a massage in the spa," Katie announces as she leaves. "She'll be back in her room in fifty-five minutes. She no longer wants the DND. She wants all calls directed to the spa. *Nothing* should go to the room, or voice mail. She will come down here and kill you all if it does. Someone needs to unblock her phone."

"Would have been nice if you told us that sooner," Rodney calls after her.

"Agreed," Trina chimes in.

Katie flashes us the finger and walks out of the office.

"Kendall?" Wanda calls out from the other side of the room. "Can you do me a favor?"

"Uh-huh," I say.

"I have to call my roommate in two minutes," she says when I come over to the fax desk. "We have an emergency. Can you be fax operator while I take my break?"

"Sure," I say, faking a smile.

I hate being fax operator. Everyone does. Fax operator is just about the worst gig in the department. For a while, Kirk set up a fax schedule to stop the out-and-out screaming fits we would pitch if we found ourselves doing faxes two days in a row. But some crafty operator would always manage to get out of it by scratching her name off the schedule, or taking her break during the hour it was her turn to do faxes. Finally, Kirk gave up and just started telling people it was their turn to do it, threatening to write us up if we refused.

Kirk doesn't ask me to do faxes often. I tend to screw them up because, according to him, I "don't pay attention."

Wanda, as usual, has left the faxes on the desk in complete disarray. There are about twenty faxes that need to be collated, folded, logged and stuffed into envelopes. And to make matters worse, all five machines are steadily rolling.

"Kendall," Rodney calls out. "You have a call."

"No calls," I say. "I'm crazed already."

"It's urgent. I just passed it to you."

I curse him, and he laughs.

"Keep it clean, keep it clean," he says, doing a pitch-perfect impression of Kirk.

"Fax operator Kendall," I say.

The voice on the other end is young. She tells me she works for Sam Ripper, the notoriously difficult film producer who stays at the hotel once a month. She's about to send me a forty-five-page fax that is *very important*. Every fax Sam Ripper has ever received since I started working here has been *very important,* and his assistants have a knack for driving fax operators insane.

"I would hold off on that if I were you," I tell her. "The fax machines are crazy."

"It's urgent," she claims. "He has to receive it in twenty minutes."

"Well . . . ," I start.

"Please." She sounds like her life depends on it.

The forty-five-page fax that has to reach Sam Ripper's room in twenty minutes rolls out of one of the fax machines ten minutes later. Wanda is nowhere to be found. I drop everything, grab it and start to count the pages before his assistant calls again.

"Kendall," Trina calls out. "You have a call."

"Shit." I put on my headset and take the call.

"Fax operator?" Sam Ripper's assistant says.

Impatiently, I tell her which pages of the fax are missing. She offers to resend the entire fax. I try to convince her to only send the pages that are missing, but she's near tears and says she doesn't want to take any chances. The second time the fax comes in, even more pages are missing. The girl asks me to shred both faxes and look out for the fax again because she's going to resend it. I toss my headset on the desk and take a deep breath. I want to kick Sam Ripper's ass.

"1700, 1700," Rodney says. "What did that girl say we had to do with these calls."

"The spa," Trina tells him.

"Oh, damn," Rodney swears. "I sent it to the room. I think it was a hang up, though. I should have stayed on."

"*What happened to all the faxes?*" I shriek when I return to my desk with Sam Ripper's third forty-five-page fax that is now five minutes late.

"What faxes?" Rodney asks, leaning back in his chair and frowning at me.

"All of the *other* faxes I stuffed into the big envelopes that I never logged into the fax log because Sam Ripper's assistant has been driving me up a wall for the past twenty minutes!"

Trina and Rodney stand up and look at me over their cubicles. I'm breathing hard, panicked. Faxes must be logged; otherwise, we have no record that we ever received them. And that guy who just got that fax from his doctor in Beverly Hills with his test results could sue if the hotel Page delivers it to the wrong room. It doesn't matter that Front Desk routinely recommends guests not receive obscenely personal faxes from people like their doctors or divorce lawyers.

"Fuck!" I drop into my chair and call Front Desk. Sage answers. He tells me the Page has already left to deliver the faxes, but he'll send someone else down to pick up the fax for Sam Ripper.

"You okay?" he asks.

"No," I say before I disconnect him.

"Hey, Kendall," Trina says. "I got Ripper on the line. He wants to talk to the fax operator."

I look up slowly. "Can you tell him . . . can you tell him that a Page is on his way to pick it up?"

After a second Trina says, "Kendall?"

"What?"

"He wants to talk to you."

I stand up and glare at Trina. "I am really overwhelmed right now. I have about twenty faxes that are MIA, and Sam Ripper's fax is still sitting here. Where the hell is Wanda?"

"He's pissed," Trina informs me casually. "He wants to talk to you, and then he wants to talk to a manager."

I've never been on the other end of a call from Sam Ripper, but the last operator he insulted locked herself in the bathroom and cried hysterically. I take another deep breath and prepare myself. "Pass it over."

"Here goes," Trina says.

"Fax operator Kendall," I say.

"Fax operator?" He has a soft, feminine voice.

"Yes."

"This is Mr. Ripper in room 3712. I was expecting a fax five minutes ago."

"Yes, sir," I say, confident that Sam Ripper's reputation has exceeded him. "I've just called a Page to pick it up and deliver it to you."

"No, fax operator," he says softly. "No. Did you hear what I just said?"

I think it's a rhetorical question, so I don't answer.

"*Hello? Fax operator*? Did you hear what I said?"

"Yes, sir."

"What did I say?"

I bite my tongue. "You're expecting a fax . . ."

"No," he interrupts, voice raised. "I *was* expecting a fax. Five minutes ago. Now, I don't need it anymore because my conference call is over. And all of the names and numbers that were needed are no longer needed anymore."

"I'm very sorry, sir," I say slowly, calmly, softly. "Would you like to speak to my manager?"

Sam Ripper is still quiet, but I can hear him breathing. A time bomb ready to explode. After a minute he says, "Yes."

I put him on hold, rip my headset off. "*Where's a fucking manager?*" I scream.

Trina offers to page Kirk. When he calls back, she tells me to pass the Sam Ripper call to Front Desk. I do. And then I wait. Ten minutes later, Kirk strolls into the office and looks directly at me. I lean back in my chair and hold his gaze, ready for an argument.

"Why are you doing faxes?" he asks.

"Wanda's on break."

"Wanda had an emergency and left for the evening." He looks around the office, then back at me. "Did you put Mr. Ripper's fax in the shred pile yet?"

I shake my head. Mr. Ripper's fax is in my bag. I plan to give it to Amy the next time I see her.

"Why don't you discard Mr. Ripper's faxes in the shred pile and come back to your desk?" Kirk suggests. "We'll let someone else handle faxes."

He sits down, types his password into his switchboard and starts taking calls. I watch him and wait for something else. But he doesn't look at me again.

I say, "What did Ripper say to you?"

Kirk looks up from his switchboard and stares at me. I recognize pure hatred in his eyes. But I don't know if the hatred is directed at me, or Ripper, or this job.

"Don't worry about what Mr. Ripper said to me," he says. "We'll just make sure to pay closer attention to his incoming faxes next time."

I stand up, grab the two Ripper faxes I didn't swipe and leave the office. As I pass Rodney, he grabs my hand and squeezes it. The gesture warms my heart for a second. It's like Rodney's trying to say we're all in this hell together, and I'm not living through it alone.

*   *   *

A guestroom at the hotel is meant to be a guest's sanctuary. It doesn't matter what size it is, or what floor it's on. The hotel's goal is to give its guests a better home away from home. A home they'll want to come back to again and again. And most guests do.

Boasting curtains so thick that a room can replicate the dead of night in the middle of the day, why wouldn't they? The hotel claims you will never sleep as well as you sleep here, and most people attest to it.

Sometimes Sage will slip me a key for a room that hasn't been booked, or a room that's expecting a late-night check-in. He usually joins me. But there are some nights I just want to be alone. I just want to feel like I've merited a seven-hundred-dollar-a-night hotel room.

Sage gives me the key to a room on the twelfth floor. It's a late-check-in room, so his friend from Housekeeping has given us four hours. I change into a blue smock as soon as I leave the office. In the hotel lobby no one even gives me a second glance. The blue smock makes me invisible to everyone, including my fellow hotel workers.

As I wait for the elevator, a young woman appears and waits with me. I try not to pay any attention to her, but I become very aware that she keeps staring at me. Finally, I look over, and she smiles.

"This is going to seem like a very weird question," she begins.

"Yes," I say with a fake smile. "I do work here."

She chuckles lightly. "Obviously." She points to the smock.

"Can I help you?" I ask coldly.

"Are you Kendall?"

I look down. The other thing I refuse to wear besides my uniform is the hotel nametag. I look at her again and frown.

She does not look familiar. She holds out her hand. "My name is Rae Jensen. I'm engaged to Jack Sullivan."

My mouth drops open. I'm sure of it. "You're . . . what? I'm sorry. I didn't . . . you're? . . ."

"Rae Jensen," she repeats slowly. "Jack Sullivan's fiancée."

Oh Lord, she really did say that.

And what immediately comes to mind is Saturday night. My hands at Jack's waistband, searching for a button to pop open. *And how sick was that?* I was going to have sex with him. Or drop to my knees. That's how into him I was on Saturday. And now the whole trying-to-kick-me-out-of-Nick's-room scene makes sense. The bastard. Unlike me, he knew he was getting married.

"Oh." I flush. "Gee. Hey. How are you?"

She smiles. "Jack told me you work here. And I saw a picture of you. A Polaroid."

"Right." I nod, thinking back to the moment when Jack asked if he could keep a couple of the pictures. "From Saturday night. At Nick's. You know Nick?"

"I think we're having dinner with him later."

"Great." I realize I should shake her hand. I do. "Nice to meet you."

"Same here."

Rae's light-skinned. Possibly biracial. She's the same height as me, well-built. An athlete, I decide. Gymnastics? Rowing? She has long, curly hair and a pleasant face. Her eyes are enormous and light brown like Jack's.

They match. How adorable to have matching eyes with your fiancée.

What strikes me, though, is that she isn't outstandingly attractive. She's plain. She's normal. She's very casual in a sweatshirt that says BAR HARBOR across the front of it, khakis and white tennis shoes.

"Why don't you come up?" she asks tentatively, looking the smock over again. "Jack's upstairs. He would love to see you."

"Well," I say awkwardly. "I am on my way *up*. But I have business to take care of."

She nods. What a sweet smile. This can't be the *cunt, cunt, cunt* Katie was speaking of.

"It's weird to know someone who actually works *in* a hotel . . ." Rae's voice fades. She glances at me, then lowers her eyes, knowing the damage has already been done. I agree with Katie all of a sudden.

"Well, now you know me," I say tightly, and she nods in agreement.

The elevator arrives. The worker in me hits her floor first, then mine. We share an odd smile, this one not so sweet, and I find myself dismissing my actions with a stupid lie. I say, "I know which floors all of our guests are on."

I can tell she doesn't believe me. I wouldn't.

We smile; say little. Little to say. When I step off the elevator, I catch her checking out my shoes.

"Tell Jack I say hello," I call out as the doors close.

When I enter the room I know Sage is already here. He always manages to remind me why turndown service is a good thing. When I started working here, I felt nothing but outrage when guests would call for Housekeeping because they hadn't received turndown service. I'd look at Wanda or Rodney and say, "Is it really a difficult task to pull back a comforter?" Then Sage showed me the Art of the Turndown and I quickly understood its allure.

I walk into the room. Only the bedside lamp is on, shining soft light over the pillows. The radio is tuned to an easy listening station, and music plays softly to invoke an immediate feeling of relaxation. One corner of the comforter is pulled back to form a perfect triangle. And a single Godiva chocolate is nestled snugly on the pillow.

Sage comes out of the bathroom, body covered by one of the hotel's plush, terrycloth robes. He grins when he sees me.

"Thought that was you," he says.

"Soft."

I cover Sage's hand with my hand, but he flicks me away and continues the light, tortuous dance up my leg.

"You're beautiful. You really are." He slides his fingers up higher. Stops. Our eyes meet and he smiles, teeth covering his bottom lip, eyes crinkling. "Nice."

"You think?"

"I think." His eyes sweep over my body, stopping here and there to take parts of me in. He makes a low sound in his throat to indicate appreciation. I can't help but smile. I like to be appreciated.

For an hour, we lie in bed and play.

"I wish I lived here," I say dreamily.

"Mmm," is Sage's answer.

"I had a bad day," I tell him.

He stops kissing my earlobe and whispers, "We're making it better."

We take a bath in the Jacuzzi. The Jacuzzi, in my humble opinion, is worth the price of the room alone. I lie with my back against Sage's chest. I keep my eyes closed and pretend we belong here. Sage listens as I tell him about Sam Ripper.

"Just waiting for Kirk's reaction," I conclude. "He's going to make me suffer. I know it."

"Ripper is insane," Sage says, taking a drag from his cigarette and balancing it on the edge of the tub again. "He gets off on intimidating people. Kirk knows it. That's why he didn't flip out."

"Well, Kirk gets off on hassling me."

"No, he doesn't," Sage says.

"You're defending my boss?"

Sage nods, his chin bumping into the back of my head. "Yes."

"Why?"

Sage is quiet and I wait. He lifts one of his legs so that his knee comes out of the water. He shifts a little.

"Do you even know how abused Kirk was today?" he asks after a minute. "If he was going to make you suffer, he would have done it the minute he saw you."

"It wasn't my fault." I sit up and turn to look at him. "Ripper's assistant kept sending this fax and there was no way it would have reached him in time."

Sage stares at me. He picks up his cigarette again and takes a drag.

"I know," he says. "Kirk knows. That's why he took the blame. That's why I don't think you should be so quick to assume the worst in him. I mean, he's a dick, yeah. But he's just doing his job."

I know Sage is right, but I still feel ticked off. I stand up, get out of the tub, drip water all over the bathroom floor.

"And you're angry because?" he asks, watching me dry off.

"I'm not angry." I wrap the towel around my body and watch him smoke, arm draped over the side of the tub, cigarette ashes landing on the floor. I lean against the doorframe and wait for him to finish up.

"I'm not taking sides," he says. "I always take your side anyway."

The telephone rings. One ring. Sage answers, then tells me Housekeeping needs the room sooner than they expected. I imagine the guest standing in the lobby, desperate for a shower, enraged because his room isn't ready.

Sage and I dress in silence. As he checks the room to make sure we haven't left anything behind, I say, "I'm sorry I came off angry. It isn't you I'm angry with."

"No problem."

We slip out of the hotel through the lobby instead of the employee exit. I have the hotel smock stuffed inside my bag. We part on Fifth Avenue like two strangers who just happen to work together.

When I come into work the next day I'm feeling out of sorts. I didn't get much sleep. My upstairs neighbor dropped something heavy above my bedroom at three in the morning. Awake, I couldn't stop myself from thinking about Jack.

And Rae.

Jack was a badass, yeah, but he never hurt anyone intentionally. Especially not me. Not someone he was dating. Though I'm surprised I even matter, I know why he'd hurt me now. I don't know why he'd hurt Rae.

The mystery bothers me. I don't want to think of Jack as the typical guy. A guy who goes after what he can get even when he's got something serious. A guy women develop complexes over. He was never that.

In the office, Victoria—back from vacation—is scolding Chelsea for missing seven wake-up calls. I take my seat and sign into my console.

There's really no excuse for missing wake-up calls in the morning. Because the first thing the morning operator is supposed to do before the overnight operator clocks out is run the morning report, which lists every guest who requested a wake-up call the day before. It's very simple.

"You can run the report until your fingers turn blue," Chelsea is saying. "They aren't there."

I try to tune them out by listening to a call between a television producer and her husband. Their son has gone missing again, somewhere in California. But Victoria's voice is like Kirk's: impossible to ignore.

Victoria trained me, and she's my least favorite telephone operator in the department. On my first day of work we ate lunch together in the cafeteria. She spent the entire hour talking about the other operators, warning me which ones would eventually ruin my reputation if I befriended them. Funny, since all of the operators Victoria warned me about are the only operators I can stand.

Most people know that the one person in the office who talks about everyone else is the one person in the office you can't trust. No one has ever turned Victoria on to that concept, so she still thinks the rest of us don't know what she's telling the new operators when she has lunch with them on their first day. I always get a kick out of the fact that the new kids can never look me in the eye when they come back from lunch with Victoria.

"Well who *the hell* forgot to input all the wake-up calls that came in before seven yesterday?" Victoria screams. "Don't you all know by now that you input wake-up calls as soon as you get them? How many times do I have to tell you not to write them down on a piece of paper? Damnit. Where's Kirk? I'm going to get Kirk down here right now."

I release the call I'm listening to and pull my headset off. I have this vague memory of Katie handing me a piece of paper and asking me to input her wake-ups. And then Wanda had to make that emergency call to her roommate. And then Sam Ripper tried to rip me a new one. I remember looking at this piece of paper at the end of the night and wondering what it was.

"Shit," I say.

Victoria and Chelsea look at me. Chelsea looks hopeful, which almost makes me want to say I broke a nail or something. Victoria is looking at me with utter contempt.

"That was my screwup," I tell Victoria.

Chelsea lets out a huge sigh of relief and returns to her cubicle. Victoria, meanwhile, looks like that cartoon bull with smoke coming out of its ears.

"I screwed up," I say again. "I'm sorry."

Victoria swallows hard, unsure of how to react to my confession. Then: *"How many times do I have to tell you to input wake-up calls the minute you get them?"*

"Actually," I begin, then think twice about bringing Katie into this. It's a good thing Katie's off today. Otherwise, she'd wait for me after work and threaten to kick my ass.

"Do you know who didn't get his wake-up?" Victoria shrieks. *"Do you?"*

I shake my head calmly. "No, Victoria. I don't know who didn't receive his wake-up this morning."

"Mr. Carl Lakefield didn't get his wake-up this morning," she howls. *"Mr. Carl Lakefield."*

"The designer?" I say, like it's no big deal.

"Do you know what that man said to me?" she screams, outraged by my nonchalance. "That man said things to me I can't even repeat here in this room. You don't want to know the things that man called me. And do you know what we had to do? We had to pay for that man's first-class flight to Paris because he missed the first one. Thousands of dollars! Kirk is mad. He is mad, mad, mad. He should fire your ass. He should. In fact, that's what I'm going to tell him to do."

She storms out of the office, brandishing the morning report ferociously. I just stand where I am, trying to figure out if

I should disappear until things calm down or wait around for the outcome.

"At least you admitted it," Chelsea says from her cubicle.

"Excuse me?" I say.

"At least you admitted it," she repeats. "I wouldn't have. I would have pretended I didn't know a thing."

"Well, maybe you're smarter than I am," I say, returning to my cubicle.

"Fifteen calls holding," Kirk says. I jump and disconnect the call I'm listening to. I look at him. He's staring at his monitor. I take another call. The guest in room 510 is having phone problems. I tell her I'll be up in ten minutes. Kirk watches me get up, pull a new phone from the storage cabinet and start to program it.

"Kendall, what are you doing?" he asks.

I stop myself from asking him what he thinks it looks like I'm doing and say, "I'm programming a phone. The guest in 510 needs a new one."

Kirk looks around the room. "Rodney, would you take care of that? I'd like to talk to Kendall in the conference room."

"Me?" I say, feigning total innocence.

He nods, looking at his monitor again. Then he points to the door.

The conference room is next to the office and across the hall from the General Manager's office. It's a big room with a long table where every department has weekly meetings. When Kirk requests an operator's presence in the conference room, it means she's done something wrong, or she's fired.

I sit at the opposite end of the table, and Kirk stares at me for a minute.

"Would you take a seat closer to me, please?" he asks.

I move closer, keeping one seat between us.

"Kendall," he says solemnly.

"Kirk," I say, just as solemn.

"What's up?"

"What do you mean?"

"Everything okay at home?"

"Yes."

"You're sure?"

"I said yes."

"Were you on a personal call?"

"When?"

"A few minutes ago."

I think about it. "I don't think so."

He picks up the phone on the desk and dials a number. "Maria, would you run a phone report for me on Kendall's console."

If Maria runs the report, Kirk will see that the calls I've answered today weren't disconnected once they were directed to the proper rooms.

"Shit," I say. "Okay. I made a call. One call."

"Never mind," Kirk says into the phone. "I'm sorry to bother you."

"That sucks," I say. "That you would ask *her*. I know I fucked up big time, but she's on the phone all day and she doesn't even have enough respect for you to wait until you leave. And you never reprimand her."

"Have I given you the impression that you can talk to me that way?" he asks. "We aren't friends."

I stare at the table.

"And this conversation isn't about Maria," Kirk states calmly. "This is about you. Maria and I have discussed her conduct privately."

Maria and Trina are notorious for making personal calls while Kirk is sitting at his desk. They talk for hours, regardless of how many calls are on hold. Kirk never says a word. The last time he did, he almost got fired.

"How old are you?" he asks out of the blue.

I look up at him again. "What?"

"How old are you?" he repeats slowly.

"Early thirties," I say. "Why?"

He shakes his head. "You don't act thirty. You act younger."

"Oh, and you're a vision of forty-one every day that I'm with you."

"Not exactly," he concedes. "I'm sure there are plenty of thirtysomethings like you."

"You better believe it."

"I'm just glad I don't know them." He writes something down in my file.

"What right do you have to say something like that?" I ask. "Everyone I know is like me."

"Your world is small," he says simply.

What do you say to such a nasty, below-the-belt jab like that?

I say, "Your world is smaller."

He smiles. It's a tiny, condescending smile. "You think so?"

"I think your friends are probably more like me than you know. They probably never felt comfortable enough around you to be young."

He loses the smile. "This is getting personal, and that's not why I asked you here." He looks at my folder again. "I'm writing you up."

"You know the Ripper thing wasn't my fault," I tell him immediately.

Kirk doesn't say anything, just stares at me.

"And while I'm real sorry about the wake-ups, I think it could have happened to anyone. It's not like I did it on purpose."

"Another fax—not Mr. Ripper's fax—is missing," Kirk says. "When we checked the log this morning, we couldn't find it. In fact, no faxes were logged when you and Wanda were handling them."

I nod. "I can explain that."

"I'm sure you can," he says. "Very well, too. But I don't want to hear your explanation. The fax was delivered to the wrong room. Obviously not your fault, but a Page's mistake. Still, we can't retrieve the fax from the incorrect room because we have no record of who else received faxes at that time. We have no idea how many other people received an incorrect fax because they may have simply thrown them out, or checked out of the hotel before opening the fax—"

"The Page showed up while I was collating the Ripper fax . . . ," I begin.

"What the hell happened here last night?" His voice cracks, the first sign that he's about to lose his cool. Part of me wishes he would. Lose his cool, that is. It can't be healthy that he's got all this pent-up rage boiling inside him. I don't like him very much, but I don't want him to give himself cancer. I also don't want him to snap one day and take all his violent anger out on an innocent like me.

"Look, Kirk," I begin.

"Don't 'Look Kirk' me," he bellows, and I jump. "The guest in 1700 missed two very important calls last night that were supposed to be directed to the spa. She's demanding a complimentary week in the hotel. Mr. Ripper, a *VIP-return-guest,* never received his fax. Mr. Lakefield, another *VIP-return-guest,* never received his wake-up call this morning. And Lord knows how many other guests didn't receive the correct faxes last night. We can't exactly send out a memo asking all guests who received faxes last night to meet us in the conference room so we can sort this thing out. Can we?"

"Well, no. That would be . . ."

"Do you have something else on your mind besides the hotel?"

Trick question.

"Wanda asked me to take over faxes just as I was going to input the wake-up calls last night," I explain. "And then I got caught up with the Ripper fax, and the Page took the faxes before I could log them, and then I completely forgot about the wake-ups when I was finished. In all fairness, though, that 1700 thing had nothing to do with me."

Kirk officially wants to kill me. I can tell by the look on his face.

"I think you're being really mean to me. But I'm sorry," I say sincerely. "I'll do whatever to make it up to you. You want me to call the guests personally and apologize?"

My apology seems to calm him down a little.

"Luckily, there was only one major wake-up call we missed," he says. "The other guests were very understanding, and we offered them complimentary breakfast in the restaurant for as long as they plan to stay here. But we can't afford mistakes like this."

"I know. I'm sorry."

He folds his hands in front of him and leans forward. "Technically, I don't need three write-ups to fire you."

"I'll do better," I say.

He stares at me, waiting. But I don't have anything else to offer.

"The entire department suffers when you decide you don't care," he says.

"Hit me over the head, why don't you?"

He frowns.

I need this job. I need to pay my bills and rent. "I understand."

He stands up and gives me one last look before he opens the door. "And put on your uniform. *Please.*"

Outside, I smoke a cigarette.

Three limousines are parked in front of the hotel. A crowd has gathered across the street, anticipating a superstar sighting. I lean against the wall next to the employee entrance and watch the doorman, Chester, help a family of four into a waiting cab. He tips his hat at me once they're whisked away.

"Nice evening," Chester says.

The doormen are the most pleasant people in the hotel.

"Yes."

"Break?" he asks.

"Not really."

He raises his eyebrows. "They'll be looking for you soon. Should I plead the fifth?"

"Not if they offer to pay you," I say, and he laughs.

Another guest walks out of the hotel, and Chester escorts him to the curb. I watch Chester, how he grins at the man, who is at least twenty years his junior, how he bows submissively when the cab arrives and the man puts a couple of dollars in the palm of his hand.

God, that makes me sad.

I don't want to be here when I'm fifty, bowing submissively to some rich thirtysomething after he tips me five bucks. I don't want someone else's five dollars to make a difference.

I turn away, saddened.

A few months ago, I considered transferring to Concierge. I think I'd be good at Concierge. True, my bedside manner isn't terrific. But I've always believed that your surroundings create you. And Sage is always saying he thinks I'd be great at it.

Chester's phone rings. He picks it up, and uh-huhs whoever is on the other line. When he hangs up he winks at me.

"You a fan of John Travolta?" he asks.

"When I was seven."

"He's on his way down. Coming through the employee entrance."

"I didn't know he was staying here."

"It's about to get crazy."

I don't want to get caught up in the drama of a celebrity exit. "Thanks for the warning," I say.

As I take a last drag on my cigarette, a cab stops in front of the hotel. Jack, all snazzy in a black suit and leather jacket, gets out as Chester holds the door for him. He's having an intense conversation on his cell phone. He doesn't look up. I watch him swagger past me and through the hotel's revolving door.

Without thinking I toss my cigarette and follow him inside. The hotel's lobby is bustling with businesspeople preparing for business dinners and meetings in this world of marble and impeccable service. Everyone's smiling tightly. Content, yet tense.

Jack weaves through the crowd easily, never acknowledging anyone around him.

We turn into the elevator bank. I don't look at Front Desk. I don't care which agent is on duty, don't care if a manager is standing there watching me. I'm focused on Jack, his cell phone, his leather.

Jack presses the call button, then looks up to check if an elevator is on its way down. When he sees me, his mouth drops open a little. He isn't sure if he should smile.

"You asshole," is all I can manage.

The smile doesn't make an appearance. All business, he half turns and tells "Roger" he'll get back to him. Then he clacks his phone shut and stuffs it in his jacket pocket. He doesn't look me in the eye.

Can't?

Won't?

What would I see in those eyes if he could look at me? I wish I knew. Wish he would look at me and say something that will make it all make sense. So I can move on like I thought I had. So I can get over what happened and get back to work.

He doesn't say anything. When an elevator arrives he watches its occupants exit, then makes a move to get in.

"You're just going to walk away?" I ask.

He holds the elevator door open and meets my eyes. "I don't know what you're hoping I'll say."

"Hoping?" I balk.

He kind of rolls his eyes and steps in. I block the doors from closing. "Why'd you come on to me?" I ask in my best *duh* voice. "You're engaged."

"I wasn't going to go through with anything." He does the *duh* voice just as well.

"Then why?"

Three people push past me and get into the elevator. One annoyed look from all three of them prompts Jack to get out of the elevator and let it go. He looks around to make sure no one else is in our general vicinity, and then he says, "I wanted you to remember something fabulous. That's all."

I wanted you to remember something fabulous? That's all?

I curb the urge to kick him and walk away. It's not like me to walk away from something ugly without an uglier comeback. But I do. Even when he calls my name and I hear the regret and apology in his voice, I keep walking. I don't want to look at him again. I don't want to see the meanness that has taken up residence in his face. I can't believe I'm the reason for it.

Following me, he calls my name again. I quicken my pace and head outside. I plan to keep going, even if it means I have to jump into one of Chester's cabs and take it around the block. I don't want to know this new Adult Jack anymore. And maybe this means I'm stuck in the past, unable to accept change in the present, doomed to be young forever. So be it.

Jack catches up to me as soon as I step outside. He grabs my shoulder so hard I yelp, then I turn around and kick him in the shin.

"*Fuck.*" He bends over and grabs his leg. "*Christ,* Kendall."

"Hey, hey, hey," Chester chides as he comes over to see what's happening. He puts his hand on my back. "This guy bothering you, Kendall?"

Jack looks up and frowns at Chester. "Got some ice?"

Chester recognizes Jack immediately. His hand jumps off my back like my shirt is on fire and he's just been burned. "Mr. Sullivan. Certainly, sir."

I roll my eyes, irritated with Chester for being such a kiss ass, but even more irritated with myself for understanding why he has to be. Tips keep most of the hotel's staff alive, not friendships with coworkers.

I squat next to Jack. He glances at me, then turns his attention back to the front door in search of Chester's return with soothing ice.

"Really needed me to know I'm not good enough for you anymore, huh?" I sneer.

"Can't take it?" He looks at me again, then holds out his hand for the makeshift ice pack Chester has impressively found in less than a minute. He holds the ice to his shin, smiles at Chester. "Thanks. What time are you off tonight?"

"Sir, I'm off in an hour."

Jack nods. "I'm good here for now. I'll see you before you're off."

"Sir." Chester backs away, taking his place at the front door again like one of the lions standing guard in front of the New York Public Library.

The exchange leaves me feeling slightly dizzy. When did Jack become this person? This Hotel Personality.

"You're jealous," Jack observes.

"Of what?"

"Me," he says. "What I have. What I am."

I stare daggers at him. "Don't flatter yourself."

He snorts, concentrates on his shin again.

"You invite me to dinner," I say. "*Hound* me. I knew there was something off about that."

"What the hell are you creating in your brain, Ken?" He looks up, irritated.

"You hate me."

"I wish." His voice is soft. I'm sure I've misheard him.

"Where'd you learn about cruelty? Your girl? She doesn't seem that mean, or angry." My voice cracks. Best if I stop now, I think. "Someone taught you how to hurt people."

"You did," he says harshly.

I stand up so quickly I'm embarrassed. To cover it I point at his leg. "I didn't kick you that hard, Jack. Stop being such a drama queen."

I fly through the employee entrance, past Security. Just as I'm about to go down the stairs to the office, Sage calls my name.

"Break?"

I hold up my pack of cigarettes and notice my hand is trembling. "Quick. Illegal."

"Me, too." He holds up his own pack. "And I want to get a look at John Travolta. He's coming out in a minute. I missed him when he checked in."

I nod, stare at the floor, try to stick my cigarettes in my back pocket and miss. I'm hot and edgy and upset.

"What's all this?" Sage says softly, capturing my hands and holding them until the trembling subsides. "What's going on with you?"

I move into the stairwell, and he follows. I lean against the wall.

"I screwed up," I say.

Sage tilts his head and waits for me to explain.

"Kirk wrote me up for missing some wake-up calls."

"That was you?" he says. "Shit."

I nod. "That, and the faxes."

"You were never good at faxes," Sage says, trying to be supportive.

"Just had it out with a guest, too."

Sage quiets me with a soft peck on the lips. Right. Not a good time to tell him about Jack.

"Do you know how much it cost them?" I ask. "Thousand bucks, maybe?"

Sage frowns. "What are you talking about?"

"That designer. Victoria told me the hotel had to pay for his trip to Paris."

"Um, bullshit," Sage says. "We paid the fine so he could take the next flight. That was about a hundred dollars."

"No," I say, shaking my head. "Victoria said we paid for the flight."

"She lied." He laughs.

"I was feeling really guilty."

"Well." He shrugs. "In all honesty, you deserved to feel guilty."

"Yeah."

He chuckles, shakes his head, then starts to leave me. "I'm going to catch Travolta."

"Sage," I say seriously.

He stops.

"Do you think I'm a loser?" I ask.

"Absolutely not," he says too quickly. He leans against the wall next to me, hesitates. Then, "Define loser."

I give him the finger.

"You're not a loser," he says. "Why would you ask that? Because you missed a couple of wake-ups?"

"Seven."

"I was being generous."

I shrug. "Just a question."

He grasps my hand, kisses it. He knows me better than that. It's never just a question. And I can tell by the look in his eyes that he wants to grab me and hold on tight. But there's something in my face that tells him not to.

"Let me take you for a drink after work," he says.

"Okay."

"Wherever you want to go."

"I have to get back," I say.

He squeezes my hand before he lets go of it. I turn away and head down the stairs.

"Kendall."

I stop, but I don't turn around.

"Don't let them get to you," he says. "It's just a job."

I turn back slightly and smile. "I know."

Gary's smoking a cigarette in the kitchen when I come in. All of the lights are off except the one in the hall.

"Smell like piss to you?" I ask before I close the front door.

"The cat upstairs," he informs me, pointing up. "Have you met him? He likes to piss in front of our door, apparently."

"I met him."

"He is a Nasty. Little. Fuck."

I close the door, lock it, make a mental note to complain to Betty about Hercules pissing in front of our door. "You're home."

Gary blows a stream of smoke into the air, eyes squinting at me in the dark. Then he sighs deeply, and I can see him rest the back of his hand against his forehead. "I want you to hear it from me."

I turn on the kitchen light, panicked. "What? What happened?"

He looks solemn, but not grief stricken. I calm down.

"Sweetie . . . ," he begins.

"Gary. What? Please."

"Sweetie, Jack's engaged."

Relief floods my body. I want to laugh, even though I don't

think there's anything funny about Jack's engagement. Better than a fatal accident, or an eviction or a robbery.

"That all?" There's a hint of annoyance in my voice, and he hears it.

"Oh, right," he says defensively. "You would have killed me if you heard it from someone else."

"When did you find out?"

"Nick told me this morning. I didn't call because I wanted to tell you in person."

I don't tell him I already know, because I don't want to get into what happened today. How awful that scene was in front of the hotel. If Chester had tattled, or if a manager had witnessed any of it, or if a guest had complained, I would have lost my job. I shake my head. Jack still has the power to make me stupid.

Gary watches me closely as I move past him and open the refrigerator. "So you knew? You listened to his calls?"

I pull out a Budweiser and open it. "No. I don't listen to his calls. I didn't know."

"Well . . . you're . . . indifferent."

I take a long swallow from the beer, then shrug. "I don't care."

"Yeah. Uh-huh." Gary's wearing a smirk. "Maybe Nick and Amy didn't notice, but *come on.*"

I meet my roommate's eyes. In so many ways he knows me better than anyone else. And it's very annoying.

"Come on, what?"

"You go to the bathroom. Jack disappears. You're both gone for like twenty minutes. I'm not an idiot." He ticks each comment off on his fingers so that the only finger left standing is the middle one. "The vibe between you and Jack is bigfatsexualtension."

I open my mouth to counter.

"I don't want to know," he cuts me off. "That girl is about to get herself married and I wanted to be the first person to break the news to you. Nothing more."

"Okay," I admit. "Maybe a little sexual tension."

Gary winks, then he taps his cigarette in the sink. "I know, sweetie. I know."

Something about the way he winks at me reminds me of the Gary I used to stay up all night with to gossip.

"For a split second I wanted to go to bed with him again," I say.

"Then you didn't go to bed with him." An eyebrow shoots up.

"Go to hell."

"Well, how do I know?" he says.

"Is this why you're not staying at Nick's tonight?" I ask, exasperated. "To break the news to me? To bust my balls? Because . . . damn, Gary. Twenty minutes? You think we could have done it in twenty minutes?"

Gary gives me one of his *you never know* looks, then says, "Jack is at Nick's."

He tosses this off like it's no big deal. But it is a big deal. Considering what happened today.

"Why?"

Gary shrugs. "I think he's fighting with Rae. The fiancée."

"About what?" I know I sound too interested. Gary knows as well, because he pauses and gives me a suggestive look. I back up a little, look down at the beer in my hand.

"Rae showed up at the hotel Wednesday night."

"Really?" I pretend I don't know.

"Uninvited. And from what I've heard, it sounds like they've been fighting for a while. Calling the engagement off, and then back on. Not that I give a shit."

"Exactly," I say, looking at my beer again.

"So she shows up," he continues. I look up, interested. "And he's got all these business meetings, and she's all pissed off because he's ignoring her, or whatever. You would understand that more than me. And they have this huge argument tonight, and he leaves the hotel and comes to Brooklyn to 'have a drink with Nick.' So they went to some bar to catch up. To *talk*."

"Why Nick?" I ask.

"Thank you," Gary snaps. "That's exactly what I said. The ladies are best friends because they make more money than they used to? I don't think so. I think he was hoping you'd be there."

"Stop." I roll my eyes, but part of me gets an unwanted thrill from this assessment.

"Listen," Gary says, moving closer to me. "I have to tell you something."

"What?"

He doesn't say anything for a minute. Then, "When Jack called us a few months ago, he wanted a hotel recommendation. Nick insisted he stay at the house, but Jack wanted to be in the city. For meetings. So, Nick told him about your hotel, said Jack should call you and ask for a discount."

"That's not funny."

"It was a joke," Gary says. "Nick didn't think he would stay there. He figured it would be a deterrent."

We stare at each other. He pushes some hair out of my face. I say, "It wasn't a deterrent."

"It was, at first," Gary says. "He didn't want to stay there. Nick mentioned other hotels in the area, and Jack ultimately decided to stay with Nick. And then we didn't hear from him. And then he just turned up in New York. At your hotel. It's not Nick's fault."

"I wasn't going to blame Nick." I stand up and start to pace the floor.

So, it wasn't a coincidence. He knew I worked at the hotel all along. He knew he'd run into me. He probably planned out the way he wanted everything to happen.

"Don't," Gary says.

"What?"

"Don't read into it."

I nod, like I'm going to heed his advice and everything will be forgotten in the morning. He stares at me for a long time and I stare back, expressionless.

"We do this thing with memory," Gary says. "We idolize people we once loved and haven't seen in forever."

"Believe me, I haven't *idolized* Jack."

"Okay. Idealized."

I suck my teeth. "It means the same thing."

"No, it doesn't."

"Well, I haven't done either."

"I don't know, Ken." He sounds doubtful and touches his chest. "Who's the last guy you let in?"

I stare at his hand on his chest, mortified. "You mean in my heart?"

He nods.

"So not about Jack," I say.

"Well, Nick and I think he's staying at the hotel because of Sully. And you."

At the mention of Sully's name I feel sad. Despite everything, I really should have sent a sympathy card.

"Sully liked me," I note.

"Yeah," Gary says. "And, well . . . Sully's death . . . impending marriage . . ."

I nod.

"All conspire to make a man—"

"Got it," I cut him off.

"We were thinking along the lines of the Twelve-step Program. Four and eight, actually." Gary and Nick spent a few months of their lives following the Twelve Steps of the Twelve-step Program to become better people. They aren't alcoholics, but they decided to live like recovering alcoholics for a while. It didn't work. They didn't become better people. But occasionally one of them will implement a step in our everyday lives, try to explain away someone's actions. "It's like, you make this inventory of yourself, and then you make amends to all of the people you've hurt."

"Not reading into it much?" I say.

Gary shrugs. "Nick's theory."

"Jack didn't hurt me."

"You hurt him. I know. I was there. But he never faced it. He left it unfinished. You both did."

I stop pacing. "It's been nine years."

"Well, yeah. But . . ."

"You and Nick think he stayed at the hotel to see me?"

Gary nods. "Obviously."

"To hurt me back?"

"No," Gary says. "To see you."

"To? . . ."

"I don't know what he came to do. He's getting married. Maybe one last fling?"

"That could make things complicated."

"Only if you have a fling with him," Gary quips. Then he grabs my hand. "You wouldn't . . ."

I pull my hand away. "No. I haven't been . . . *he's* been hounding *me*."

Gary nods. He knows.

"The beer thing is really taking off," Gary says. "He's looking for a New York distributor. I don't understand the logistics of it. Nick said it's really complicated. There's tons of money to be made here if Jack can get it to work out. He doesn't want to leave it for someone else to take care of."

"That sounds like him," I say, thinking Jack always liked New York and never wanted anyone else to take charge of the things he cared about.

"You want my honest opinion?"

I nod.

"He's here," Gary says. "He wants you to know it. He wants you to see what he's done. Wants *us* to see it."

I'm quiet for a long time. Gary waits.

"Well, he's shown us." I'm flippant.

"Exactly," Gary agrees. "Now he can go fuck himself."

I have trouble getting back to sleep. I lie awake, wondering what Jack and his fiancée have been arguing about. Stupid me. I still can't stop thinking about him.

I listen to Gary tiptoe around the apartment. Nick hasn't called to say he's home yet. When I hear the fire escape outside my bedroom window rattle, I jump up to close my curtains. But I'm not fast enough. Our eyes meet, and I scream. A man in a red sweatshirt and dirty jeans puts a finger over his mouth to shush me. He doesn't have a gun, or a pipe or a stick. I tilt my head, stare at him, fascinated by his audacity. Then I mouth the words *fuck* and *you* at him.

Gary opens my door. "What's the matter?"

"Some guy is on the fire escape."

Gary grabs the phone from the living room and dials 911. We wait, listening to the man on the fire escape struggle to open our upstairs neighbor's window. Part of me feels like we should do something to stop him.

"Maybe we should ring her doorbell and warn her?"

Gary thinks about it. "Would it be such a bad thing if—"

I flash him a look and he stops midsentence.

"Bad thoughts," he admits.

"Very bad," I say.

We hear the sirens soon after. A police car stops below, a door slams. Gary and I watch the man climb back down the fire escape. We walk over to my window, raise it a little and listen.

"Yeah, yeah, thank God you're here, Officer," the man says hurriedly. "I'm locked out."

Gary and I look at each other.

"You live here?" the officer asks.

"Yes," the man says. "My wife and daughter are asleep. I don't have my key."

"Can you buzz them?" the officer asks.

"She sleeps like a log," the man answers quickly.

"Do you know anyone in the building who can verify that you live here?"

That one takes a little longer to answer. Gary and I wait eagerly for the handcuffs to be produced, then we look up at the ceiling when we hear Betty bound down the stairs above my bedroom. She stomps across the floor, opens her living room window and screams, *"Carter."*

"Ma'am," the officer calls up to her. "Do you know this man?"

"Yes, he's with me," Betty tells the officer warily. Obviously, she's been through this before. "I'll buzz him in."

Betty sounds resigned, testy. Like a woman saddled with a man who is too much to handle. Gary and I sit on my bed and listen to the various sounds we've never had to deal with before. Betty walking across the floor above, the tinny sound of her voice through the intercom downstairs telling Carter to hurry up, the door opening, Carter bounding up the hallway stairs and entering the duplex, the door slamming, chairs sliding across the floor, dropping.

"Fuck," Gary says.

At least Gary has a boyfriend he can stay with.

The strange noises last for ten more minutes. Then we hear Betty and her husband go upstairs. I shake my head, trying to clear it. I take a deep breath.

"It's just newness," I say. "Once they're used to the apartment, the night noise will go away."

"Yeah," Gary agrees.

We're quiet, settling into the sudden silence.

"Do you want me to sleep in here tonight?" Gary asks.

I don't answer. I think he's asking more for himself than me. He slips underneath my covers, the side closest to the window, and closes his eyes. When I get into bed next to him, he wraps his arm around my waist. This is familiar. Gary in my bed, keeping me safe in the middle of the night several hours after Jack has hurt me.

"Gary," I say.

"Hmmm?"

"What does she do?" I ask.

"Who?"

"Rae."

"She's a caterer."

I snuggle closer to him, my ass rubbing against his crotch.

"What if," I begin, "the Jack-Nick friendship isn't a phase?"

He doesn't answer.

After a minute I say, "Gary?"

He's pretending to be asleep. I nudge him.

"Hmmm?" he says.

"Will you choose me or them?"

Still, he doesn't answer me.

"I chose you over Jack," I remind him.

His arm tightens around my waist like a silent apology. "I love you," he says after a minute.

"I know." My voice is far away.

everything you know is wrong

Evil never rests, Gary tells me.

The new addition to our wacky upstairs neighbors doesn't have a job. Gary has learned from the twentysomething couple on the third floor that he's just been released from an eighteen-month stint in drug rehab. Nice.

The man in Betty's life is a drug addict.

Since his arrival—via the fire escape over a week ago—I've had very little sleep. I'm a light sleeper, and this man named Carter Robinson doesn't sleep at all. I've learned pacing is big with addicts. So is insomnia. It's not the pacing that wakes me up, though; it's the constant moving of furniture at three in the morning. The pacing just *keeps* me up.

I've complained twice. Once by banging on the ceiling with an umbrella, and once by cornering Betty in the hall before she left for work. The umbrella banging motivated Carter to do an alarming, fifteen-minute tap dance. And cornering Betty proved to be equally futile.

Mussed and hurried, Betty and the kid glared at me the morning I burst out of my apartment and accused Carter of waking me up for the fourth time in a row.

"I live alone," Betty informed me brusquely.

"Okay . . ." She caught me off guard with that. "But . . ."

"I live alone," she repeated. "And we own a duplex. We sleep on the second floor. I don't know what your problem is."

"Not sleeping," I said as she grabbed the kid's hand and pulled her down the steps. "That's my problem. Four nights in a row because the man who isn't upstairs is constantly dragging furniture above my bedroom."

They continued to trundle down the stairs, pretending to ignore me.

"And your daughter is still jumping up and down at six in the morning," I called. "Also above my bedroom."

I heard something. A muffled response?

"And Hercules is still pissing in front of my door," I screamed.

Two weeks of living under Betty Blacksmith—this horrid woman who surreptitiously became president of the co-op board before she even lived here—her kid, and this Carter Robinson person who doesn't exist has taxed my nerves. I'm perpetually on edge, wishing Gary were home more often to commiserate with. Wishing I had a boyfriend of my own to spend peaceful nights with in his apartment.

"She's the president," Gary reminds me whenever I call him at Nick's to complain. "She isn't going to listen to reason. Nick says you can stay here for a few days if it's so bad."

Staying at Nick's hasn't been an option all week. Pre-Jack, it would have been. Post-Jack, I stay clear. Because Jack and Nick are *friends* now. According to Gary, "If the ladies aren't meeting in the city for drinks, Jack and that disturbingly quiet fiancée are popping by for dinner."

Jack and Rae are still living at the hotel. After ten days, it's no longer a "stay." It's living. And I've been avoiding him. We haven't spoken or run into each other accidentally since the debacle in front of the hotel.

Gary avoids getting into any deep conversation about Jack and Rae and why I've been avoiding them. He probably thinks I'm uncomfortable around Rae and mourning the fact that Jack isn't available for the reunion-sex we both seemed so primed to jump into a short time ago.

Today I have a call for Jack. The guests in room 1700 have been quiet. Katie still refers to Rae as a cunt, but there haven't been any major mishaps. I put the call through without an ounce of desire to listen to it. But the call comes back to me, and the caller complains that Jack's voice mail is full. I offer to take a handwritten message, but he hangs up in a huff.

"The guest in 1700 has twenty-seven unchecked messages," I announce. "Twenty. Seven. Are we concerned about this?"

"No," Katie spits.

"Why don't you call the guest?" Kirk suggests, cutting his eyes at Katie.

"Why would I . . . what?"

"Call the guest and alert him that his voice mail is full," Kirk says. "Even though his phone has a message indicator, he may not realize what it's for."

I stare at him. "The man's been here for a few weeks already. I'm sure he knows—"

"I forgot to mention it yesterday, Kendall," Kirk interrupts me. "Mr. Sullivan sent a note to Mr. Schmidt commending your work."

Mr. Schmidt is the General Manager.

"What work?" I ask.

"I don't know," Kirk admits. "I'm sure he appreciated your help with his telephone a couple of weeks ago. And maybe he appreciates your phone manner."

Next to me, Rodney snorts.

I turn back to my switchboard, feeling odd. What's Jack playing at? I wonder. What's this game?

A minute later, Rodney taps me and whispers that I have a call.

"I don't want to talk to him," I whisper back.

"You don't want to talk to Sage?" Rodney sounds scandalized. He doesn't know my relationship with Sage is intimate, he just knows Sage is my hotel best friend.

"Oh. Yes. Pass him over," I stumble.

He passes Sage's call over.

We're running back to the hotel. Sage is trying to catch me. Every time he comes close, I duck out of his reach, and he stops and starts laughing hysterically. We're a couple of kids having fun between responsibilities.

I see the man in the suit pacing in front of the employee entrance first, and I stop running. Sage stops as well and pulls me into a gentle headlock.

I push him away.

"What?" Sage looks at the man. "You know him?"

"I'm not sure."

I think about disappearing around the corner because I'm wearing my uniform with hideous black stockings and white sneakers. And Jack is wearing a black suit and black trench coat; his black shirt is open at the neck. He looks mature, not to mention dangerously sexy.

He stops pacing, watches us for a second, then half waves.

Sage and I cross the street.

"Sage, this is Jack," I say. "Jack. Sage."

Jack and Sage shake hands tentatively. Sage backs up but doesn't go inside. Jack checks out my uniform and then looks at the ground. I flush and smooth my hands down the front of my skirt.

"I had a meeting," Jack offers. "I saw you turn the corner. Thought I'd say hello."

This is an obvious lie, since both Sage and I saw him pacing in front of the entrance. I don't say anything. Sage stares at him steadily.

"We still have fifteen minutes," Sage says, glancing at me. "We're going to the cafeteria. You're welcome to come with us."

Jack shakes his head.

"Everything's free," Sage continues. "We can set you up with a great lunch."

Jack looks at me and waits for me to say something. When I don't, he turns back to Sage and says, "Think we can have a second?"

Sage's eyebrows knit together in a frown. The way the two men stare at each other is a slight turn-on. I think I'll have to step in and pull them apart any minute. But I know it's wrong to think that, to want it. So I look at Sage imploringly. Don't want him to protect me. Don't want to end my lunch break breaking up a fight.

"Nice to meet you, man," Sage says finally, holding up his hand to slap Jack's. He points at me. "We're still on for later."

He leaves and I look at Jack, eyebrows raised, waiting for him to start this conversation he needed to be alone with me to have.

"Still giving me the silent treatment?" he asks.

"You don't think you deserve it?"

He smirks. "I'm not going to say yes to that."

We stand in silence too long. I say, "The whole thing was evil. Awful. To me and Rae."

He nods, serious. "I took it too far."

"So this is an apology?" I ask.

He looks a little surprised. "I . . . yeah," he says slowly. "I'm sorry."

"Good." I step back, ready to disappear. "Maybe I'll see you around."

"I didn't actually see you," he admits.

I stop, come back reluctantly.

"I've been waiting. I called your office from a pay phone. Someone said you were out on your lunch break."

"Why'd you call from a pay phone?"

"I kept calling from my room, but you never picked up. I didn't think it would be appropriate if I asked for you. I mean, a guest asking for you . . ."

I nod. "You're right."

"I haven't seen you," he says. It comes out like a sigh. A big regret. Another admission.

"No. I've been busy," I lie. "Working extra shifts . . . and stuff."

"We went to that gay bar in your neighborhood over the weekend," he says.

"Excelsior. We like it there."

"Decent beer selection."

"Yeah."

"Gary said you'd probably stop in. I was looking out for you."

"Jack," I say.

"You like it here?" he asks, cutting me off.

"Sometimes," I say. "I don't read *Hotel World,* if that's what you mean."

He laughs. "No. Just. Do you like it?"

"It's okay. I mean, I'm working in the hospitality industry. I wouldn't say that's one hundred percent my style, you know?"

"You like the people you work with?"

"Why are you asking?"

"Curious."

I think of Victoria, who is working the evening shift for another operator. I've been itching to get her back for lying to me about Carl Lakefield, but I haven't had a chance.

"I go to war some days," I say, and then I shrug. "It's just a job."

"Then why are you doing it?"

I stare at him for a minute, then I shake my head. "Your questions."

"What about them?"

Impatient, I say, "I'm going to lose my temper if you keep asking them."

"I'm not supposed to ask you questions?"

"No," I snap. "You're not supposed to be here. What are you doing here?"

He leans against the wall, props a foot up on it. Cool and casual. Unfazed by my anger. "I'm staying here—"

"In New York, Jack. At this hotel. Why'd you stay at *this* hotel?"

He stares at me intently, but doesn't answer.

"We haven't spoken in nine years," I say softly.

The expression on his face is unreadable. He moves away from the wall, watches some people cross the street and go inside the hotel. Then he leans against the wall again and stares at the ground.

"Still," he says.

"What does that mean? Still."

For a second, he looks hurt, and I'm struck by it, and just how quickly he's able to cover it. I see his jaw set, and after a second he starts to walk away.

"Jack," I call out. And I hear it in my voice, the urgency that makes him stop.

"Look, I'm sorry if seeing me bothers you," he says, coming back, avoiding looking in my face again. "I shouldn't have stayed here."

"It's not the seeing you part," I say. "It's . . . why? Why did you want to see me? Hurt me? Why did you try to? . . ."

"I don't know."

"Am I a question?" I ask bluntly. "I mean, you getting married and all. Am I something you need answered?"

He tilts his head and looks at me, face filling with understanding and relief. "Maybe."

I'm struck by his honesty. I shouldn't be. He was never afraid of the difficult questions. So, now *I'm* afraid. Of how his answer makes me feel. I don't hate it, but I want to hate it. I want to hate him. For being evil and owning up to it. And I don't want this brief moment alone with him to turn everything upside down. I've carved out a good place for myself here, in this world. No one can get in to bother me or make me feel things I don't want to feel.

"I don't want to be that," I say coldly. "It's not cool."

He nods, eyes glued to my face. "Okay."

We're quiet for a long time, watching people go in and out of the hotel. I know I should get back to my break. Sage is probably waiting for me in the cafeteria, legs jiggling like a man hopped up on major doses of pure caffeine.

"Are you with that guy?" Jack asks. "Sage."

"Yes."

He looks down, nods. For a second, I wish I hadn't lied.

"He's nice."

"I do want to see you," I say abruptly, meaning it. "It's just . . . I don't have much to say. Not after what happened at Nick's."

He nods. "I'm sorry."

This time it isn't a false apology, and it's nice to be apologized to.

"I accept."

His eyes focus on me again, and then he moves forward, hand rising up to touch my face as though he's going to kiss me. I pull back, unsure if it's what he's really about to do. His cell phone rings and I laugh. Nervous laughter. And he looks like he really regrets what was just about to happen.

He says, "Hang on a second," and answers the call.

I start to head back inside, but he puts the call on hold.

"It's business," he tells me.

"I have to go, anyway."

He catches hold of my arm. "I didn't mean to . . . ," he starts.

"No problem."

He just stands there.

"I'll go first." I back up. "Don't worry. I didn't take it personally. I'll pretend it never happened."

"Ken," he says.

"No, really." I disappear inside the building.

In the office, I sit at my cubicle and stare at all the calls holding on the switchboard, and I concentrate on pretending the thing with Jack never happened. But for the first time, in a long time, I feel something for someone who isn't just a voice in a faceless conversation, and the pretending isn't working.

"Would someone help me answer these phones?" Katie asks.

Thirty-five calls holding. I've seen it hit seventy when Kirk was out sick. That time, the General Manager came in to see if we were all dead.

"Hold on," I say, grabbing my headset. "We can handle this."

Maria and Trina hang up on their personal calls and we start answering expertly. Connecting, disconnecting and apologizing to the guests who say, "Is there anyone working here?"

It's a mad rush until Wanda comes in to start her shift. We have a break for a minute, and I slouch in my chair.

Katie comes over to my cubicle and offers me a package of Pepperidge Farm cookies. Soft-baked. Chocolate chip macadamia. My favorite. No one has told her about the wake-up call debacle.

"Thanks," I say.

"Good job," she tells me. "Couldn't have handled it without you. You're so good at this."

I toss the package of cookies on my desk when she walks away and slouch deeper in my seat.

It's just a job.

A job I'm really good at.

Sage and I ride the train downtown. He's quiet. Still angry that I missed him in the cafeteria earlier.

Tonight we're on the guest list for a new club called Therapy. The Texan is supposed to be there. When we walk out of the Twenty-third Street station he says, "How was lunch?" very casually.

"Nice," I tell him. "You were with me for most of it."

Before he can say anything else, we spot Amy and her date waiting across the street. She sees us and starts to wave frantically.

I wave back.

A black skullcap fits snugly over Amy's small head. The rest of her hair flows wildly past her shoulders. The man with her is tall, and very well built. He has sandy blond hair that's slightly long and covers one of his eyes. They're both wearing black dress pants and turtlenecks.

When the light changes, Amy runs across the street and hugs me. Her friend takes his time. Amy hugs Sage as well. Sage doesn't hug her back, just looks surprised.

"You must be Sage," she says.

"You must be Amy."

Amy introduces us to Jonah.

"So, what's the occasion?" she asks when all of the introductions are finished. "Why are we on the guest list? Therapy is a very hot club."

"No occasion," I say as we start to walk in the direction of Tenth Avenue. I've never invited Amy or Gary or Nick to a club before, never admitted to any of them what I used to do when I went.

Tonight is different. I have no problem admitting that tonight I'm trying to appease Sage. Not that he's been a real ballbuster about the whole meeting-my-friends thing. He only asked that one time. I can feel it coming, though. A tidal wave of demands he doesn't have a right to make. And I don't feel like having that argument.

Not now. Not tomorrow. Not ever.

Amy slips her arm through my arm and pulls me back. "This is the guy you're sleeping with?"

I nod.

"Cute."

"Yours, too. What happened to the Russian?"

The last boyfriend I met was a big-time DJ named Gorvic, or something equally as Slavic and vampiric as that. I only met him once, and I wasn't impressed.

"Remember how I used to say he always had a different girl on his arm before we started dating?" she asks.

"Vaguely."

"Well, I started to realize I was that girl. The girl I always laughed at. I was the butt of my own joke. I was girlfriend twenty-five. No name. Just twenty-five. I hated that feeling."

"Jonah looks like a good thing," I tell her.

She nods, agreeing. "I knew you'd like him."

"I do," I say, even though I've barely met him.

Inside, I feel overwhelmed and a little tense. I haven't been to a club in four months. Amy and Jonah head straight for the dance floor and say they'll find us later. Sage offers to find us a place to sit. I offer to buy Sage a drink.

I stand at the bar trying to be seen, and when I am, I spend five minutes shouting at the bartender.

"How much is a glass of wine?"

"Nine-fifty," the bartender shouts back, annoyed.

"Nine-fifty! What about Bud?"

"We don't carry Budweiser," the bartender sneers.

I think of another inexpensive beer I can stand. "What about Red Stripe."

"Seven-twenty-five," the bartender says through clenched teeth, like she's really had it with me now.

"Shit." I hand her a twenty. "Seven-twenty-five for Red Stripe. Give me two."

I bring the drinks back to Sage, who has secured a booth at the edge of the dance floor. "Fifteen bucks for two Red Stripes," I tell him. "Plus two bucks for tip."

"I'll get the next round," he promises, taking his drink.

We watch the people on the dance floor.

"You're quiet," he shouts after a while.

"Yeah," I shout back.

"What's on your mind?"

"Nothing."

"That guy?"

I look at him. "What guy?"

"The one at lunch. Who was he?"

"I went to school with him," I say. "He's in town for a while."

Sage eyes me. "He looks familiar. Like somebody I checked in."

I nod. "He has a pretty common face."

"No he doesn't."

I suck on my beer.

"You fuck that guy?"

I don't answer.

"You sleep with him?" he asks again.

I still don't answer. But I look at him.

"He's a guest at the hotel," Sage says. "His wife's staying with him."

"Fiancée," I correct. "And I went to school with him. It was a coincidence that he stayed at the hotel."

"A coincidence?"

"Yes."

Sage stares at me for a long time. "You sleep with him?"

"Like ten years ago, yeah."

Sage looks away.

"Aren't you married?"

I regret saying it the second it comes out of my mouth. There's always been an agreement between us: Don't use the marriage. Sage puts his beer down and leans back in his seat.

"Sage," I say.

He sighs, looks at me. "Being the jealous one is just as awful as being the object of the jealousy," he tells me.

"But you really have no right. You know?"

"It's just my way."

"Yeah." I nod. "But we're friends first. Right?"

He ignores the query. "You sleeping with other guys . . ." He shakes his head.

"Not sleeping with him."

Amy and Jonah come back from the dance floor sweaty and giddy. Amy zeroes in on my drink.

"Can I borrow a sip?"

"Borrow?" I hand her the beer.

She gulps the beer thirstily. She offers some to Jonah.

"Beer dehydrates," Jonah informs her.

"I usually don't drink beer," she tells him self-consciously. "I just needed something wet in my mouth."

Jonah invites her to dance again, but she declines. She sits between Sage and me and tells him to go out without her. He does.

"So, I met this guy at a party the other night," Amy tells us loudly. "You won't believe this guy. He's perfect. And the way we met? It was like a scene in a movie when the music stops, and the lights dim and the two main characters only see each other across the room. I have a scene like that in one of my scripts."

"We're talking about your friend out there on the dance floor?" Sage asks, amused.

Amy nods, then she looks at me. "I could love this guy, Kenny. You know what I mean when I say that? Love? He's the one. I'm sure of it."

I squeeze her leg and smile. "That's great news," I say.

"So, you work with Kenny?" Amy asks Sage, inching closer to him.

He nods, inching away from her a little bit.

"Do you meet a lot of celebrities?"

Sage nods again.

"What do you think of Jennifer Connelly? Do you like her?"

"I don't think she's ever stayed at the hotel," Sage tells her.

Amy nods. "Well, if you ever see her address, would you keep it for me? I've written a script for her. It's a great script. I think she'd like it."

I watch Jonah dance with a couple of very attractive men in

tight shorts. I check to see if Amy's catching any of this. She isn't.

"I also have a script for Don Cheadle," she's saying. "Do you know him? Great actor. I would love to sleep with him."

"What would your boy Jonah have to say about that?" Sage asks.

Not a lot, I'm thinking. Jonah is now sandwiched between a different man and a tall, shapely drag queen with big blond hair.

"Uh, Amy," I say. "Maybe you should join Jonah on the dance floor?"

Amy stops asking Sage questions and follows my gaze. She squints at Jonah dry humping the drag queen, looks thoughtful, then stands up and says she'll go dance with him for a while.

An hour and two more beers later, Sage is desperate to get out. The music is too loud and the kids are too young and the beer is way too expensive. I'm pretty fed up as well. The club scene hasn't been my favorite scene since I got out of it. To add insult to injury, Sage has accused me of being "someplace else" and isn't speaking to me. And I can't bear to watch Amy try to keep Jonah's attention a second longer. The man is obviously gay.

I tell Sage I'm going to the bathroom and I'll meet him outside.

The bathroom is vile, as most club bathrooms are. There are men and women clutching drinks, smoking pot, snorting coke and pissing in stalls without doors. I stand in the middle of it all, feeling strangely calm, strangely safe.

I take a couple of deep breaths, and then the Texan walks in.

Damn. To be young, rich and famous. I see famous people

all the time at the hotel. Mostly they look normal, or like they've had too much plastic surgery. But it's the young ones that always get me. They're just so damn beautiful. No one should be as beautiful as they are.

He's with a few guys who look more rowdy than anything else. They stop near the sink next to me and look around. I think about introducing myself and offering to buy him a drink, but the group doesn't seem approachable.

For one thing, they're drunk. They're laughing and pushing each other around. Being predictably male and ridiculous. The Texan gives one of the guys a powerful shove and the guy knocks into me, nearly taking me down.

The Texan snickers. No one apologizes.

I open my mouth to say something but think better of it. These kids live for bar brawls. It gets them in the papers and makes them feel tough. I thought the Texan was different.

When his hand lands in a puddle of putrid water on the sink's counter, he stares at it for a while.

"Fuck," he curses and looks to his friends for help.

This just disgusts me. There's a stack of napkins right next to him, but he's so used to having the tiniest chore completed for him that the idea of reaching for a napkin himself hasn't crossed his mind. It hasn't been conditioned to.

One of his friends grabs a couple of the napkins for him and hands them over.

For a second, he just stands there holding the napkins. I wonder if he needs someone to help him out with the drying of his hands part. Does he have people to wipe his ass, too?

Finally, he cleans up and tosses the dirty napkins on the sink.

I wish I hadn't witnessed any of this. And it's not like tossing napkins on a sink or needing them handed to you are heinous crimes. Not like I've never littered before or wished someone would take care of me. Not like the bathroom is all sparkly and clean. Not like I have this illusion that celebrities have a higher moral ground than the rest of us.

It's just that I've been listening to his personal calls, and I've learned he's sensitive. One of the only people in the hotel I can actually claim that about. He's an advocate for the environment, talking about trees and the rain forest and the possibility of gorillas becoming extinct. Talking about it like he *really cares*. And he seems to like people.

Outside, Sage is smoking a cigarette, waiting for me. He asks if I'm okay, because he thinks I look sad. I don't tell him about the Texan. I don't know that he'll understand. I don't even understand. Not really. I should have known the Texan was full of shit, and it bothers me that I thought he might not be.

"Amy says she's going to stay at your place tonight," Sage tells me. "She has a key."

"You can still come over."

He doesn't say anything.

"Please come over," I say, verging on sounding kind of desperate. But I know he won't. I know the exact minute he decided he wasn't going to. I take his hand. He resists at first, and then he squeezes tightly.

"I can't. Not tonight."

I don't push him. It's best that he doesn't know how much I don't want to be without him right now. All of a sudden, I'm needy. And Sage is the only person who is consistently there when I get like this, ignoring the vulnerability, knowing not to point it out. There's something about this—about feeling needy and being aware of it—that scares me.

Doomp!

Amy opens my bedroom door, letting harsh light from the living room seep in. "What the fuck is that?"

This morning there's the *doomp*ing I've almost become accustomed to. Loud and disconcerting. I stare at the ceiling and wait for it to stop. But it doesn't. I sit up, look at Amy and concentrate.

The kid upstairs is jumping off the staircase, running back up the stairs and jumping off them again and again and again. What the kid is doing jumping off stairs at . . . I check the clock . . . a quarter past four in the morning is baffling. But here it is. Happening above my head.

"Okay," Amy says. "You need to go up there and do something about this."

"It'll stop."

"It hasn't stopped," she says. "It's been going on for fifteen minutes. It's just getting louder."

I don't bother to get dressed. I slip on a pair of shoes and go upstairs in my pajamas.

The small area in front of my neighbor's doorway is like a

garage sale. I rarely have a reason to come up to the fifth floor, so I can't say that it hasn't always looked like this. But something tells me this is a Betty Blacksmith Special.

There's a tacky white wall unit, circa 1985, holding up the wall, partially blocking the stairs leading to the sixth floor. A tall, dead plant is in the corner, sitting atop piles of yellowing magazines and newspapers.

I navigate my way through the mess and ring the doorbell.

It takes Betty about three minutes to come to the door. I wait. She fumbles with the locks—there seem to be at least seventy of them—and pulls the door open. Her hair is tangled around her face like a crow's nest. She's wearing a crumpled sundress.

"*What?!*" she barks.

I haven't made a lot of friends in the building. I leave the making-friends-with-neighbors thing to Gary. There are a couple of women who have knocked on my door in search of sugar or flour or oil. We've talked about trivial things in the hallway, like books we've read or movies we've seen. We've discussed getting together for coffee or dinner but have never followed through.

Overall, I like it here. The people are pleasant, private, considerate.

Yet now, at half past four in the morning, I'm standing here, staring at the evil that is my upstairs neighbor. And here is the little kid, the rodent, the pest I want to squash with my bare hands.

"Your child's jumping," I say.

Betty rubs her eyes and jabs her hands through her hair. "No, she isn't."

"Well, yeah, she is. I have company, and she woke us up."

"*You* woke *us* up."

I look at the kid. I'm sure she's going to step in heroically any second now and explain how desperate she's been for "mommy time." How the jumping off the stairs at four in the morning, while admittedly a very bad decision, was a desperate cry for attention. How it won't happen again.

The kid clutches her mother's dress and stares up at me fearfully. Betty looks down at her.

"Honey, were you jumping?"

Without hesitation, the kid shakes her head no.

"*NO?*" I'm horrified. "Tell your mother the truth, kid. You were jumping right above my bedroom, weren't you? I have witnesses."

"*Madam,*" Betty hisses. "She just said she wasn't jumping."

I meet Betty's eyes. "You're going to take the word of a child over mine?"

Betty doesn't dignify my question with an answer.

"Look," I say, doing a damn good job of not losing my temper. "Since you've moved in you've been pretty excellent in the noise department. You. The Kid. Red Sweatshirt Guy who doesn't exist. And Gary and I have been pretty excellent at giving you the benefit of the doubt. Being new and settling in and all. But every night you've been here, you have managed to pull me out of a deep sleep at some insane hour, and it has to stop."

Betty is dumbstruck. Completely. Utterly. Dumbstruck. *Who the hell do you think you are?* her look says. *You peon. You . . . subletter.*

"Do you know who I am?" she asks in a quiet rage. "I'm the president of the co-op board."

I nod, unimpressed. "I know. That's why I'm shocked by your lack of respect for my quality of living."

Pow! Her head kicks back like I've just coldcocked her.

"My child was not jumping," Betty snaps, then slams the door in my face.

I ring the doorbell several times, to no avail. Then I kick it once. This proves to be a big mistake, since Dina, the woman on the other side of the floor, has come out to check what's happening. I don't know Dina very well. She's an "artist," though Gary and I believe a better description for her is "psychotic." We've witnessed her vicious and foul arguments with her ex-husband early in the morning. She has a daughter who is a little older than Betty's.

I smile at her. She glares at me.

"I was just—"

She slams her door shut before I can explain.

Amy's curled up in my bed when I come back downstairs.

"Did you tell her?" she asks groggily.

"Yes."

"The kid's still jumping."

"I hear it," I say as I get back into bed.

The jumping resumes for about ten minutes. Amy groans into my pillow the entire time. I start to get out of bed again, but it stops suddenly. And then there's complete silence.

In the morning, there's a flurry of activity that wakes us up. Amy buries her face in the pillow and wails. "Can we hurt them? Can we? Please?"

I take a shower.

"Look," Amy says when I come out of the bathroom. She's holding up a sheet of pink construction paper. I take it.

I'M SORRY I MADE NOISE is scrawled sloppily across the paper in black crayon.

"That's adorable," I say, looking at the apology note. "Kids always come through."

Amy sucks her teeth. "Children are not innocent."

"Right," I say sarcastically, tossing the note in the garbage. "They're guilty."

"Don't throw that out." Amy points to the garbage can. "It's an admission. You may need that in the future."

"For what? A trial? We'll put the little brat on the stand and cross-examine her? Then when her little lip starts to quiver and she looks at the judge with her huge, little girl eyes—"

"We lost sleep," Amy reminds me. "Someone has to be held responsible for that. Why not the little person who terrorized us?"

I wave her ridiculous notion away, then remember the Sam Ripper fax I kept for her.

"It's missing a couple of pages," I say, pulling it from under a pile of Gary's magazines. "But I think you'll find enough names and numbers to get you through your next job hunt in L.A."

Amy takes the fax and looks it over. Ever since I started working at the hotel, she's been asking me to jot down phone numbers and addresses of producers, directors and actors. She hopes to find the right Hollywood insider to read one of her scripts.

She breaks into a grin. I'm aware the Sam Ripper fax has a ton of "inside information" in it. Amy now has the private office numbers for executives at Dreamworks, Fine Line, Fox Searchlight, New Line and several other film companies.

"Why do they fax stuff like that?" she asks.

"Probably because they believe if you pay seven hundred dollars a night for a room, you should be able to trust that the employees aren't going to steal your faxes," I say.

"Why don't they just put fax machines in the guest rooms?"

"You can request a fax machine," I explain. "But that means you have to retrieve and collate your own faxes."

Amy snorts. "Then they deserve it," she concludes.

I start to boil water for coffee.

"I don't want tea," Amy tells me grumpily.

"Not making tea. Making coffee."

Amy wrinkles her nose. "With a teakettle?"

I show her the box of coffee singles. "Coffee."

"I'm not drinking that crap coffee."

"Coffee singles are time saving and economical, and not bad at all," I tell her.

"We need real coffee," she argues. "We had a bad night."

I roll my eyes. "This is perfectly decent coffee."

Amy says she wants to treat me to *real* coffee before I go to work. Starbucks coffee. As a rule, I don't drink Starbucks coffee unless I'm with Amy. It's too expensive for my budget.

"Don't think poor," Amy warns me.

"That's kind of hard when you're treating me to coffee with seven of my dollars I could use for a MetroCard."

On our way out of the building, we see Betty struggling to open the driver's side of a beat-up Toyota Corolla. As usual, the hair is wet and stringy. A pile of manila folders sits precariously on top of the car's hood next to a cup of morning coffee or tea. The kid is jumping up and down.

Until she sees me, that is. She stops, eyes wide with terror, bottom lip hanging so low it's nearly hitting the ground.

"*That's* the wildebeest making all the noise?" Amy asks when Betty looks over at us and half-waves. "*Oh, please.* You can take her."

"Someone told Gary she comes from western Pennsylvania," I say, half-waving back. "Real backwoods."

"Mountain trash," Amy surmises. "You can take her."

"A bit rough around the edges, don't you think? Seems like she's been fighting for decades."

"Yeah, fighting off her father and brothers," Amy snickers. "Let's go beat up the kid then."

She starts to cross the street, but I catch her arm.

"Right," I say. "Something new and relevant to add to our CVs."

"Say good morning, sweetie," Betty instructs the kid loudly.

The kid continues to look shell-shocked.

"Thank you for the note," I call out to her with a nonthreatening smile. "I really liked it."

Slowly, the kid's mouth closes.

"She knocked," Betty informs me. "But you wouldn't open the door. I told her to slip it under."

"She didn't knock," Amy says defiantly.

"I must have been in the shower," I tell Betty.

"She didn't," Amy insists.

Betty dismisses me with an unbelieving look as she finally gets the car door open. She gets in. The kid finally slips out of shock and waves in slow motion, a tentative smile making its way across her face.

Cute.

"Get in the car!" Betty shouts.

Amy and I sit on the ground in front of the local Starbucks and drink our three-dollar coffees in silence. I marvel at us. Just sitting on a dirty sidewalk in our decent clothes, not talking.

I'm also marveling at the number of familiar faces walking hurriedly in the direction of the train. Off to work, the way I should be. Some of them nod, alarmingly. It means I'm familiar to them as well.

"You know how you never notice anything?" Amy asks.

"No."

"Well, you never noticed how often Jack looked at you that night at Nick's." She's staring at me solemnly. "I know we're not going to talk about it, but I just wanted to tell you that."

"That came out of nowhere," I say, sipping my coffee.

"I was hoping it would prompt you to tell me about Jack's fiancée."

"Oh," I say, meeting her eyes. "Forgot to mention it. Sorry. How'd you find out?"

"I crashed at Nick's the other night," she tells me. She doesn't have to add Jack and Rae were there. "She's not as pretty as you are."

I chuckle, shake my head. Such a best friend thing to say.

"No. Really. I know that's not where we're going with this, but I thought you should know."

"Where *are* we going with this?" I ask.

Amy shrugs. "What do you want to know?"

Again, silence between us. The number of people hurrying to work has diminished. I'm late.

"What'd you talk about?" I ask.

"Beer," Amy answers immediately. "Boring as hell. He was never this boring in college."

Amy met Jack by accident. She and I were coming out of class one afternoon, and he was waiting for me. He acknowledged her with a slight nod and told me he'd be waiting outside. He stuck his cigarette back in his mouth and walked out of the building.

Amy watched him retreat, bottom lip curled into her mouth. This was her first impression of him. Brief. Not wonderful. Definitely not boring. A few days later I asked him if he'd meet my friends, and he made it clear he didn't want to. But Amy kept hounding me. And even though she promised not to tell Gary and Nick I was seeing some badass from the dorms in Southwest, or "the zoo" as students and employees referred to them, I knew Amy would tell them eventually. A payback for not introducing Jack to them sooner. And I knew what my friends would say.

Why would a nice girl like you date a guy like him?

"Is she nice?" I ask.

"Not really." Amy shrugs. "Kind of boring, too. Quiet. Nothing we said interested her. And she kept getting catering calls, which was annoying. You know she's a caterer? She kept getting up and taking the calls in the other room, and then she'd come back and say something inside-jokey to Jack about her clients. She would laugh and he would look embarrassed. It was all very painful. I pulled a Kenny. I told them I had a headache and went to bed early."

I smile a little.

"What did you think of her? I know you met her at the hotel. She made sure to tell me that."

I finish off my coffee and stand up, tell Amy I'm late for work. Amy stands up, too, but she doesn't let me go.

"What'd you think of her?"

"She didn't have time to make an impression on me," I say. "We were on an elevator."

Amy takes my empty coffee cup and dumps it in a nearby garbage can. We start to walk toward the train.

"She said you seemed unhappy," Amy tells me quietly. "She asked Jack if you were always that unhappy when he dated you. I thought it was obnoxious."

I almost stop walking, then think better of it. I don't want Amy to know how much Rae's impression of me stings. I shrug like it's no big deal.

"Jack said you used to be happy. He said he agreed. That you don't look the same. Are you unhappy, Kenny? I mean, I think I know you better than most people, and I never get that impression. Maybe a little unsatisfied in the love department, but I thought Jack and Rae were being kind of cruel."

I shrug again, like I don't care.

"I think they were jealous," Amy says.

"Probably," I toss off lightly.

The truth is, I haven't allowed myself to love anyone the way I loved Jack in college. We were young. Love is meant to be honest and raw and unguarded when you're young. I don't trust myself to feel that kind of love for anyone now. I don't trust my friends to allow me to.

That's not to say Jack and I would still be together if I'd ignored the crew's warnings about Jack's inappropriateness as a boyfriend and his lack of everything that's needed to be someone's future. I don't even know if I'd still love him if I'd given us a chance. I just have this question.

Do I regret not letting us find out if we would have lasted?

I've been asking myself this question for the past two weeks, and it bothers me that I don't have the answer. It bothers me that I know I'll never have the answer.

I watch Victoria at the dry-erase board, writing out instructions. Standing in the front of the room, on her toes to reach the top of the board, she's a painful reminder of just how stupid we all look in our uniforms.

"Mr. Davis has just checked into the Presidential Suite," Victoria announces loudly. "Now, I don't know who this man is, but he's obviously a superstar. If you don't put his calls through the way he wants them, you're going to deal with him and his manager and Kirk. After what happened with the wake-up calls the other day, I don't want anything to do with it. Because *no one* pays attention. Davis is paying six thousand dollars a night to live here for a few days, and I don't want to hear about how you don't know how to put his calls through or spell his name or whatever . . ."

I lean back in my chair and look at the board. Victoria watches me, which makes me stare at the board longer than I need to. We've been hating each other, and I've been desperate to get her back for lying to me about the Carl Lakefield plane ticket.

"You have a problem?" she asks me.

"Um," I say, not taking my eyes off the board. "You think you could rewrite that a little neater?"

Victoria's eyes narrow. "What?"

"Neater," I say slowly. "So I can read it. And you spelled *disturb* wrong."

I turn back to my switchboard, aware that Victoria hasn't moved but is, instead, giving me the evil eye.

"You can't read that?" she shrieks. *"You can't read it?"* Because you can rewrite it yourself if you can't read it."

I know I should let this one go.

I stand up and look at the board again, squinting. Victoria, on her way back to her desk, stops and looks at me.

"Hmmm," I say, fighting a grin. I just love that look on her face, which I can see from the corner of my eye. Her mouth all poked out like an angry child, her eyes narrowed, and the usual cartoon smoke floating out of her ears. "*I* certainly can't read that." I look her in the eye. "And *disturb?* D-I-S-T-U-R-B."

Victoria goes back to her desk and slams her chair around.

"People need to get some manners in here," Victoria starts. "I swear I'm going to tell Kirk how you all treat me. I come in *early* and I work late because you can't get yourselves together. And I get treated like this. I'm not going to come in here anymore, and I'm not going to train the new people anymore."

"Good!" I say. "We'll celebrate after work. Drinks are on me."

"Victoria," Maria warns. "Keep your voice down. The guests can hear you."

"I don't care," Victoria shouts. *"I don't care."*

I get a call from Cheryl, Victoria's office buddy. She whispers, "Apologize."

"No," I say.

"You started it," Cheryl accuses. "And you know you can read that board. So just apologize, otherwise she's going to call Kirk and he's going to leave his meeting early and take it out on all of us."

Cheryl's from the South, pushing sixty. She thinks she deserves respect because she's old and has worked at the hotel longer than the rest of us. In my world, respect is a two-way street. If you don't give, you don't receive.

I disconnect the call.

Cheryl stands up and looks at me over the partition that separates us. She's a heavy, good-looking woman with reddish-brown hair. She has small, beady eyes that sear you when you get on her bad side. She can cause a world of trouble without ever leaving her desk.

"You okay over there?" she asks sternly.

"Slight headache," I answer. "Got any Advil?"

Cheryl gives me one of those looks, the look that says *I'm watching you.* Everyone in the hotel knows about Cheryl's looks. Even Sage. But I don't back down. It's true that Cheryl can make my life hell here. She has Kirk in check, and for some scary reason, Mr. Schmidt even listens to her. All she has to do is tell them I listen to calls, and I could lose my job. But the truth of the matter is, Cheryl knows I'm not above snitching on her.

For the next couple of hours before Cheryl clocks out, I'm subjected to hearing the operators on the other side of the room whisper about me. When I get a call for the fax operator, I clear my throat and say, "Cheryl, I'm passing a fax call to you."

Cheryl doesn't say anything, and I don't pass the call. Part of me knows she won't take it. She never takes calls when she's doing faxes.

I repeat, "Cheryl. Someone on the line was expecting a fax twenty minutes ago. I'm going to pass the call to you."

"I have two speeds," Cheryl thunders. "Slow and leave me alone. Don't send that call to me, child."

I bite my tongue. Kirk never gets on Cheryl's case about answering fax-related calls when she's doing faxes. So, getting into it with her over a fax call isn't worth it. I get up, go over to the fax log and check to see if the fax has been received and picked up by a Page. It has.

I go back to my seat, assure the guest that his fax will arrive momentarily.

A few minutes before Cheryl leaves for the day, I stand up and look at the dry-erase board again.

"Okay," I say. "I have Mrs. Davis on the phone. And I can't figure out if the instructions are to put her through without screening, or if the DND applies to his wife as well. And if the DND is only on between seven in the evening and eleven in the morning, how can we screen calls from nine in the morning to eleven at night? And even though this chick says she's Mrs. Davis, she doesn't know his alias, so what should I do? Victoria?"

There's silence on the other side of the room, and I wait. I can hear Maria and Cheryl whispering, telling Victoria that I'm lying, and not to take the bait. But Victoria can't help who she is.

"Pass the call to me," Victoria says finally. "Hurry up. You had that woman holding for five minutes."

I pass a random call to Victoria.

"Mrs. Davis?" Victoria says in a voice dripping with honey. "I'm sorry about that. There was a mix-up with . . . excuse me? Oh, I'm sorry. I thought you were holding. *How may I direct your call, sir?*"

I munch on the bag of Pepperidge Farm cookies Katie left for me as Victoria curses me viciously and puts her headset away. She comes over to my cubicle and points her finger in my face. "You want to play games with me, little girl?"

"Little girl?" I say, inching away from her finger. "Victoria, you're like three years older than me."

"You want to play games?" she repeats, eyes narrowed and ugly. "You want to see how fast your ass gets fired? Because I'm ready to show you."

There's only so much of Victoria I can take, so I tell her to shut the fuck up before I make a formal complaint to the General Manager. Not a huge deal in my world. Because everyone in my world knows I'm just talking shit. But in Victoria's world, everything is taken literally, and what I've said is the equivalent of saying I slept with her boyfriend and I'm going to have his baby.

She starts to cry and scream and tell everyone she's leaving. Cheryl has to grab all of her bags and escort her to the cafeteria for water.

I love it.

"You all suffer without me," she huffs as she storms out of the office.

Everyone is silent.

Nearly twenty minutes later Maria stands up and looks at me over the partition.

"You should try to be nicer, Kendall," she says evenly. "You never know when you'll need friends."

There are two things you can do at the hotel once you've been employed for a year: vacation at sister-hotels for free, and transfer. I've yet to have one of my requests to stay at a sister-hotel approved. I've never inquired about a transfer.

Molly Hay is the assistant Human Resources director. She's petite and curly and perky and sweet. She's surprised to see me in her office. She doesn't ask if I have an appointment. She says, "What can I do for you, Kendall?"

I tell her I'd like to apply for a transfer, and she raises her eyebrows.

"Do you know what the process is?" she asks.

I shake my head no.

"All you have to do is fill this application out." She pulls a one-page application out of a drawer behind her. "It takes five minutes. You're on your break, right?"

I nod.

"Okay. You fill this application out. I'll review it. And then I'll ask Kirk for a written recommendation. It's as simple as that."

"Great," I say, taking the application.

"You've been here a year?" She types something into her computer. "Oh. Definitely. You shouldn't have a problem. As long as the department you're interested in has an opening and you haven't been written up more than once . . ."

"So far, so good," I tell her.

She smiles blandly. "May I ask why you want to transfer, and which department you would like to transfer to?"

"Certainly," I say. "I believe it's time for a change. I don't want to answer phones anymore. And I'd like to transfer to Concierge."

Another bland smile. "You'd answer phones at Concierge."

"Yes," I say slowly. "But it's different. I wouldn't be defined by answering telephones."

She grimaces. "Do you speak any foreign languages, Kendall?"

"English feels pretty foreign sometimes," I joke.

"Concierge requires at least one language other than English," she says seriously.

"I can get by on Spanish."

She shakes her head. "You can't just get by at Concierge."

"What about Front Desk?"

"What about Room Service Order Taker?" Molly suggests. "Or Reservations? Why don't we start small?"

I stare at Molly for a long time. Her smile becomes uncertain, and she lowers her eyes after a minute.

"Okay," I give in. "I'll try Reservations."

There's a voice-mail message from Amy when I return to my cubicle. She's in room 1700.

With Gary and Nick.

With Jack and Rae.

She says, "Come up when you're off work. We can't start the orgy without you."

I wondered why Rodney was smirking when I walked in. Creep. Listening to my messages. Now he thinks I'm sleeping with the gay soap opera actor in 1700, not to mention the gay soap opera actor's pseudo-girlfriend.

Doesn't matter. I'm not going up there.

"Passing a call to you," Rodney says quietly.

I think about letting this *Sullivan, Jack* call go to voice mail again.

"Can't talk," I say when I pick up.

"Where are you?" Amy pesters. "We're waiting."

"I'm working," I snap.

"Should we order room service without you?"

"What? Yes. I'm not coming up."

"You have to," Amy says.

"Give me one good reason."

"Food," she says.

She recites everything they're planning to order from the

room service menu. Enchanting goodies like roast duck, red snapper and crab cakes. I've never eaten the hotel food, which is different from the cafeteria food. Everything the guests consume, including everything on the room service menu, is prepared by the hotel's award-winning chef and her assistants. The hotel cafeteria food is prepared by twenty-year-old high school dropouts who don't have any aspiration to win a James Beard Foundation Award.

It's tempting. Eating thirty-dollar duck sandwiches on someone else's dime in one of the hotel's deluxe suites. But pride's got me looking at this like a shameless pauper begging to be fed by her ex-boyfriend.

"I don't think so," I say.

"He's trying to impress us," Amy says. "All of us. But the one of us he's trying to impress most isn't here. She's refusing to pay any attention to him."

"If you mean me, you're wrong. I've paid too much. . . . *Are you saying all of this in front of him?*"

"I'm on the bathroom phone." She sounds giddy all of a sudden. "I love this hotel."

"I have to go."

"Kenny," Amy barks. "Come upstairs. Don't be a chickenshit."

As soon as I disconnect the call, Rodney tells me he has the Texan on the line. He's going to pass the call to me.

"No," I say quickly. "Don't."

Rodney raises his eyebrows, but he doesn't ask.

Amy's waiting for me outside. We don't say anything when I come out of the employee entrance. I light a cigarette, and we walk to a public courtyard a few blocks away. Amy sits on a bench and reaches out for my cigarette. I sit next to her, and we share for a while.

"Jack used to feed me," she says.

"I remember."

"He only fed me because he loved you," she continues. "He told me he didn't trust me. He was very straightforward."

"I know."

"But he watched my back when I was stupid. Because you loved me and he loved you."

"Yeah. I know." I sound annoyed because I don't want to be reminded about how much Jack loved me. I don't want to be reminded of the things I loved most about him. Like his protective side. I used to hate it that Amy accepted food from him. Not like he had a ton of cash when we were in college. He did the occasional mechanic job in South Hadley and Greenfield, and then he'd promptly spend the money on food and beer for Amy and me. He never liked to see us hungry.

"They had these tiny crab cakes when I got there," Amy says. "To hold us over until you came."

I take a drag from my cigarette and continue to stare straight ahead.

"With a remoulade sauce to die for," she adds. "You know I don't eat crab."

I've had the crab cakes in the cafeteria. Leftovers from Grand Ballroom parties. We do get to try hotel appetizers on occasion. Anything left over from a Big Event is transferred to the cafeteria. Employees are always on the lookout for treats on Big Event days. It's kind of pathetic, actually. That getting your hands on the hotel leftovers has become competitive.

Someone with an in, like Rodney or Sage, gets a call from the cafeteria. Next thing you know, Rodney is running out of the office and returning ten minutes later with a chef's hat full of mini crab cakes and tea sandwiches. Kirk is meant to stop him from doing it, but he likes the treats just as much as the rest of us.

"They also had miniature quiche," Amy says. "With ham and asparagus. I don't eat asparagus, Kenny. You know that. But I ate like twelve of them. I shudder to think what that's doing to my ass right now."

My Work Life and Real Life are converging. It isn't supposed to be this way. My friends aren't supposed to be dining happily in one of my hotel's suites. They aren't supposed to know this part of me.

Leave it to Jack.

Amy changes the subject. I welcome the change. She says she's going to Los Angeles in three months if she can come up with enough cash.

"Gotta keep plugging away," she says. "I asked Gary to come with me."

I laugh. Gary and Los Angeles wouldn't mix. He doesn't favor sun or beaches or plastic. "What did he say?"

"No."

"I'm not surprised."

"He would do well there," Amy muses. "He'd get a job writing for television in a minute."

"It'll happen for you, too," I tell her.

"I don't write as well as Gary," she admits. "I don't have the same oeuvre he has. He can actually show scripts. What have I finished?"

I squeeze her leg. "You'll do it."

She stares at me for a long time. And then she turns away. "God, we're bored, aren't we?" she says, reaching for my cigarette again.

We drift into the soothing, gardenia-scented lobby of the hotel, with its mirrored walls, glossy marble floors and twelve-hour live pianist. I catch a glimpse of us in one of the mirrors and realize we look short. Not only short, but young.

We're all wrong.

And there's more to our wrongness than height and youth, but I can't put my finger on it. Maybe it's our clothes. How can you tell we aren't wearing the latest fashions touted in *Vogue* magazine? How can you tell Amy's shoes are straight from Payless and my shoes are three years old? I don't know, you just can. It feels obvious.

As we wait for an elevator to whisk us up to the seventeenth floor, I glance casually at Security, and then at Front Desk. I stare at both desks a little too long, daring someone to recognize me and ask where I think I'm going. But that moment doesn't come. Even without the blue smock and the uniform, I'm invisible.

I follow Amy to Jack's door and take a deep breath before she knocks. I think about grabbing her arm and telling her the truth. I don't want to go in there. I don't think I should see Jack again.

But the door flies open before Amy rings the bell, and I'm sure Jack looks disappointed to see us.

"Kendall," he says.

"Yeah. Just us." Amy walks past him without a proper invitation.

I stand in the hall and wait for the invitation. Jack doesn't issue one. He steps aside to make more room for my entrance.

"I thought you were Room Service," he says as I walk inside. "I'm waiting on coffee."

"This late?"

"Doesn't keep me up," he says, closing the door.

Amy has already shed her jacket and joined Nick on the plush sofa in the living room area. Nick is holding out a fork to Amy, who takes it into her mouth and groans at the food's tasty goodness. Gary is standing by the window, sipping on a glass of wine, and Rae is channel-surfing from a plush chair next to the sofa.

Jack picks up the phone and punches a button.

Rae rolls her eyes. "You're so impatient, honey. It's only been five minutes." She notices me and smiles. "Hello."

"Hi," I say.

She rubs a hand over her hair, which is pulled into a sloppy ponytail. She's wearing sweats and sneakers and looks like she's just in from a run. Still, she manages to look like she belongs in the suite more than I do. "Would you like a drink?"

"No, thanks," I say.

"You can have some of my wine." Amy holds up her glass.

I can tell she likes this lifestyle. Her cheeks are glowy and flushed. She can't stop grinning. And what's not to like? Endless amounts of expensive food brought to her by a man in a white uniform. No bill to pay.

"There's absolutely no fat on this duck," Nick tells Gary. Gary looks over his shoulder at Nick and raises an eyebrow.

They like this lifestyle, too.

I feel ambivalent as I watch my friends, who look very comfortable and happy. I hope the charms of pricey food and enormous guestrooms don't blind them to the faults of the people who can afford them. Because here's Jack, tapping his foot impatiently because the Room Service Order Taker has put him on hold. And it just reminds me so much of the people I despise who stay here.

He stops tapping his foot when he realizes I'm noticing it. "You want something from Room Service?" he asks.

"No, thanks." I move deeper into the room and look around as though I haven't been here before. "Nice room."

Jack stares at me for a minute. I glance at Rae, which seems to jog his memory a little. He nods. "Thanks."

"You're welcome."

"I didn't think coffee could be a situation," he remarks, hanging up the phone and looking annoyed. Then he shrugs, resigned to his fate of having to wait like everyone else in the world. It's one of the things that amazes me about people with cash. They believe in magic. "Guess you can't expect much when you pay the help five bucks an hour."

I flush. There's an ugly silence. Everyone is glaring at him. I catch Rae giving him a pointed look, and then they both look at me. And I'm spotlighted. Expected to say something to smooth the awkward moment over and make it okay for stupid people to say stupid things.

"You are such a brute," Rae says affectionately when I don't make it okay. She smiles at me. "He has a tendency to sound . . . privileged. He doesn't mean anything by it."

"I'm suddenly relieved," I say flatly.

Nick clears his throat, uncomfortable and afraid I'm going

to say something evil and drag this scene out. "No biggie," he says lightly.

I say, "Starting salary is ten dollars an hour, in case you're interested. After three months it's raised to twelve. Every year it goes up about fifty cents. Not nearly as much as you make, Jack, but it doesn't give you a right to assume less money means inferior to you."

"I used to make five dollars an hour," Jack says.

I raise my eyebrows. "You remember."

A knock on the door. Jack holds my gaze for a few seconds longer, then opens it. I recognize the Server immediately. He's a young man from Ecuador who is often in the cafeteria the same time Sage and I are. We've taken to smiling and waving at each other, even though we've never bothered to exchange names.

When he sees me, he pauses. No uniform. No smock. I'm not here as a worker. He nods slightly, unsure if he should say hello.

"Hey," I say, overly friendly. "How's it going?"

He glances at the others, doesn't answer my question. He's afraid to engage in idle banter with me in front of actual guests. I guess I can't say I blame him. Not after Jack's little outburst.

But Jack's guilt over saying something stupid is my Room Service Server friend's gain. A nineteen-percent gratuity has already been added to Jack's room service bill, which will later be charged to the credit card the hotel has on file, yet Jack hands the guy a twenty. The fifteen-dollar carafe of coffee and the ten-dollar bowl of fresh strawberries have just cost Jack a lot more than most of our richest guests would be willing to pay.

"Why did you do that?" I ask after the Room Service Server leaves.

"What?" Jack starts to pour the coffee.

"A twenty-dollar tip? He's lucky if he gets five bucks from guys who make twenty million dollars a picture."

"He's been up here three times, Kendall." Jack sounds tired. "He deserved it."

"And you forgot to tip him before," Amy points out cruelly. "When we had the crab cakes and quiche."

"You want coffee?" Jack looks at me warily. "It's decaf."

I shake my head.

"Ken," he says. "Come on. You can have something."

His tone implies an intimacy between us that no longer exists. I immediately look at Rae. She's staring at me, wondering if I'm someone she should pay a little more attention to. I suspect she had the answer to that question before she even came to New York. And the suspicion gives me a slight chill, reminds me why I shouldn't have come here.

"Yes, have something Ken," she says, going for the bowl of strawberries and holding it out to me. "We don't want you to starve."

"I'm good," I say. "I had a snack before I left the office."

Rae puts the bowl back on the table. "Do you work in Sales? My cousin is Sales Director at The Regent in Nevis."

"I'm a Telephone Operator."

"Oh. Right," she says. She picks up the brightest, plumpest strawberry in the bowl and bites into it. Then she chokes. "Damnit." She tosses the rest of her strawberry in the garbage can. "They're not sweet. I'm not eating them."

"Call Room Service and complain," Jack suggests in his tired voice.

"I don't want to complain," Rae huffs.

"Why not?" Jack glares at her. "It's what you're best at."

I stare at the bowl of very big ten-dollar strawberries to avoid witnessing the silent battle waging between Jack and Rae. This could get ugly. And since we're already somewhat aware of the debacle that is Jack and Rae's engagement, we all know this little spat might lead to yet another breaking off of it.

I concentrate on the fact that the strawberries look absolutely delicious. The kitchen would never send mediocre strawberries to a guest. I'd vouch for that.

Now I want to taste one.

"We can't keep ordering shit," Jack tells Rae, clearly losing patience. "We'll have a twelve-hundred-dollar Room Service bill by the time we check out."

"*So*," Rae spits.

"So, you're not paying for it."

Rae drops into a chair next to the sofa Amy and Nick are occupying quietly. She fixes Jack with a relentless stare. And Amy watches Rae from the corner of her eye, almost like she's afraid Rae is going to sprout fangs and devour the closest person to her.

"They look good," Gary comments idly from his place by the window. He glances at Nick, and then me. Nick looks at me as well. I know what they're thinking. They want to try one. Or they want me to try one first. But they know I'd be enraged if the strawberries turn out to be as delicious as they look.

I look away from them. I don't want them to tempt me into grabbing one and biting into it. The hotel strawberries aren't an easy thing for a hotel employee to come by. The chef never puts them out in the employee cafeteria when she has extras. I know from Sage that she keeps them and eats them with the pastry chef. I've always wanted to try them. Still, I hold back.

Every day I walk past carts of half-eaten twenty-four-dollar hamburgers and barely touched fifteen-dollar salads on my way to the cafeteria, and I think it's such a waste. I look at Rae and the way she folds her arms across her chest and pouts and looks very upset because Jack is no longer willing to indulge her in front of his friends.

I want a cigarette. I pat my back pocket in search of one.

Rae watches my hands. "Do you want one?" she asks.

"One what?"

"A cigarette," she says. "I assume that's what you're looking for. I'm desperate for a smoke. Why don't we have one on the balcony?"

I hesitate, not exactly wanting to spend time alone with her. She watches me. Slowly, I stand up and follow her outside. I guess I can handle a minute with her if it means I can get some much needed nicotine in my system.

Outside, she hands me a cigarette.

"Nice view," I say.

Rae merely glances at the spectacular view of New York City's Park Avenue from the seventeenth floor's balcony.

"Unfiltered," she warns, lighting her cigarette, then handing the lighter to me. "I gave up coffee for carrot juice three months ago. I'm still neurotic. I said fuck it and started to smoke."

I take a drag from my cigarette.

"So, what's it like working in a hotel?" she asks, then decides to answer her own question. "Like working anyplace else, I would think."

"Yeah," I agree.

"Though I did see Britney Spears this morning," she appends. "It's probably cool to talk to famous people every day."

"Not really," I say.

She laughs. "So celebrities don't have all the answers?"

"To life's questions?" I ask. "No."

"No cure for cancer, or AIDS, or depression?"

I shake my head and genuinely grin, though I think she has a lot of nerve disrespecting the celebrities. "In the end, they're all the same. You hope they aren't. They say they aren't. But they are. All the same. And you become less enthusiastic when your favorite actor's name comes up on your switchboard."

She smiles, looks a little fascinated.

I add, "But it's really the average guest who disappoints me the most."

"At least it's not boring," she says. "I bet there's a lot of juicy shit floating around."

"You do find out things," I admit. "Things about yourself . . . and other people."

She stops pulling on her cigarette.

"Like?" she asks.

"Can't say." I shrug. "Confidentiality issues and stuff."

She eyes me, a slight grin playing on her face. She drops her cigarette and steps on it, blows the rest of the smoke out of her mouth through closed lips. She looks at me again.

"Then what else?" she asks me.

"People don't realize when they call a hotel they aren't speaking to Front Desk. They don't realize there's a whole department of telephone operators hired and trained specifically to direct their calls."

"You're kidding, right?" she says after a minute.

"No."

"And that's significant?"

"When you're a telephone operator, yes."

"I'll be honest with you," she concedes. "I always think I'm talking to Front Desk when I call a hotel."

"I know." I smile and she smiles. "To millions of people we don't exist."

"Why do something that millions of people think doesn't exist?"

"Everyone needs to do something."

She nods. She takes out another cigarette, considers it, then puts it away again.

"So," she says, "tell me about Jack in college."

I blow smoke in her direction, squint at her. I knew this was coming. Why else would she want to share a cigarette with me?

"Why?"

"Why?" She laughs. "Because I'd like to know what my future husband was like when he was twenty."

"Then maybe you should ask him," I say.

"Yeah. Ask me." Jack's standing by the door, hands stuffed in his pockets.

"You won't be honest," Rae accuses sweetly.

"He was quiet," I tell Rae. "He was antisocial."

"I could argue that," Jack says.

"Try," I challenge just as Nick comes out on the balcony to join us. Unaware that we're in the middle of something, he pats Jack's back fraternally.

"So," he says. "You're doing it."

"What?" Jack watches me drop my cigarette on the floor next to Rae's. Right. Housekeeping will get it. I move past them and go back inside, suddenly hungry for a bite of duck or red snapper.

Inside, Gary and Amy are sitting on the sofa, finishing the last of the wine and food. I take a seat between them, gently take a tiny piece of duck from Gary's hand and put it in my mouth. Cold, but delicious.

"We have our eye on a place," Jack is saying as they all follow my lead and come back inside.

"Great," Nick says. "Details."

Jack is watching Rae fiddle with her cell phone. When it rings, she disappears inside the bathroom. Jack waits until the door is closed before he looks at Nick again. "It's taking a while. Brooklyn costs more than I planned to spend."

"Can't afford Brooklyn?" Amy says facetiously.

Jack glances at her.

"Maybe you should check out of the hotel," she quips.

"I can afford it." Jack's voice is sharp. He looks down, and I think he didn't mean it to be. "I wasn't expecting to spend that kind of money to live there."

"And it's a big step," I say. "Moving to a new state."

"Not really," Jack counters. "You don't want to live in New York the rest of your life?"

"I haven't thought about it much," I say.

"Have you ever been to Maine?" Rae asks, coming out of the bathroom.

Jack looks up at her. Watches her closely as she takes a seat near him.

"No," I say.

"Why don't you come?" she says. "We live fifteen minutes away from Acadia National Park. The hiking is amazing."

"I don't hike," I say.

"Jack said you love to hike."

"Used to."

"You should come," Rae insists. "All of you. Maybe for Christmas? We're spending Christmas in Maine this year. You all would love Maine."

We all share a look. No one says anything.

Rae's cell phone rings again and she rolls her eyes. "The Parker wedding rehearsal," she tells Jack. "I told them to call the room."

Jack watches her go back into the bathroom. We sit in uncomfortable silence for a moment. Nick looks at Gary. Gary looks at Amy and me. A signal it's time to make our exit.

"It's that time," Nick begins. "We all have to get up early . . ."

Jack nods, seems to be looking at the wall behind us. "Okay."

We look at our watches and move to stand when Rae storms out of the bathroom, picks up the guestroom phone and punches a button.

"*Hotel operator Katie*," she chokes. We settle back in our places, deeming it rude to escape in the middle of Rae's apparent freak-out. "Yeah. You can help me. Is there a reason why my colleagues have to call my cell phone? You don't know? Well, I know. It's because you people have slapped a Do Not Disturb on my line without my fucking permission."

"Rae, calm down," Jack says calmly.

"Yeah, why don't you check that out," Rae tells Katie. She looks at me as she holds. "I'm sorry. I know it's your department, but some of your coworkers are complete idiots."

Jack says, "Come on, Rae," and looks completely dejected.

Rae glances at him, then her eyes turn back to me. "I'm sorry."

I don't say anything, just stare at her.

"I hope you're not as rude as they are when you talk to us," Rae continues, then turns her back to us as she speaks into the phone. "Right," she says. "You need to change it, then. I missed some *very important* calls."

"Look," I say to Jack as I rise to my feet. "I can't stay."

"Are you sure you want to go?" Jack says.

I'm at the door, pulling it open. Jack's right behind me.

"Never been so sure about anything in my life," I say lightly.

Jack follows me into the hall. "Maybe we can—"

"Probably not," I cut him off as I turn to look at him.

"I said a fucked-up thing before," Jack admits quietly.

"You did," I agree.

"I should go, too," Amy says as she joins us in the hall.

"I didn't mean anything by it."

"You ready, Kenny?" Amy asks, squeezing past Jack. She flashes him a sweet smile. "Thanks for dinner and everything."

Jack doesn't take his eyes off my face.

"Come on, Kenny," Amy persists.

Part of me is struck by the way Jack is looking at me. There's pain in his eyes. I can see it clearly. But I'm not sure if it's pain from now or pain left over from before. I'm also struck by how sad and alone he appears to be at this moment. And an unnerving thought enters my mind.

I want to kiss him.

Now. Here.

"*Kenny.*"

"Yeah." My voice almost catches in my throat.

Amy loops her arm through mine and pulls me to the elevator. Jack's still standing in the hall, watching us.

"This is just wrong," Amy's mumbling as she hits the elevator button. "Wrong, wrong, wrong. Why were you looking at him that way? And why is he still standing in the hall watching us?"

"I wasn't looking at him," I mutter.

The elevator arrives. A male voice calls out, "Hold it!" Gary and Nick, running to catch up with us, hop on. The elevator doors close.

"What a raving lunatic bitch!" Amy says it first.

"Oh, my God," Gary says.

"She wasn't *that* bad," Nick defends.

"You're such a kiss ass," I say.

"And you aren't?" Nick shoots back. "Oh, wait a minute. You're just superior."

"*What?*"

"You were acting all superior," Nick elaborates.

I look at Amy and Gary for confirmation. Gary just raises his eyebrows. Amy stares at the floor.

"Superior in what way?" I demand.

"I can't explain it," Nick says. "You had this whole vibe going on. Like people who work in hotels are better than people who stay in them."

"Was I the only one who caught the condescension in the room? The five-dollar-an-hour line?"

"You're sensitive because you're embarrassed by your job," Nick accuses.

"That's unfair," I snap. "And untrue. This job kicks my ass on a daily basis. Being subservient to these ingrates twenty-four-seven is no picnic. Maybe I'm slightly bitter, yes. Never embarrassed."

"Oh, *please*," Nick scoffs.

The elevator doors open.

"Jack didn't mean to say what he did," Amy offers as we move into the busy lobby toward the exit. "Heat of the moment and all that."

I stop in my tracks.

"You guys suck," I say.

We ride the train to Brooklyn in silence. I don't say anything to Gary and Nick when they get off first. I ask Amy if she's coming home with me, and she declines.

"I can't get any sleep at your place these days," she says.

An hour before I clock out, Sage visits the office with two pints of Häagen-Dazs ice cream and four sterling silver spoons from the hotel kitchen. He offers one pint to Wanda and Rodney. He pulls a chair over to my cubicle, hands me a spoon, and we start to eat the ice cream wordlessly.

We don't say a word about our club night, and I don't spill the beans about my decision to leave PBX and transfer to Reservations, or my visit to Jack's suite the evening before. Between spoonfuls of ice cream and phone calls, Wanda and Rodney gleefully fill him in on yesterday's argument with Victoria. I tell him I think I was too harsh on her.

"She deserved it," he says.

"How do you know?"

"She has that look."

Rodney howls with laughter. "That look," he repeats. "Doesn't she?"

"It's not even the way she looks," I whisper to Sage. "It's the way she looks at *me*."

"Not just you. At everyone. You just happen to be the only person here willing to do what the rest of us want to do."

"I wanted to be cruel to her," I admit. "I don't even understand why. It doesn't feel good to be cruel to people."

"Can we keep the spoons?" Rodney asks Sage.

"Yeah," Sage says. "No one will realize they're missing."

Sage sits with me until I end my shift. I let him listen to the calls he's interested in. And Rodney keeps him entertained with the lives of the hotel guests he's been following. When I clock out, Sage invites himself over to my place. He says he thinks we need to talk.

The front door of my apartment opens before I put my key in the lock. Jack steps out and we freeze, shocked to see each other. And then Jack blinks and holds out his hand to shake Sage's.

"Nice to see you again," Jack says.

Sage nods. "Same here."

"I'm patching up a hole in your kitchen ceiling," Jack explains. I notice his sleeves are rolled up to expose muscular arms and a tattoo of a pint of beer. Weird. "Gary said you'd be out late."

"Well, no," I say. "I usually work until seven."

"Water was pouring out of the light fixture in the kitchen when Gary came home," Jack tells us awkwardly. "He called Nick. I was there. . . ."

"Gary isn't into patching things up," I tell them. "Not that we ever have to patch things up. What happened?"

"I'll let Gary explain it," Jack says. He holds up a ratty five-dollar bill. "I'm just going to buy ice. We've kind of set up shop in there."

"Thank you," I say as Jack walks away.

"No problem," Jack calls back.

I hesitate at the door. It's only slightly unsettling that Sage is about to meet Gary and Nick. More than slightly. Everything is coming together. No longer converging, but merging. Work. Life. Sex. Friends. Old Boyfriends. Secret Lovers.

"You're about to meet the other people I like," I warn Sage.

Sage raises his eyebrows, interested. "I'm ready."

Inside, Gary's standing on a ladder, checking out Jack's patch job. He's wearing cutoff sweatpants and a T-shirt that says LOVABLE across the front of it. Nick, still in his suit from work, is holding the ladder steady, begging Gary to be careful. Rae's sitting on the sofa, flipping through a magazine. They all look surprised to see us when we walk in, as though I don't actually live here.

"The Bitch Upstairs left her apartment with a full sink of dishes and a running faucet," Gary says bitterly, then waves at Sage. "Hey."

"Any other damage?" I ask.

"Isn't this enough?" Gary snaps.

Nick looks at me expectantly, waiting to be introduced to Sage. But I'm still upset with him about last night. I ignore the look. So he holds a hand out to Sage, and they shake.

"I'm Nick."

"Sage."

I stare up at the patch job. Jack has painted the area a different color white than it was originally. Or maybe our ceiling is just dirty.

"Is she going to pay for the damage?" I ask.

Nick and Gary laugh.

" *'It's probably your pipes,'* " Gary does a pitch-perfect imitation of Betty's mountain-trash accent. " *'The subletters are the root of all the problems in the building.'* "

"She didn't say that."

Gary looks at me. "Honey, please. She also said, in not so

many words, that we wouldn't be here much longer. She only wants owners living in the building."

"Who does she think she is?" I say.

"I know you," Amy says, coming out of the bathroom. She gives Sage a hug as Nick and Gary watch them curiously.

Rae stands up to meet Sage. "Me, too," she says. "I know you."

All eyes turn to Rae and Sage, and we wait for Rae to continue. My first thought is, Oh my God, they've slept together. And I don't get that rumbly, scared feeling I would normally get if I thought my boyfriend was cheating on me. It's pretty much a given that Sage is still sleeping with Paula. I just get that sharp-pain-through-the-heart feeling I normally get when I think my friends are going to find out a secret I've been keeping from them.

If Rae blurts out that she sought comfort from Sage after a particularly nasty argument with Jack, and it's no big deal because the hotel staff routinely sleep with guests who are open to that, my friends will look to me for the truth. I'll tell them yeah, some hotel workers sleep with guests. Not for money. Mostly for the ego boost. Mostly to feel worthy of a good lay with a wealthy sucker. And then they'll call me later and ask if I've ever done it. Slept with a guest. And I'm not a great liar. And they've known me for a long time. They can pretty much tell when I'm lying.

But I'm being selfish right now. It's really Jack who will suffer if she admits it.

"You're . . ." She snaps her fingers. "You're my Front Desk Guy at the hotel."

I start to breathe again, surprised I was holding my breath.

"Yeah," Sage says. "You look familiar."

"We've been there for a while," she says. "Room Service says, 'The usual?' when I call in the morning."

Sage tries to laugh with her.

"We would love an upgrade. Think you can pull some strings?"

Sage looks at me. He could pull strings, but he wants to make sure pulling strings for this person is okay with me.

"Can you upgrade a Deluxe Suite?" I ask Sage, truly curious. It takes my mind off the fact that *I can't believe she's asking*.

"You're in a Deluxe Suite?" Sage looks at Rae. "I thought you were in . . ."

". . . 1700," she finishes.

Sage looks at me. "That's not a Deluxe Suite, Ken. That's a Superior. An upgrade would be a Deluxe Suite."

"Oh." I shrug. "How big is a Deluxe Suite? Because the Superior was enormous."

"Take the tour," Rae tells me. "I've already taken it twice. I can't get enough of seeing the Presidential."

I've never seen the Presidential Suite on the top floor. I didn't even know the hotel gave tours.

"What's your rate now?" Sage is asking.

I walk away from them and go to the kitchen. I don't want to hear them discuss the hotel. If I told Sage what she did with the strawberries yesterday, he'd walk away, too.

"We're making piña coladas," Gary tells me when I pull a couple of bottles of Sullivan Brew from the refrigerator. "Jack went to buy ice."

"We'll have beer," I tell him.

"Actually, I'll have tea." Sage cuts off his conversation with Rae and passes me a bag of tea leaves. "Surprise drug testing in a few days. Need to piss that shit out."

Gary climbs down the ladder and glances at the others in the living room. "Oooh, drug testing. They still do that?"

Sage nods. "I have a friend in Security who gives me a warning. It's very random, but Security usually gets a heads up a week earlier."

"What about our Ken here?" Gary puts his arm around me. "Is there a tea to piss out heroin?"

The way Rae is staring at me makes me want to tell her Gary's joking.

"They don't give a hoot about the operators," Sage tells Gary. "They could snort heroin off the switchboards and no one would spend the cash on the testing. Front Desk is . . . different."

"That's so sad," Rae says. Her tone makes the hair on my arms bristle.

Gary takes one of the beers and leaves the kitchen. "Finally," he says to Sage. "Heard a lot about you. Been dying to meet you."

"Same here," he says, giving Gary a hesitant smile. He's cute when he's shy.

"You can drink beer and tea, no?" Gary asks.

Sage takes the beer. "Yeah."

Jack walks into the apartment. He inches past me and sticks the bag of ice into the freezer. I try not to look at him. Rae asks Sage if he speaks Spanish, then launches into what seems like a very serious conversation with him in his native tongue. Gary frowns and slips away. Jack glances at me.

"She's trilingual," he tells me.

"Ahhh," I say, unimpressed. I think he's waiting for me to ask what the third language is. I don't. It's probably French.

We watch Sage and Rae for a while, and I wonder what's going through Jack's mind. How cute Sage is struggling with his native language because he's nervous? How pretentious Rae is for engaging Sage in a conversation in Spanish? Maybe Jack's wondering what's going through *my* head. That I don't want to kiss him as much as I wanted to last night because now I've moved on to wanting to see him naked?

I hate it that I'm thinking this, and that I'm so aware of sharing kitchen space with him. I'm so aware that he's standing next to me, not making any move to leave. And all of a sudden, I'm twenty again. And Jack is standing in some random kitchen, talking to his friends, ignoring me, even though we've just spent the last five hours in his room kissing. And I'm standing three feet away from him, also trying to pretend he doesn't exist, but having a hard time because I want him to kiss me again.

"How many piña coladas am I making?" Jack asks loudly, and I nearly jump out of my skin.

"Five," Nick tells him.

He would ignore me for hours.

At first, neither one of us was eager to tell our friends we were together, but Jack wouldn't have cared so much if they all caught on because we were holding hands or kissing in public. And that was the Thing in the very beginning. Public. It riled him that I wouldn't let him touch me anywhere but in his room or in some out-of-the-way staircase. Like I was embarrassed by him. Like I wanted to hide him.

For a while, he pretended he wanted the anonymity as much as I did. He showed up to parties he assumed I'd be attending with my friends. Parties I'd mention in passing because part of me wanted him to be there, too. He would pretend he didn't notice me, flirt with other girls and occasionally take a phone number. And then he would brush up against me, touch me *here* or *there,* and it would drive me absolutely crazy. When I was ready to introduce him to my friends, he didn't want to meet them. He'd said it was never about The Meeting. It was about me, and why I wasn't ready.

"This is great beer," Sage says, looking at the bottle Gary gave him moments earlier.

"Thanks," Jack says, opening a few cabinets and finally finding the blender.

Sage stares at Jack for a minute, not understanding why Jack thanked him.

Nick says, "Jack is Jack Sullivan. Of Sullivan Brew."

"Oh." For the first time since they met at the hotel, Sage looks mildly interested. "You make beer?"

Jack nods.

"How'd you get started?" Sage asks. "Take a class?"

I think Rae rolls her eyes, but I'm not sure. She turns away from Sage and stares at Gary's album collection lined against the wall.

"You can't really learn how to brew formally," Jack tells Sage. "I read a lot. It's really all about reading and self-teaching. In college I visited microbreweries on the weekends. And listened. And I homebrewed. I played around until I got things right."

"Cool," Sage says, nodding. "How long did it take you to get started?"

Jack tries to answer Sage's question and make a batch of piña coladas at the same time. Gently, I push him out of the way and take over. And as he discusses the basic facts about his business—hops, grain, malt and more hops—I start to remember the way he used to touch me. Like my body was a precious material he didn't want to soil or tear.

"How are those coladas coming?" Nick asks, and I realize I've been blending them for a long time. I stop, pull out five wineglasses and start to fill them with the mix. I avoid Jack's eyes, almost like I think he'll know what I've been thinking if he sees them.

Conversation is suddenly all about beer. Jack answers Sage's questions carefully, with as few words as possible, and Rae throws in an occasional snide remark, which Jack ignores.

"Draught sales are the best because you're serving the freshest product," Jack is saying now. "But I wouldn't want to close up shop in Maine. That would mean moving the entire operation to New York and relocating all of my key people, who don't want to live here. Like I said, we have a great head brewer. And Rae and I still have the house in Bar Harbor."

"Just wish you didn't specialize in the dark stuff," Sage tells him.

"So you're not wild about the stout?" Jack asks, grinning.

Sage shakes his head, kind of smiles. "Not too crazy about the dark beers. But I can go either way if it's good."

Jack nods.

"You like blondes," Rae says.

Sage glances at me and winks. "No. Not really."

Jack catches the wink and looks down, uncomfortable. Sage notices.

"What about you?" he asks Jack, his voice a little more formal than before. "You prefer dark?"

"It really depends on flavor," Jack says, still looking down. "We do a very dark imperial stout every year. I like that dense, coffee flavor you get from them. Rae likes the yeasty beers, a little sweet."

"What's the alcohol content in one of your stouts?" Sage asks, and I stare at him like he's an alien. How is he all of a sudden a beer connoisseur?

"We do about twelve percent," Jack answers.

Sage whistles.

"To be a good stout," Jack says, "it should be high in alcohol strength."

"Let's not stay," Amy suggests quietly.

"I have company," I say.

"Well, I think I'm going to kill myself in a minute," she whispers. "I don't want to talk about beer all night."

"Change the subject," I tell her. I smile when I realize Rae is watching us.

"And you do well with them?" Sage asks.

Jack shrugs. "We mainly brew pilsners."

"Americans like yellow beer," Sage says.

Jack looks impressed. "Yes," he agrees. "That's very true for some reason."

His cell phone rings. He takes the call in a corner of the room. Involuntarily, I watch him. He speaks softly, taking his glasses off to rub the bridge of his nose. Then he looks over at us and says his cell phone is losing its battery. He asks to use our phone.

Gary immediately offers his bedroom for privacy, and Rae follows. Sage joins me in the kitchen, makes the cup of tea I forgot about.

"You okay?" Sage asks quietly, and I nod.

A few minutes pass. Rae comes out of Gary's room and sits on the sofa. She doesn't look happy. I wonder if I looked like that when Jack didn't pay a sufficient amount of attention to me. Lost. Pouty. Resigned to being the loser in the situation.

When Jack comes out of Gary's room, he sits next to Rae. She puts her hand in his lap. For some reason—a stupid one, I'm sure—I can't take my eyes off of them. Jack looks up, sensing me, and I finally look away.

After a minute, Rae says she isn't feeling well. The couple is going to call it a night. Gary tells Amy and Nick they should go for dinner anyway. I think there's a sigh of relief from Sage.

I thank Jack for patching up the ceiling before they leave. Rae turns back, says something to Sage in Spanish.

"Your new best friend," I say to Sage as I close the door.

Sage grabs me before I can lock it, kisses me on the back of my neck and presses me against the door. "Jealous?" His mouth comes down on my ear, teasing it mercilessly with his tongue.

"Sage . . ." I push back a little, but he leans into me with more pressure.

"Tell me how much you want me."

"No. Damnit. Sage."

I'm not into playing submissive, and he knows it. But there's a reason for this game. Sage knows I'm thinking about Jack. He knows I'm wishing Jack had me pinned against this door. He knows it's what I've been thinking about all evening. And he's racing to make the images of Jack leave me before they become embedded in my brain. Every nip at my ear, at my neck, is a desperate attempt to remind me of Sage. And I feel awful about it. Guilty as hell.

But I can't give in to him, because I hate pity. Would never want anyone to have sex with me because they feel sorry for me. I can't do it to Sage.

I stop resisting him and he lets up on me. I turn, back flat against the door. When he pulls back completely, I keep my eyes closed so he can't look in them. I'm afraid he'll be able to see that I'm being unfaithful.

He kisses my lips softly. I open my eyes after a minute and smile at him. I can see him searching my face.

"You want another beer?" I ask.

"A Sullivan Brew?" I can hear it in his voice now. A question leading to another question. I open the refrigerator and pull out a bottle of Budweiser for myself.

"More tea?"

"No."

"What did you want to talk about?" I ask.

He doesn't move away from the door, just stares at me like I've said something incredibly hurtful. "What?"

"You wanted to talk about something."

He shakes his head. "Forget it."

We do the usual nighttime rituals like brush our teeth and put on our pajamas. When I come out of the bathroom, Sage is looking through the drawer he keeps some of his clothes in. Like he's taking an inventory of what he keeps here.

"What are you looking for?" I ask.

He ignores my question, gets into bed, pulls aside the comforter invitingly so I'll get in next to him. Then he rolls over on his side, his back to me.

"Sage," I say. He doesn't move. "Jack was my boyfriend in college. And I loved him."

Finally, Sage turns over and lies on his back. He stares up at the ceiling, listening.

"But that was nine years ago. And if you're sensing some kind of tension . . . well, I think that's normal. We were very close. And it just ended one day. We woke up and it was finished."

"Why did you pull away from me?" he asks the ceiling.

"That had nothing to do with you. Or him."

"Let's drop it," he snaps.

"Hey," I say, annoyed. "I'm not the one who picked it up, ran with it and slammed you over the head with it."

Sage looks at me. I hold his gaze for a long time, watch the features in his face soften. When he starts smiling, I can't help but smile back. He nuzzles his face in my stomach and blows on it, making fart noises and spraying spit all over the place. I laugh and start to relax, and I start to like him more than ever because his voice feels good on my body and it makes me laugh.

He holds me so tight I can barely breathe and I try to pry him away, but he won't let go. And then he's sleeping, snoring lightly on my belly button, and I rub his head. I think we bond momentarily while he sleeps, and I think I love him in a different way, not only sexually. I feel good with him, the way I feel with my other friends.

Stupid thoughts of Jack are banished from my brain.

In the morning, the kid jumps off the stairs above us.

"I hear children," Sage moans. I snuggle close to him, but he pulls away and gets out of bed.

"Where are you going?" I reach for him, but he disappears into the living room.

"Is this all you have?" he calls out from the kitchen. "These fucking coffee singles?"

"Come back to bed," I say. He doesn't.

In the kitchen, he's dipping a coffee bag in and out of a mug of water he's just removed from the microwave. I try to pull off his T-shirt, but he stops me. He holds my wrists and stares into my face.

"I don't think we should do this anymore," he says sternly.

"What?"

"We shouldn't do this anymore," he repeats.

"Do what?" I try to kiss him, and he tightens his grip on my wrists. I pull back, understanding. "Oh."

He lets go of me and leans against the sink. "Me and Paula are going to try to work things out," he says softly.

I step back. "That's fabulous."

He reaches for me, but I back away further.

"Why didn't you tell me last night?" I ask. "I mean, you didn't have to stay. Why did you stay?"

"I was going to, but it didn't seem like the right time. You had that whole thing going on with Jack, and I didn't want to leave—"

"What *thing*? That wasn't a *thing*. What are you talking about?"

He sighs. "Forget it."

"I'm sorry," I say. "This isn't about him. It's about Paula."

"You knew this was going to happen."

I nod, look him directly in the eye. "Every day."

"You knew it."

I smile delicately. "Every second I was with you."

There's a long silence. I know this isn't what he expected me to say. And even though he knows me pretty well, knows how I react to most things, he's imagined the way this scene would play out.

It wasn't this. What he's waiting for is resistance. Or more questions. Or one question. He's waiting for me to say, Are you sure you want to end this?

What I don't tell him is that every time he mentions his wife I expect him to tell me they've worked it all out, and they're getting back together. I do. I expect it. Because sometimes I'm a realist.

He pulls the coffee bag out of the mug and dumps it in the garbage. He takes milk and sugar. He stares at me while he stirs. "You're okay?"

"Yes." I nod reassuringly. "I'm really happy for you."

He comes with me to the sofa. We sit. I put my feet in his lap and ask him a bunch of questions about how it happened. He answers the questions, even the one about how he'll explain being here last night. And then he stops talking altogether.

"What?" I say.

"Did you think we could do this forever?" He sounds annoyed.

"Yes. Or until you and Paula got back together."

He pushes my feet away. "You never expected more?"

"No. Maybe once or twice. Briefly."

He stands up, brings his coffee to the kitchen and pours it into the sink.

"What?" I ask. "You want me to be angry? You want me to expect something?"

"*Yes*," he snaps. "I wanted you to. Sometimes. Jesus."

"I've always wanted you to work things out," I tell him honestly. "I didn't think there was another option."

He turns around and looks at me. "When I thought we were serious . . . me and you . . . when I thought we couldn't avoid being serious, you pulled away. I thought it was your way of saying I shouldn't give up on her. So I didn't. Even though I wanted to."

I don't know what to say.

In the beginning, with Sage, when I didn't know he was married, we were honest about everything else. We didn't want to love anyone, didn't want to be serious. We were companions, for lack of a better word. And then he told me he was married, and working things out with Paula, and my ego was bruised. But I knew it was just my ego. The second time Sage and Paula separated, I knew what I was getting into. I didn't expect anything, so I was rarely disappointed. And I'm just a little bit thrown, I guess, by this sudden confession.

"I had no clue," I say.

"I wanted to ask you if there was even the slightest chance we'd get serious," he continues. "I don't know why I didn't. I guess I knew what you would say."

"I didn't know."

"I love my wife," he says.

"I know you do."

"What I feel for you is different than what I feel for her."

"I know." I stand up, go to him in the kitchen. "I feel strongly about you, but it's not in a way that makes me want you to leave your wife."

He looks baffled. Then he closes his eyes, covers his face with his hands and sighs heavily. I've said the wrong thing. I take his hands away from his face.

"What?" I say.

"Shit." He shakes his head, looks away from me. "I'm in love with you."

I drop his hands, and then I scramble to take them back because that was the wrong thing to do at that moment. He won't let me touch him again. Just shakes his head and leaves the kitchen.

"I'm okay," he says.

I watch him. I don't know what else to do.

"I know you're not in love with me. I've always known."

"Oh, Sage."

"It's better this way," he decides, not looking at me. "Working it out with Paula. It's less complicated."

"Yeah," I agree, playing along. "Me and complicated don't work well together."

He attempts a smile, but he only manages to look really sad. It almost breaks my heart, but mostly I feel relieved. Then I feel angry with myself for feeling relieved. I'm hurting him, and there's nothing I can do to stop it.

As he gets dressed, I remain exiled in the kitchen drinking coffee and trying to work out what else I can say. I've never been good with endings.

He comes over to me, and we hug for a long time. But it isn't the same. I know it'll never be the same with him again. It isn't like the last time he broke up with me. The last time, he wasn't in love.

When he leaves, I press my head against the door and close my eyes.

Occasionally, the owners in the building get together and have parties: fixing-the-boiler parties; putting-the-air-conditioner-in parties; taking-the-air-conditioner-out parties. Recently I've learned from Gary these gatherings aren't parties at all. They are the Co-op Board meeting.

Tonight's Co-op Board meeting is happening in the apartment across the hall with Lisa and her James-Van-Der-Beek-look-alike boyfriend, Craig.

I curse myself for not making plans with Gary or Amy or anyone else in my phone book. Because if there's anything in life more painful than a tooth extraction without Novocain, it's Betty Blacksmith's too-loud-to-be-natural cackle right outside my door.

Betty and I have yet to mend fences.

Hercules, the cat, is still pissing in front of my apartment, and Betty is still denying it. Red Sweatshirt Guy was on the fire escape again last night. No one called the police this time, but I was tempted. And according to the twentysomething couple on three, Betty has been saying that people who sublet have no rights and are the root of all the problems in the building.

Which, now that I think about it, is better than being the root of all evil.

I call Amy to take her up on one of the blind dates she's always trying to set me up on. Mrs. Goldstein answers the phone on the first ring.

"Hi, Kendall, how are you?"

"I'm fine, Mrs. Goldstein. How are you?"

"Fine, thank you. Amy's not home. She's out on a date."

"Oh? With Gorvic?"

There's a slight pause. Shit. I didn't mean to say Gorvic. Mrs. Goldstein doesn't know about him.

"I thought his name was Jonah . . . Stanley? What was that boy's name we met tonight?"

"I don't know," Mr. Goldstein says in the background.

"No, Kendall. I think she went out with Jonah tonight. What the hell is a Gorvic?"

"Oh. Okay." I avoid the question. "Well, I won't keep you, Mrs. Goldstein. Tell Amy I called."

"You're in for the night then?"

"Uh, I think so."

"Oh. What a shame. It's Saturday night."

"Okay, Mrs. Goldstein," I say. "Don't forget to tell Amy I called."

"I won't. Goodnight."

I slink past Lisa and Craig's door, sneer at it just as Betty laughs so loud the walls shudder. I meet Hercules on the first floor. He howls at me, and I stick my tongue out at him. When I open the front door he darts out, racing past Dina's daughter—whose name is so pretentious and unpronounceable Gary and I simply call her the Brat—and the kid from upstairs. They stare at me, a little frightened.

"My cat," the kid, whom I have ungraciously dubbed the Rodent, squeaks.

"Oh, shit." I run after him. The kids hold the door open so they can watch me. Hercules is sitting on the sidewalk. "Hey, kitty. Stay right there."

Hercules tilts his head, licks his paw casually. I get closer and Hercules goes rigid, watching me intently. Then he lashes out at me with his paw and I pull back, narrowly missing a bloody paw attack.

"Kid," I say. "Wanna help me out here?"

I turn back to see the Rodent and the Brat leaning against the building, looking kind of bored with the whole thing. I decide, at this moment, children are evil.

When I turn back to Hercules, he darts away. I follow him for a minute, but he jumps into a garbage can overflowing with smelly, rotting food. I step back, hands held up in surrender.

"You're on your own, Herc," I say. I smile at the kids sympathetically.

Their eyes are unnaturally black and unrelenting. Like *Children of the Corn,* or some other horror movie with kids possessed by demons.

"Sorry I couldn't catch him," I say in a sickeningly sweet baby voice. They just stare. "He's very, very fast."

They look at each other, then back at me.

"Well, maybe we can try again later?" I offer. "Cats never go very far from home. They are resilient little creatures."

Blank stares.

"I have to go," I say, moving on. "I'll be back soon."

At the corner I turn back. The two girls are still watching me walk away.

*   *   *

I end up at Excelsior, the bar Gary and Nick love to hang out in. Through the blinds, I see Nick sitting at the bar, sharing light conversation with the bartender. I search for a glimpse of Gary or Jack, a reason to go in, but Nick and another man are the bar's only patrons.

I don't go in.

The truth is, when I'm around Nick these days, I feel alone. I become self-conscious and anxious. Even though I say very little to him, I still worry I'm saying the wrong thing. And because I hate anyone who cares what people think, I hate myself and how I feel when I'm in his presence.

What he said to me the other day in the hotel doesn't help either.

I sit on the ground next to the bar and wait for the possibility of Gary. I light a cigarette. I don't recognize Jack until he squats in front of me.

"What are you doing out here?" he asks.

"Hanging."

"Are you going in?"

"Maybe."

He looks around. And then he takes my cigarette and puts it out on the ground between us.

"Why'd you do that?" I ask.

"Because you smoke too much."

"You think?"

"Yeah."

"Well." I take a pack of cigarettes from my jacket pocket and tap one out into the palm of my hand. I stick it in my mouth. "The rest of the world didn't stop smoking when you did."

"Touché." He sits on the ground next to me.

"So, back in Brooklyn," I say.

"Just for drinks. You know your boyfriend almost got us an upgrade?"

"Oh?" This is news to me. Sage and I haven't spoken since the other night.

It's been a tough week, actually. Without Sage, I realized how alone I really am in the hotel. For one thing, the office was divided into my foes and friends, and it became clear that I only have three friends. Word that I'm an evil bitch managed to spread around the hotel, so the only people who would speak to me besides Wanda, Katie and Rodney were the workers on the half-day program: an elderly man and a mentally handicapped teenager.

"We were going to a one-bedroom Deluxe Suite on forty-six," Jack continues. "But a celebrity booked it last minute."

"Darn," I say.

"I like it there. But I think it's time to move on."

"I bet."

"Found a brownstone in the neighborhood I like."

"Oh, that's great."

"This brownstone," he says. "It's nearby."

"It's not a huge neighborhood."

"Aren't you cold?" he asks.

"No." And I almost smile.

"Sully used to do that. Sit outside when it was cold. Never bothered him."

I nod. "I remember."

He leans his head against the wall behind us.

"I know about Sully," I say. "Nick told me when it happened."

He closes his eyes briefly, then turns to look at me. "That was the family emergency I mentioned when I first saw you. You seemed not to be aware of it."

"I know. I . . . it wasn't . . . something . . ."

His eyes don't move from my face. I give up trying to come up with an excuse. He waits.

"I'm sorry," is all I can come up with. "I don't . . . I was wrong not to contact you."

He turns away now, closes his eyes again.

I stare at the ground. "How's that going?"

"What?"

"The mourning."

He doesn't answer right away. And then he says, "I feel like a child again. Angry, confused, hurt, alone. I miss him a hell of a lot."

"He was always there for you. Even when you didn't think you needed him to be."

Jack chuckles softly. "You could have said good-bye to him. He loved you, too."

Oh God. "I know."

"Why won't you look at me?" he asks.

I look at him. "I'm looking at you, Jack."

He used to look at me like I was the only woman in the world, the only woman he would ever love. He doesn't look at me like that now. Of course. I wouldn't expect him to. But there's something cold about the way he looks at me now that unnerves me. I don't like the way it makes me feel.

He swallows hard. "About the other day," he begins.

"Forget it."

"No."

"You're so formal," I say.

"Not really."

"Just around me, then?"

He smiles, looks down for a second. "Maybe. I do feel a certain weirdness when I'm around you." He looks directly in my eyes again. "What about you?"

I don't like the way my stomach feels, but I don't admit that. And the thing that bothers me most is that I was never nervous around Jack. I don't understand why I am now. I'm nervous at the thought of him, at his presence next to me.

And then, just like that, I know why I'm nervous. I'm nervous because— *oh, hell*—I care what he thinks about me. I wish I were more than I am. I want him to go away and never come back. But at the same time, I just want to keep sitting here with him. Having him to myself. I want to ask him to tell me a story about his life. A story I missed.

I've been dreading this moment since I ran into him at the hotel.

"I don't feel any different around you," I say slowly.

There isn't time for him to react because his cell phone rings. He takes it out of his pocket and looks at the tiny screen. He puts it away again and says he doesn't answer his cell phone after eight in the evening, unless it's Rae.

I'm glad for the distraction. I say, "I hate Amy's cell phone. I think I can hold out for another three years before I decide I need one in my life. I was able to hold out on call-waiting until I moved in with Gary."

He laughs.

"And now I can't live without it."

"Call-waiting with caller ID," he puts in.

"Exactly. I have to know who's calling me while I'm on the phone with someone else. Very sad."

Abruptly, he stands up. "I should get in there. I'm already late."

He holds out his hand to help me up. I take it.

"Why don't you come back to the bar? We'll talk."

I'm tempted, but I think of Nick sitting there, waiting for him to arrive. I think, *This is so Jack*. Being the center of attention like this but not realizing it. He actually believes we would have a minute to talk. Besides, I didn't bring enough money to buy a drink.

"Take care," I say, and I touch his arm. He covers my hand with his and holds it there for a second.

When I start to pull away he says, "I did stay at the hotel because of you."

There's *emotion* in this brief statement, a crack in the wall between us. It throws me off course for a second. I freeze. And there's a long, electrified silence. Then he lets out a short laugh, rolls his eyes.

"Just thought I'd get that out there, in the middle of nowhere, so it could lead to nothing."

I laugh, too. I'm relieved. Some of the tension disappears.

He smiles. "I'm not buying a place in Brooklyn because of you," he adds. "But I did stay at the hotel so I'd see you. Gary and Nick, well, they've always been very vague. About you. I'd ask and they'd say things like, 'Ken's great, living in a different place these days, but you know Ken.' And I'd want to tell them I didn't. Not really. I didn't know you. Not the way I wanted to."

I nod, smiling, ready to jump into the shallow end of the pool and be trite and dismissive. But the lightness of the moment has left his eyes, and I get nervous.

"I came here to gloat," he admits. "And then I got here and I saw you and I sat at Nick's dinner table and felt this tide of anger overcome me. I wanted to hurt you. But wanting to hurt you didn't last."

"Jack—," I start.

"And that was the thing," he cuts me off. "It was brief. It scared the fuck out of me. And annoyed me. I don't want to brag or make you feel awful about anything that happened between us. It's not worth it."

"Well, thanks," I say awkwardly.

"We'll probably be seeing more of each other. And I think we should be friends."

No sudden declarations of love. No angry accusations about our past. Relieved, I grin. He grins, too. Then he takes off his jacket and holds it out to me. I stare at it. It's a gorgeous leather jacket. Dark brown, distressed, giving the impression it's very old, but I know it's very new and expensive.

"Take it," he says. He holds it out to me. "I know you're cold. I can . . . you're shivering."

I continue to stare at the jacket. I remember this part. Why I loved him. He was kind and cared if I was cold.

"Maybe we shouldn't see each other again," I blurt. "I know. Hard. Since we oddly, disturbingly, all of a sudden have the same friends. But. We can work at it. Not seeing each other."

I look at him and he looks shocked. "I don't get it."

"It's better," I assure him. "Really. For me, especially."

His new smile is rueful, accompanied by a slight nod of resignation. "Okay," he says. Then he holds out the jacket again.

I shake my head. "No. I'm five minutes from home."

"You're sure?"

"How would I get it back to you?" I ask, and he sees the point I'm making.

"Okay," he says. "Take care."

We part. At the corner I turn back to watch him enter Excelsior. And I imagine him laughing with Nick and the bartender. I want to laugh with him, I decide. But I know I'm too late. He's laughing with someone else.

The moment I put my key into the lock, Lisa and Craig's door opens. A chorus of good-byes crashes out of their apartment, and Dina ushers her brat out. The Brat stops short when she sees me, eyes wide and mouth gaping open. Dina bumps into her.

"Sweetie?"

"I just remembered something bad," the Brat says ominously.

Dina leans forward to look into her child's face. Her child is still gawking at me. And what Dina sees in that tiny face alarms her.

Fear. *Her child is afraid of me.*

Slowly, Dina looks up to meet my eye. I begin to sense something corrupt in the air. I stare at Dina, and then I look at the Brat. She wrenches herself away from Dina's grip and runs up the stairs. Dina looks to me for answers, but I don't have any. She runs up the stairs behind her daughter.

Okay, I think, that was weird.

Gary comes out of his room when I enter the apartment.

"Want to hear something funny?" he asks, though from the tone of his voice I don't think what he's going to tell me will be funny.

"I don't know. Do I?"

"Someone let your neighbors' stupid cat out and the thing got hit by a car."

A lump lodges itself in my throat as I remember Hercules dashing out of the building when I opened the door earlier.

"Is it dead?" I ask.

"No," Gary says. "Hurt. They're at the animal hospital on Seventh. Everyone's been in the hall all evening. Even the people we know hate them." He shakes his head. "Hurt someone's cat, no matter who they are, and they get disgusting amounts of sympathy."

I sit at the kitchen table, pull a cigarette from my jacket pocket and light it. Hercules is not dead. That's important.

"What?" Gary asks.

"He's not dead. The cat. That's good."

Gary shrugs. I swallow hard. It's really not my fault. *They* locked him out of the apartment. I tried to catch him.

"What?" Gary asks again.

"Nothing. What are you doing?"

"Watching you sit there in your jacket," he says. "Is something wrong?"

"No." The Hercules thing isn't worth mentioning, though that kid's face from a minute ago is haunting me. I look at Gary. He's still watching me, frowning. "Looked for you at Excelsior."

"Nick there?"

I nod. "I didn't go in. Are you feeling okay?"

"Tired. Cranky. Didn't want to see Jack."

"Oh, Jack was going to be there?"

"Yeah." Gary reaches for my cigarette. As he takes a drag, I slip out of my jacket. "I think it's nice that he's here and all, but I don't feel that burning desire to reconnect with him. Like you keep saying, it's been nine years. And I thought he was a bitch the other night. At the hotel."

I take my cigarette back, eye him wearily. "But you didn't feel the need to back me up when Nick said I was sensitive."

"I didn't feel the need to get into it," Gary says. "*I* was going home with my boyfriend."

"Okay. Whatever." I put the cigarette out on the empty plate in the middle of the table that has been serving as our ashtray for weeks. Gary sits across from me.

"If it makes you feel better, we're fighting."

"You and Nick?"

He nods. I pull out another cigarette and hand it to him. He picks up my lighter and lights it.

"I talk to him and I feel like I'm from another planet," Gary complains.

"And this fighting is a result of? . . ."

"I didn't love what he said to you."

"Neither did I."

Gary sighs. "When we're sitting around there's something there. Something that separates us from them."

"Them? Nick and? . . ."

"Jack," he says. "Nick works sixty-five hours a week. Jack's a beer expert and always working. And Rae is on call twenty-four hours. And I'm just Gary at Sam's Coffee Shop, who writes scripts he may never sell."

"And I'm just Hotel Operator Kendall." I shrug. "What's your point?"

"That. *What is the point?* You work your life away so you can get into your fifty-thousand-dollar car and drive to your million-dollar house where you spend a total of eight hours before you have to drive to work again. You retire when you're seventy and die from heart failure a couple years later. What's the point of the rat race? So you have two years?"

I take his hand and squeeze. "Geez, Gary. Who gives a shit?"

"I do," he says. "Every time I'm in a room with Rae I have to field questions about my plans for the future. I'm over thirty. This is my future. And what pisses me off most is that she wouldn't understand that I'm happy. You think I want to work at Sam's the rest of my life? No. I never look forward to going in there. Doesn't mean I'm unfulfilled. I get happy when there's a smile on Nick's face. I get happy when you laugh. A great fucking cup of coffee in the morning can make my day. Tell that to Rae or Jack or Nick? They look at me like I'm crazy."

"Again Gary, who cares? You don't have to apologize for not

having the same definition of happiness and success they have. I don't."

"You do," Gary says softly.

"I don't."

He nods. "You apologize. Whenever Jack's in the same room with you."

I let go of his hand. "I do not."

"You do."

"When?"

"The other day . . . ," he begins.

"Give me fifty examples."

"Ken." He sighs again. "You defer to him without realizing it. I see it. Amy sees it. You come into every contact with him defensively."

"That's not me saying I'm sorry."

Gary lowers his eyes, shrugs.

"Believe me," I insist, "it isn't."

"Do you still love him?" he asks.

"Hello? Nine years. Long time to hold a torch."

"Fuck that," Gary says. "People are apart for twenty years and never fall out of love."

"Well. No."

"I'm sure you're aware of this, but you've never loved anyone else." He considers this. "Well, maybe this Sage character. But it's not the same."

The mention of Sage upsets me more than it should. I stand up.

"Okay," Gary says. "I'm going to admit something to you, so you better listen, because I'll never admit it again."

I roll my eyes. "Gary—"

"You and Jack? Your relationship was a wonderful, complicated, horrifying mess. The fights and the breakups and the kissing and the passion. We all knew you loved him. But you were twenty, Ken. You were too young and too good to be part of such a hurricane. He was too serious. And, yeah, you're older. And part of me is wondering why you would need a Jack in your life right now. The other part of me knows he still loves you. I can tell by the way he looks at you. I can tell because he's here. So I'm admitting for all of us—me, Nick and Amy— that we were wrong to persuade you to let him go. We had no right. I wish we had let you make your own mistakes."

"I need to get some rest while your neighbors are still out with their cat," I say.

"Yeah." Gary sounds disappointed. "Maybe they'll stay out all night and give us a break."

I kiss his forehead. He latches onto my arm so I can't pull away.

"I'm not going to talk about Jack," I tell him. "I'm not going to think about him, or see him again. We've already discussed it, Jack and me. We agreed it's better this way."

Gary lets me go. I avoid looking him in the eye.

"Love you," he says.

"I love you, too," I say.

The neighbors didn't stay out all night and give us a break. They stomped into their duplex after midnight, dragging and dropping things until two in the morning. When Gary banged on the ceiling with an umbrella, they banged back.

Sunday morning was strangely quiet. Not a sound above until ten. By the time the little Rodent bounced down the stairs and started running across the floor, both Gary and I were dressed.

Gary was going for a late morning run, though I suspected he was really going for a late morning run to Nick's. I was simply going out. I had a craving for Starbucks coffee. I spent the entire morning in a cozy armchair in a corner with an abandoned copy of *The New York Times*.

On my way back into my building, I held the door for an exiting Dina and Brat. They passed through in silence, which irritated me enough to call out, "You're welcome!" Dina turned back and scowled at me. I scowled back and slammed the door.

Lisa and Craig were on the second floor, placing fliers in front of everyone's door. They didn't say a word as I passed them, but I could feel the eyes of the perky blond couple burning holes in my back as I walked up the stairs. On three, the fliers had also been placed in front of every door. On four, each door had a flier except my door, and Lisa and Craig's.

Knowing instinctively that the lack of a flier in front of my door was a slight by Betty's minions, I picked one up in front of my other neighbors' door. HELP HERCULES HEAL, the flier read in a flowery font that was barely legible. JOIN YOUR NEIGHBORS ON MONDAY NIGHT AT EIGHT AS WE HELP PRECIOUS HERCULES RECUPERATE.

When Kirk asked me to work tonight, Monday night, the night of a huge music award show that has returned to New York City, I jumped at the chance.

Working the occasional late night is not a big deal. For one thing, I'd be stupid to turn down any opportunity to make overtime. Overtime is based purely on seniority. The two women who have worked here longest always work the little overtime that becomes available. Tonight's overtime was too last-minute for everyone who has seniority over me.

Also, working at night breaks up the monotony of working with the same operators every day. The evening operators are known for being less edgy, angry and depressed than the rest of us. They work the insane eight-hour shifts that begin at four, five and six. Edgy, angry and depressed would either lead to suicide or murder.

And, of course, I don't want to be anywhere near Operation Recuperation. I even called Gary at Nick's this morning to warn him away. We're not sure what "helping precious Hercules recuperate" entails, but we both agreed it won't be pretty.

I've always wanted to work an award show night. They are chaotic and insane. They're the equivalent of a full moon on Friday the Thirteenth in hotels. Every hot musician, band and music producer stays here or five blocks away at our sister-hotel. And every fan in the world is crowded around every hotel entrance. Security has their work cut out for them. And the amount of limousines pulling into the hotel's private parking garage, then whisking away some too-famous-to-be-seen singer, is enormous.

Tonight everyone will drink too much, a couple of bands will trash their suites, and someone, probably a drummer or bassist, will overdose. Possibly die. It happens every year without fail. The sad thing is that no matter how tragic the death of the obscure musician was the year before, some other obscure musician snorts too much heroin and dies the year after. These people never learn.

And for some reason, Kirk thinks he needs more than four operators to handle the phones.

I'm not complaining. Even though Kirk has dashed my hopes of having a completely laid-back evening by deciding to work until ten, I'm happy to be here instead of home. Kirk is in and out of the office making sure all the telephones in the hotel are working, and there's an air of relaxed excitement about him I've never witnessed before.

Jeri has three bags of miniature candy bars, and Kirk has already confiscated one for himself. I've brought Pepperidge Farm cookies, which Kirk claims to love. And Rochelle is trying to convince him to treat us to coffee. He's pretty adamant with the no on that one, but he smiled when she brought it up the second time.

Despite the music award invasion, our other guests continue to be their selfish, self-involved selves. The actor in room 2710, for example, asks me to listen to the seventh message on his voice mail, copy it down, call him back and read it to him. For a second I'm struck dumb and I don't believe him.

"You want me to listen to your messages, copy the seventh message down, call you back and read it to you?"

"Yah," he says, breathless.

"You realize I have to listen to your messages, Mr. Shubano?"

"Uh, yah." Like I'm the idiot.

"Okay, sir. I'll call you as soon as I'm finished."

I get permission from Kirk, who frowns and asks if I'm sure that's what Mr. Shubano requested.

"You can call him and ask him," I say, irritated. "Room 2710."

Kirk considers. "If the guest requested it, go ahead."

I listen to Shubano's messages. The first six messages are from various actors in his current film. I'm amazed at how much pain actors seem to be in. They're all having massages, or suffering through acupuncture. Unfortunately, no one says anything juicy or significant. The seventh message—the one Shubano wants me to transcribe—is from some woman in California.

"It's me. Saw the screening. Loved it. Do you want to go to the beach Saturday?"

I listen to the message three more times. I'm sure I've missed something. I call Shubano back, really pissed. Because I've missed the opportunity to take calls from Michael and Janet Jackson, and Bono from U2.

"Yah?"

"Mr. Shubano," I say curtly. "This is hotel operator Kendall. You asked me to listen to your messages . . ."

"Oh. Right. Okay."

I read the seventh message slowly from the pad on my desk. He doesn't get the sarcasm. When I'm finished, there's a long pause.

"That's all?" he says.

"Yah. I listened to the message three times to make sure."

"Oh." He sounds completely baffled. "Well, thanks."

He hangs up, and I curse at my switchboard.

"Are all the guests on mind-altering drugs tonight?" Tonya asks no one in particular.

"Why would you say something like that?" Kirk asks, annoyed.

"Got a call for Security to go to 1700," Tonya tells him. "Some guests are complaining about screaming."

I stiffen.

"What kind of screaming?" I ask.

Kirk looks at me sharply. "Ten calls holding!" he shouts.

As I take another call, Rochelle tells Kirk she has Mr. Schmidt on the line. Kirk takes a deep breath. I think he even rolls his eyes. Tonya smiles at Kirk, and it seems to comfort him a little. He smiles back. And—the horror, the horror—I think I'm jealous! I'm jealous of Tonya because Kirk just smiled at her.

Briefly, I forget my concern for 1700 and wonder why Kirk is nicer to the evening operators. Is it because he sees less of them? Or because they're better? I've never paid attention to actual office gossip, so I don't know if the petty bullshit that rules the day operator dynamic rules the evening operators as well. I don't know if there's a Victoria or Cheryl among them. How odd that I feel betrayed by Kirk because he's more comfortable with the evening operators.

"Kirk, what's wrong?" Rochelle asks. The concern in her voice manages to raise the level on my disturb-o-meter.

I look at Kirk and panic. The color has drained from his face. He announces, in a very calm voice, that a guest has just committed suicide.

I stand up, knocking my chair over.

"I know her," I blurt. I cover my mouth with my hand, try to think of what to do. Why would Rae kill herself? She was clearly unhappy, but I didn't get the suicide signal from her. What is the suicide signal?

I want to run out of the office and rush upstairs and ask Jack if I can help. He's probably devastated, stunned, hysterical. Helpless. I want Kirk to come over and put his arms around me like a supportive boss and tell me it's going to be okay.

But Kirk's frowning at me, confused.

"*I. Know. Her,*" I repeat slowly, angrily. Would he be kinder to Tonya and Rochelle?

"It was a man," Kirk says.

It's like the wind's been knocked out of me. "*Jack?*" I ask.

"I don't know his name." Kirk looks like he's really sick of me now. He types something into his computer. "4901. Davis."

I drop my face in my hands and breathe an enormously loud sigh of relief.

"Oh, my God," I whisper.

I can feel Kirk's eyes on me. I look up.

"Oh," I say calmly. I pick up my chair, relieved and embarrassed.

Kirk stares at me for a long minute, then he shakes his head and starts to explain what happened. Apparently, the guest on the forty-ninth floor hung himself in the bathroom. All of his calls should be directed to Security. Kirk tells Tonya to write the instructions on the board.

"Why do you have to write that on the board?" I ask, sitting down.

"Why wouldn't we write it on the board?" Kirk asks.

I imagine what it would be like if it really had been Jack. How would I write that on a dry-erase board? "It's disrespectful."

The room becomes completely silent. Tonya watches Kirk for further instructions. Kirk motions for her to do as she's been told. I'm disappointed that she does.

We watch Tonya chicken-scratch her way through this one. It's so sad. Your suicide. Written on a dry-erase board so the telephone operators don't make mistakes with your phone calls.

"What happened to 1700?" I ask.

Kirk gives me an odd look, then he leaves the office. Leaves my question unanswered. Everyone remains silent. I'd like to drop my head on my desk, close my eyes for a while and wake up somewhere else.

A half hour later, Kirk is still MIA. I'm about to take my break when Sage comes in and kneels beside me. I didn't know he was on tonight. This isn't surprising, since we haven't seen or spoken to one another in a week.

"Where's Kirk?" he asks.

"I'm not sure. How are you?"

I touch him and he flinches.

"Sage," I say. I've tried not to think about him and not being able to throw my arms around him like he's mine anymore. I've tried not to deal with missing him. But it's hard. I'm not in love with him, but I need him. And that makes it worse.

"Your friend," he says coldly, "is asking for you."

"I have many."

"The one staying here."

"Jack?" My heart starts to race. "What's wrong with him?"

"He's in the bar. Drinking hard. This close to making a scene."

"What do you want me to do about it?" I ask.

"Thought you'd want to know." He stands up.

"Sage."

He doesn't look at me. "Grab your blue jacket and come with me."

"Where are you going?" Rochelle asks when I grab a blue jacket from the closet and head out of the office.

"Would you tell Kirk I took my break?" I ask the room. "I have a personal emergency."

I rush after Sage, pulling the dreaded smock on. He holds the stairwell door open for me.

"Where's Rae?" I want to know. "His fiancée."

"Gone," Sage says cryptically.

"What do you mean, *gone?*" I snap.

Once the door closes behind us, Sage pushes me against the wall. "She took a bottle opener and slashed the room's walls to shreds."

Shreds. The hotel's silk wall coverings are art. That's going to cost Jack a fortune.

"Is this about you?" Sage asks.

"Me? I don't even know what's going on." Sage starts up the stairs, but I catch his arm. "Talk to me," I say.

"Like I said, he's this close to making a scene," Sage warns. "So come with me before he gets manhandled."

"He's asking for me?"

"He's saying he's not going to leave until you talk to him. Lucky thing the manager asked me to call Security. We only have a few minutes."

We make our way into the hotel's swank bar. Lights are dim. Music is low. The bar is crowded with women and men in business suits.

And there's Jack.

Looking nothing like a threatening drunk.

I expected disheveled, drooling Jack slumped over a bottle of Johnnie Walker Blue, shouting obscenities at the world. Not sexy Jack, leaning against a wall looking cool and casually dangerous in a ritzy-hotel-badboy way. He throws back the shot in his hand, and his eyes slide toward the bar.

"Hey," he calls out. "Who do I have to bribe to get a drink around here?"

Oh, dear.

"Hey!" he calls out again.

"They've cut you off, Jack," I say softly.

He looks at me, but I'm not sure he knows who I am.

"Jack," I say.

He frowns, stares at me for a minute. I feel eyes on us, but I push my self-consciousness aside and grasp his hands.

"You've had too much," I say.

"It's the girl who doesn't want to see me anymore," he mutters, lowering his eyes.

"Yeah, that would be me." I keep my tone light, smile when he looks at me again.

"What are you doing here?"

"Heard you were asking for me."

He shifts a little, almost loses my hands but hangs on tight. Then he laughs. "Ask and ye shall receive," he says loudly. "Anything you want, they'll get it for you here."

"That's what they pay us the small bucks for," I say.

He smiles. "Can you get me another drink?"

"Nope. I'm taking you to your room."

His eyes go over me slowly, and I flush. "You're wearing a smock."

I let his hands drop. "If I leave you here, Security is going to pick you up and carry you to your room. Push me, and I might start thinking that's a good idea."

He smirks. His head lolls back and he says, "I've been bad."

"Yes, you have. And I've officially lost my patience." I look at Sage. He's standing by the bar, staring at the floor. "I'm going."

"Okay." Jack straightens and manages to place his shot glass on the bar. Sage notices that I've made progress. He looks re-

·lieved. He tells the bartender to bill everything to Jack's room, then he pulls Jack's arm around his shoulders just as Jack almost topples over.

"Why don't you take the other side?" Sage advises.

I put Jack's other arm around my shoulders, nearly lose my footing when he leans away from Sage.

"Yeah, Jack," I strain. "Try balancing between both of us."

I feel Sage pull Jack closer to him so some of Jack's weight is alleviated.

"Talk to him," Sage mumbles as we walk to the elevators.

"Why? He doesn't know who I am."

"I know who you are." Jack sounds insulted.

A few people elect not to get into the elevator with us. A man—I think he hosts an *Entertainment Tonight*–type show on cable—offers to take my half of Jack. I'd love to pass Jack off to this guy, but I know it would humiliate him in the morning. And the part of me that undeniably still cares for him, the part of me I'm quickly losing patience with, thinks Jack has suffered enough humiliation for one evening.

The man holds the elevator door open for us when we reach seventeen. I thank him and say we're lucky the band didn't have to play the award show tonight. The man squints at Jack, trying to place him, but the elevator doors close.

"We need your key," I tell Jack as we head to his room.

Jack stops, dropping his arms from our shoulders. He seems completely with us for a minute, fumbling in his pockets, pulling out a key card and handing it to Sage. He puts his arms around our shoulders again.

"You got him?" Sage asks when we reach the room. He extricates himself from Jack's grip and opens the door.

Before I can hand him off to Sage, Jack kisses me. I taste scotch and nearly gag from the potency of it. He presses me against the wall, ignoring Sage's attempt to pry him off me. I can feel his erection against my thigh, and I'm horrified and angry. I shove at him. He doesn't budge, but he stops kissing me. And for a minute he just leans on me, breathing hard.

"Jack," I say.

He backs away, eyes focused on my face. When he reaches out to touch me, I pull back. He stops, hurt.

"Let's go," Sage says to me, clearly annoyed.

Jack starts at the sound of Sage's voice. He half turns, avoids looking directly at him. "Thank you," he says hoarsely and enters his room without closing the door.

"Give me a minute," I tell Sage.

Anger flashes across his face. "He leaves the door open because he knows you're going to follow him. You're just like everyone else."

"Not really," I say. "I just don't think I should leave him like this."

"Like what? A little drunk? I've put you in a cab in worse shape."

I don't say anything.

"I have to get back," he says and walks away.

Housekeeping hasn't been here yet. The room's a wreck. I stare at the walls and silently mourn the shredded silk. I wonder how someone could destroy such expensive, delicate wall coverings. Jack comes out of the bathroom. Tugging carelessly at his tie, ripping at the buttons of his shirt. Unfazed by the room's destruction.

"Want some of this?" He holds up one of the liquor bottles from the mini bar.

"Jack. Where's Rae?"

He's struggling with the cap.

"*Do you need more?*" I shout.

He stops struggling for a second, then starts again without looking up. I go to him, cover his hands so he'll stop.

"No more." My tone is harsh. Not playing games now. Kendall Stark is not happy. Sage thinks I'm like everyone else. And why did he leave the door open when he walked in here? He was that sure I'd follow him?

Slowly, his eyes meet mine. He releases the bottle into my custody.

"What happened with Rae?"

"She, uh . . ." He moves away from me, sits on the sofa. He starts to pull the tie off again, flings it to the floor. "She doesn't feel safe with me anymore."

He lies down on the sofa, closes his eyes. Seconds later the eyes are open again, trained on me.

"Emotionally safe," he adds. "Not like she thinks I'm going to kill her."

I know exactly what she means. It's not the kind of unsafe you feel because you think your fiancé is going to attack you while you're sleeping. It's the unsafe you feel because your fiancé doesn't love you. Because your fiancé isn't even your friend. *That's* the signal she gave off when I was with her.

"She doesn't think I love her," he says.

I don't ask.

"Are you going to be okay if I leave you?" I set the scotch on the table. "I have to go back to work."

He doesn't answer.

I pull a bottle of water from the mini bar and set it on the table next to the bottle of scotch. "You choose," I say, which makes him smile.

He sits up. He grabs the bottle of water and drinks, reminding me of other nights like this. In college. When we were kids. When one of us—usually him— was too intoxicated to be left alone. Jack taught me the importance of hydration and aspirin when one has had too much to drink.

"You know," he says after a moment of silence, "I didn't anticipate being so hurt by your request."

Suddenly cranky, I say, "Please don't tell me that's what this is about."

"Okay, I won't tell you."

I bite my lip, tell myself to relax. No. I won't let him make this my business.

"There she goes," he says to my retreating back. "Would you fucking talk to me for two minutes?"

"This is what I hate." I stop at the door and turn back to him. "About you. About people like you."

"People like me?"

"You'll never be satisfied because you don't know what you want. You're all looking for something you'll never find. You have a house here and here and there, but what does that mean? What does it mean to stay here and order crab cakes and duck and champagne and send back perfect, beautiful strawberries because they don't taste like sugar? Who is it for? Who are you trying to please? What are you trying to prove? What do you get out of *driving everyone crazy?*"

His eyes flash with anger.

"You want to talk?" I continue. "About? What you have or what you don't have? Because I've heard it all before. Everyone here is the same. It doesn't impress me."

He's staring at me like I've just gone off on this inexplicable rant, which I have. He looks hurt and confused and angry.

"You think . . ." He chuckles, but he isn't amused. "That's what you think of me? I'm some mindless money machine. *You* look down on *me* because I'm here. You think I suck because I can afford to have things you can't afford. You're still . . ." He bites down on his lip and shakes his head. ". . . incredibly judgmental, Ken. That's the real reason we could never be together."

"Oh, is that the *real* reason?" I open the door, then close it again. "How do you manage to piss me off after so many years?"

"Time means nothing," he says.

"I'm not going to argue with you about a relationship that ended nearly ten years ago. It's absurd."

He laughs. "It kills you that we still care about each other."

"Oh, God."

"I've struggled to be where I am," he says. "You—Jesus—you, of all people, know that."

He chokes on this last bit.

My throat closes, and I feel myself becoming angrier. "Rae does a freak-out, leaves and now you want to do true confessions with me? Well. No. It doesn't work out that way."

He swallows hard, lowers his eyes. "Would you go?" His voice is low, tired. Much like the last time he tried to kick me out of a room.

Unlike last time, this is his hotel room. And I'm still on the clock.

Kirk is gone when I return to the office. The looks from the other operators aren't resentful, but close to it. I've been gone for over an hour. They don't know me well enough to say Kirk's going to have my ass tomorrow, but the heavy silence that blankets the room confirms it.

I walk into work with six coffees and a dozen donuts from the Krispy Kreme on Third. Kirk doesn't look up from the file he's reading. Victoria is yammering to no one in particular about moving back to England next year. Everyone else is answering phones intently. I put the box of donuts and coffee carrier on Kirk's desk. He looks up, stares at me.

Even though the employee cafeteria is rife with drinkable coffee that's free and available twelve hours a day, I've decided that actually buying the coffee is a nicer gesture. A gesture that will keep Kirk from asking questions about last night.

"Coffee?" I say, opening the box of donuts.

He looks at the coffee and donuts. Obviously, he doesn't trust them. I hand out five cups to the operators on duty, including Victoria and Maria.

"That one's for you," I tell Kirk.

Kirk looks at his watch.

"I'm not late," I tell him.

Kirk picks up the last coffee and pulls off its top. He peeks inside.

"It's coffee," I say, pretending I'm not insulted. "I didn't do anything weird to it."

He smiles meekly. "Thanks."

After a couple of minutes, Kirk steps out of the office without a word to anyone. He takes his coffee with him. I think he's going to dump it somewhere, which really bothers me. The operators leave their cubicles to grab donuts while he's gone. They thank me awkwardly.

Rodney brings me a donut. "Your friend checked out this morning," he says.

"What friend?" I ask. He doesn't answer, just raises his eyebrows and nods at my monitor. I pull Jack's name up.

Jack has checked out. I look up his Guest History for more information. *Drinks too much in bar. Monitor intake during next visit,* it reads.

"Katie's celebrating," Rodney says.

"I bet," I mumble. Katie's refrain since Rae arrived has been "the fucking bitch in 1700 wants an extra blanket again," and "the cunt in 1700 has requested all of her faxes be collated and stapled, *not folded,* for the duration of her stay," and "the fucking bitch in 1700 wants all of her faxes *after* three in the afternoon every day."

"She's been trying to get more information about what happened last night. Do you know?"

"Why did you call him my friend?" I ask suddenly.

Rodney looks at his switchboard. "What?" he says as he takes a call.

Instead of taking a call, I check my voice mail to see if Jack left a message for me. I have one voice-mail message from Molly Hay at Human Resources.

"This is Molly Hay for Kendall Stark," she says as though she hasn't reached my personal work voice mail, but some random answering machine. "I'm sorry to tell you that your transfer was denied. If you have any questions, you can call me or visit the office on your lunch break."

I pull my headset off and glare at Kirk's desk. He hasn't returned.

"I'm passing an outside call to Mr. Schmidt from that freak that stayed in 1700," Katie calls out. "Should I listen?"

"Yes!" everyone but me shouts.

What the hell? How did the incident with Jack get out so quickly? And, more important, why? It wasn't a big deal. I cringe at the thought of Katie listening to Jack on the phone. Who knows what he's going to say to Mr. Schmidt? I don't want the world to know he groveled or kissed an ass or apologized for drinking too much. I feel protective of him.

I tell Katie I have an outside call for her. I say, "I think it's your boyfriend."

"Cool," she says, disconnecting Jack's call without a second thought. "Pass it over."

I pass a random call. Less than ten seconds later, Katie says, "Stark. You passed me the wrong call."

"Did I?" I say innocently.

Rodney makes a noise at his cubicle.

"Did you fucking hang up on my boyfriend?" she booms.

"I don't think so," I say.

"That fucking guy was asking for Ilene. Doesn't fucking sound like Katie."

"Hey, hey, hey," Kirk screams when he walks in. "Keep it clean, keep it clean, *keep it clean!*"

Katie backs down, and I turn my attention to Kirk. He still has the Krispy Kreme coffee container in his hand. I bet he dumped the coffee I bought and filled the cup with the cafeteria swill. He's such a paranoid fuck. I watch him look inside the donut box, pick one out and bite into it. I stand up.

"Kirk," I say. "Can I speak to you?"

Kirk stops chewing and looks nauseous, like he knew there

was an ulterior motive for the Krispy Kreme donuts and coffee and he's sick that he fell for it. Reluctantly, he waves me over to his desk as he takes his seat.

"You denied my transfer," I say quietly.

"Yes." He wipes donut from his mouth.

"Why?"

"Because I don't believe you'd be an asset to another department right now," he says.

"Are you kidding?"

The look on his face is questioning. "You think you'd be an asset to Reservations?"

"Yes."

"Seriously?"

I consider. My next yes isn't as convincing.

Kirk sighs. "Okay. Let's go over your record for a minute. You refuse to wear your uniform unless I ask you to. You're always late. And you don't get along with any of your coworkers."

"What are you talking about?" I argue. "I brought donuts."

"You've been written up once," he says. "And I'm tempted to write you up a second time. Three strikes and you're out."

"What? Why?"

Kirk checks his monitor, announces twelve calls are holding, then looks at me again. "What happened last night?"

"I had a problem with my neighbors," I say without missing a beat.

Technically, I'm not lying. When I got in from work last night there was this unusual *thunk*ing and *gork*ing happening above the bathroom and living room. It went on until three in the morning. I banged on the ceiling with my umbrella, but the *thunk*ing and *gork*ing just got louder.

This morning everyone who lives on my block was outside making love to Hercules in his huge rehabilitation cage. This cage was enormous. And all of these people came out of their houses to see him. It was one of those you-had-to-see-it-to-believe-it moments. Betty was explaining—loudly—that the cage was for Hercules to convalesce in.

"Doesn't he look pathetic?" Betty asked everyone gathered around them. "Like a little alien? He has to wear the plastic cone around his neck so he won't lick the bandages . . ."

As I passed, the world around me went silent. Even the twentysomething couple on three lowered their eyes when I smiled at them.

"What happened *here*?" Kirk asks now. "When I left you were on a break. A personal emergency?"

"Right. There was a problem with my neighbors."

He waits, but I don't know how to continue.

"We had a little incident in the hotel last night," he says. "I've heard you were involved."

I look at my coworkers. As I suspected, they're all watching me. How does this shit get around? Who tells it? The bartender? Bartenders and cocktail servers are entirely different creatures than the rest of us. They never deign to speak to any of us, let alone spread gossip.

But what's the protocol when a fellow hotel worker—no matter how low they fall in the caste system—manages not only to sleep with a guest but to steal his affections as well? That's what this is about, isn't it? Someone thinks Jack is a random hotel guest who managed to fall in love with me.

"If you want to have this conversation," I say, "we should have it privately. Not in front of the entire office."

Kirk ignores my suggestion. "Mr. Sullivan, the guest in room 1700, had the—"

"I mean it, Kirk," I interrupt. "I don't want to talk about it here."

He's just had his answer to the question he hasn't had a

chance to ask yet. I can't tell if that's anger or amusement play-ing across his face.

"Were you having an inappropriate relationship with the guest, or guests, in 1700? For money, or any other gifts?"

Now that is just humiliating.

"No."

"Are you sure?"

I try to hold his gaze but fail. I'm not going to cry. I'm not going to scream. I know he has to do this. I know this is the standard question in the *How to Be a Hotel Manager* guide-book. I'm kind of hurt that I have to be his example.

"Kendall," he says.

"Kirk," I cut him off. "I'm not comfortable talking about this with you in front of a few people I would never confess my secrets to. But you aren't giving me a choice." My voice is soft, which throws Kirk off for a second. He loosens his tie, stares at his desk. "Jack's an old boyfriend. And I can't tell you why he did what he did last night because I don't know. But he's some-one I care deeply about. I couldn't ignore what was happening to protect my job. I've tried very hard not to mix my personal life with my life here. I think you know that. I hope you'll take that into consideration when this comes up at the next depart-ment meeting."

I go back to my cubicle without waiting to be dismissed. A minute or two passes in silence. I stare at my monitor, wonder when he'll announce there are thirty-eight calls holding.

"In the future," Kirk says sedately, "why don't you try to conduct personal matters like this outside of the hotel?"

A few operators suck their teeth in unison.

"Bringing coffee and donuts to the office one morning isn't going to do the trick," Kirk adds. "If you want to do better, *be* better. Wear your uniform. Play by the rules."

"All I do is play by the rules," I say quietly. "It never got me anywhere."

"Change into your uniform before you start taking calls," he says.

I stand up. He watches me as I head out of the office.

"You don't have any enemies here," he reminds me. "We're in this together."

Wanda's coming out of the bathroom when I return to the office. "Where'd you go?" she asks.

"I went to change into my uniform."

"For an hour?"

"What's the probability that I walk in there and he tells me I'm fired? Highly likely or highly unlikely?"

"He's not going to say anything," Wanda says.

Kirk looks up when we walk in. He doesn't say anything. Victoria is standing near his desk, talking about the guest who committed suicide last night.

"What could have been so bad?" Victoria asks. "He could afford the forty-ninth floor."

I roll my eyes and take my seat. "If only life were just about being able to afford the forty-ninth floor. You are such a moron."

"Kendall," Kirk barks. "What's happening to you?"

"What do you mean?"

He frowns like he really can't stand me anymore. "Have you taken your break yet?"

I look at him. He raises his eyebrows.

"No," I say.

"Then go," he says. "Take it."

The other operators watch me with a mixture of contempt and envy. They wish they could get on Kirk's nerves enough to merit two breaks.

*   *   *

I hear her voice the second I enter the building. It fades in and out, loud and soft. I can't piece together a full sentence. I take the steps slowly, quietly, so that she won't detect me. On the second floor I can hear her better. Her voice is piercing. She says, "She is literally tied to a chair from the minute she gets home from school until bedtime."

"You can't live like this," the other female voice says.

"What other choices do I have? The other night I tiptoed across the room a minute after midnight and she started banging on the ceiling. *He* isn't so bad. I don't think he's here that often. It's *her*."

I reach the fourth floor. Betty and Lisa are standing in front of my door. What night is she talking about? I wonder. This *other* night.

They see me. Lisa turns her back to me. Betty puts her hand on her hip and stares. I put my key in the lock, ignore her.

Inside my apartment I can still hear their voices. Whispering now.

After a moment they laugh loudly. Lisa says, "Why don't you come down and have a glass of red wine later?"

Betty cackles like a witch. "I might take you up on that."

They say good-bye, then Betty's door upstairs slams. She stomps across the floor—*doomp . . . doomp . . . doomp*—moves something heavy, and drops something even heavier.

I'm overcome by sadness and a sudden urge to be at Nick's.

I stare at Nick's house, at the darkened windows, at the sagging maple tree in the front yard. And then I ask myself what I'm doing here. Why do I still come here when I'm lost? I breathe in the cool night air and turn away, prepared to go home.

Jack is leaning against a tree in front of the house next door, watching me.

"Oh, shit. Jack." I press my hand against my chest to stop my heart from beating so loud.

Jack looks away, doesn't move.

"You're like a fucking cat," I say.

His eyes glint in the darkness when he looks at me again. A little amused?

"Kendall," he says.

"I just thought I'd stop by to see Gary and Nick."

He pulls a set of keys from his pocket and stares at them. "No one's here."

"You're staying here now?" I wonder how Gary feels about that. Nick certainly has the space. But it's Jack.

Jack busies himself with the keys. "I thought it was best to check out while I still had my dignity."

"The call to Mr. Schmidt probably helped."

He looks up. "Excuse me?"

"So Rae went back to Maine?" I change the subject.

He doesn't answer, just stares. I look at the ground, knowing I've messed up. It's going to bite me in the ass one day. I'm going to say something to the wrong person and my life as a telephone spy will be exposed. The right thing to do now is say good-bye and walk home. But he finds the key he needs and opens Nick's front door. He holds it open for me, watching me, waiting for me to make my decision.

I step inside.

Jack turns on the light in the front room, walks past me and runs up the stairs. I listen to him walk across the floor above me, stopping to turn on more lights, as I head for the kitchen.

In the kitchen several empty bottles of Sullivan Brew litter the counter near the sink. When Jack comes into the room I'm reading one of the labels.

"Thirsty?" He takes off his jacket, tosses it on a stool and pulls two bottles of beer from the refrigerator.

"How's the actual business part of your trip going?" I ask.

"Great." He opens the beer. "That part's finished. Worked out the way I hoped."

"Congratulations."

"We aren't going to be Sierra Nevada," he says, staring at the bottles he just opened. "But we'll be *available* here, which is a huge step."

"So I can walk into Excelsior and order a Sullivan?"

"No." He hands a bottle to me. This one is different from the others. The bottle is short and fat, like a Red Stripe. The label is white with fancy black lettering. *Sullivan Brew. Winter Solstice. Special Edition.* DRINK RESPONSIBLY. "Supermarkets. Delis. Sometimes a bar does a guest tap for a month or two. That helps a company get wider recognition."

I nod, taste the Winter Solstice. It's strong, bitter. There's a hint of spice. Cardamom?

"Maybe some bar owner will try it and decide he has to carry it for a month." He holds up his bottle as if he's going to make a toast, then he drinks. "This one's popular in Maine and Vermont."

"Strong." I choke after my second sip. "I already feel it going to my head."

"Fifteen percent," he tells me.

I nod again. That means nothing to me. I assume he means alcohol content. He watches me drink a little more.

"I'm sorry about last night," he says quietly.

He wasn't expecting my silence. He leans against the sink, drops his head back and stares at the ceiling.

"You want to sit on the deck?" he asks after a moment.

Outside, we stretch out on chaise longues separated by a small table. I light a cigarette and blow smoke rings at the moon. I don't know what to say to him. I'm sorry about last night, too. Got me into loads of trouble. It's like nothing's changed.

"Do you know what you want from life, Kendall?" he asks after a while.

I tap ashes over the side of the deck. Jack's staring at me when I look over.

"You can be honest," he says. "I'm not going to hold it against you."

I snigger. "Right."

"Why would I?"

"Because you can."

He sighs. "I know what Nick, Gary and Amy told you back then." His tone is still quiet. "That I had no future and I'd bring you down. I hated them for feeding that crap to you. I hated you more for listening. Because it meant you agreed."

I shake my head. "No."

"It didn't take much," he points out. "But I already told you. I'm not here to show you up."

I sit up and stare at him like he's completely lost it. "I don't blame you for wanting to hash it out and throw it in my face. I get that. I expected it the minute I saw you. What I don't get is why it took you so long."

"I don't want to hash it out." He's still calm, serious. "I came to see you. Because you matter to me."

"You came here to parade your perfect life in my face," I insist. "The perfect fiancée who speaks eighteen languages. The perfect job. The perfect house . . . you own things. . . ." My voice fades.

"She only speaks three languages," he says. "Rae. Only three."

I take a long drag off my cigarette, blow a few more smoke rings into the sky. "Okay," I say. "Well. Not anymore."

"Not anymore what?"

"Do I know what I want from life. Not anymore."

"Why not?"

"I've been thinking about how sure me and my friends were about our futures in college. Me, Gary and Amy were going to work in Hollywood. Nick was going to be a poet. We were all pretty obnoxious about it. I've also been trying to see us through your eyes."

"Oh yeah?"

"I look at Nick and wonder what I was doing when he decided to be a finance guy," I say. "He was one of my best friends and I had no idea he was interested in money. I thought he would be a starving poet his entire life."

Jack smiles.

"I realize I never had any idea what I wanted to do," I admit. "Not really. You'd ask me what I wanted to do in Hollywood and I'd say it would all come together when I got there. Because, you know, the town would see me and fall to its knees."

Jack nods, remembering.

"So I'm sorry that I made you feel like I was so much more together than I was when I was with you."

He looks touched.

I lift my bottle for a mock toast, but I don't drink. I don't want to be drunk with him. He doesn't drink either, and there's a long silence. He stares at the table between us. He starts to smile, and I smile with him, curious what he's remembering.

"I really loved you," he says, looking at me.

Now *I* stare at the table, knowing he really, really did. Love me. And it made me not respect him. Actually, there were moments when I couldn't stand it. But I can't tell him that now. I don't feel that way now. I actually miss it.

"Me, too," I say.

"Did you?"

He was, whether I liked it or not, the absolute love of my life. It made me not like myself. What did it say about me if I could love someone my friends said wasn't good enough? I can't tell him that either.

"You know I did," I say.

He finishes off his beer, then leaves me alone on the deck to get another one. When he comes back outside I'm standing, lighting a new cigarette.

"You smoke too much," he says, stretching out on the chaise longue again.

Instead of sitting on my chaise longue, I sit on his. He straightens, just a little uncomfortable being so close to me.

I say, "Are you ever tempted to start smoking again?"

"No."

I take a deep drag on my cigarette, and then I blow a huge cloud of smoke in his face. He squints his eyes but doesn't move.

"You're not tempted," I say.

"No." His voice is a little hoarser.

I smile mischievously, turn to straddle his legs playfully. I take another drag and blow again. This time, Jack leans forward and kisses me. Before I can pull away he puts his arms around me, keeping me in place, easing me down on his lap. He licks my lips gently, urging my mouth open. We kiss for a long time, forgetting where we are.

Maybe the same images that are flashing through my mind are flashing through his. Like the nights we'd spend in my dorm room, huddled on the floor, lips locked for hours. Kissing to the sounds of the Sufi music I adored so pretentiously in college. I've never wanted to kiss anyone as long and as hard as I used to kiss Jack. Not even Sage. I think I could kiss Jack forever.

When we pull apart I can feel his arousal through our jeans. I flush. He grins, pushes some hair from my face, unashamed that I can feel him.

"What?" he says in a hushed tone. "What do you want to do?"

I look directly in his eyes and nearly groan. He looks hungry and beautiful and ready to be loved by me again. It's taking all of my willpower not to grind into him, not to suggest we go to his room.

"Are you in love with Rae?" I ask.

His hands come away from my waist. He chuckles, looks down. "Well. You know me. I've only ever wanted a nice girl to love me."

I tense at how sad he sounds. I touch his cheek, lightly trailing my fingertips down to his chin.

"Are *you* in love?" I ask again.

"No." He shifts.

"Why did you choose her?" I prod.

He doesn't answer for a while. He softens beneath me, can't look me in the eye.

"Because she reminded me of you," he says finally.

"Me?"

"You were always laughing," he explains. "When I met Rae, she was always laughing."

Something about this makes me sad. For him, and especially for Rae. I kiss him again. Within seconds he's pushing into me, moaning softly into my mouth.

I pull back, searching.

"Don't look to me to be the voice of reason," he warns. "I just finished telling you I'm not in love with my fiancée."

I rest my forehead against his. He wraps his arms around me and squeezes tight.

"I never stopped loving you," he says.

"What a line, Jack," I say weakly.

"Not a line." Hands slide up my back, make me shiver. "You're shaking. You want me."

"Don't," I whisper.

"You're scared," he says, teasing the straps of my bra. "You cover it up with rebellion and snappy one-liners. But I know you...."

His words catch in his throat. He watches my hands work the buttons of his jeans and release him. We stare at him for a minute, like two inexperienced teens unsure what to do next. And then he starts kissing me again.

"You can touch me, okay?" he says. "It's okay to touch me."

His desire frightens me a little. What am I to him? What is he to me? Who is this scared, tentative Kendall? Why can't I touch him?

"Please," he urges.

I shake my head. On the edge of my tongue are the words *I can't*. But the front door opens and closes. Nick calls out Jack's name. We freeze, and then we both sigh. My sigh is from relief. Jack's sigh is from disappointment. He tucks himself away as I climb off of him and straighten my clothes.

Nick and Gary are already in the kitchen when Jack and I enter.

"Hey, Ken," Gary says when I join them.

"How long have you been here?" Nick asks.

"Five minutes," I say.

We all look at the empty beer bottles in Jack's hands.

"About ten," I revise, looking at Jack for confirmation.

Jack's dumping the bottles in the garbage, not really listening.

Nick is staring at me. I think he's staring at my lips. I have an urge to touch them because they feel sore. Maybe he can tell we've been kissing.

"I'm going to call it a night," Nick says abruptly.

"At nine-thirty?" Jack asks, but doesn't sound like he cares.

"I have work upstairs." He grabs a couple of bottles of water from the refrigerator and kisses me goodnight. Before he heads up he looks at Jack again. "You tell Ken you're going back to Maine on Sunday?"

I look at Jack, surprised. Jack is staring at the floor.

"Okay, well," Gary says, sensing something. "I guess I'll call it a night as well."

Alone again, Jack finally looks at me.

"I have to go back," he says.

I'm already at the phone, calling a car service.

Jack waits with me outside. We don't speak, which is awkward and a little silly. I step into the street, looking for my car.

"How are your neighbors?" he asks.

"The same."

"Are you going to move?"

"Some people can't just move because they have an urge to," I say bitterly.

Jack narrows his eyes at me. I'm angry because I want to talk about what just happened, but I don't want to be the one to initiate the conversation.

"Do you want to fuck me?" I blurt.

"Yes," he says matter-of-factly.

"So that's all this is about." I think I sound hurt. "Nothing else. We have sex and you go back to Maine to be with your girlfriend."

"I have to go back home," he says. "I don't . . . you haven't given me any signals."

"Signals?" I laugh as my car pulls up.

He lowers his eyes. "Yeah. Signals."

"I didn't know I was supposed to be giving off signals."

He sighs. "I have to go home, Ken."

I go to the car. I turn to look at him again.

"There are these moments," I tell him, leaning against the car door. "In my apartment. There are these rare good moments when the apartment is quiet. Really quiet. They're like mini-vacations. Twenty minutes. An hour. A whole day. And I can't imagine leaving, giving up on it." I smile warmly, remembering them. Then I swallow hard and look at Jack.

"People don't get the significance of peace and quiet until it's gone. I'm good at not knowing something special until I've lost it."

Jack straightens, and for a second he looks devastated. I get into the car and wave good-bye. As the car pulls away I wonder if I'll see him before he goes back to Maine.

I wake up with the kid. I forgo the usual moaning and groaning and reaching for the umbrella that has taken up permanent residence in my bedroom, and I drag my ass out of bed three hours earlier than I planned to. I undress and take a shower to drown out the noise, and then I sit on the bathroom floor and smoke a cigarette. I'm safe from the kid in the bathroom.

I'm early for work. Only Trina has started the shift before me. I've brought bottled water and Snickers candy bars for Wanda, Rodney and Katie. I put the gifts on their desks and start to take calls.

About five minutes later, there's a hush in the room. I look up from my switchboard to see Wanda, Rodney and Katie walk into the office together. They're wearing sweaters and slacks.

Katie flashes me a look of disgust as they take their seats. I'm wearing my uniform. Reluctantly, the morning operators on duty gather their things and leave for the day. Wanda, Rodney and Katie start their shift casually, despite the stunned look on Kirk's face.

"Rodney," Kirk says ten minutes later. "Can I see you in the conference room?"

Rodney stands up mechanically, winks at me as he follows Kirk out of the office. I watch him, alarmed. I have this sinking feeling this is about me somehow. And as though she's reading my mind, Katie stands up.

"Why the fuck are you wearing your uniform?" she hisses at me. "Are you bonkers? We can't dissent if the main dissenter has defected to the other side."

"What?" I'm clearly baffled.

She sits down when Kirk comes back into the room.

"This is lovely," Kirk says sarcastically. "But this isn't *Norma Rae,* or whatever Hollywood drama you all watched last night. Kendall, Wanda and Katie. Why don't all three of you join Rodney in the locker room and put on your uniforms? Now."

"I'm wearing my uniform," I say.

"No," Katie and Wanda say in unison.

"I'm not playing games here," Kirk warns. His eyes give me a once-over and take in my uniform. "Wanda and Katie. Go."

Wanda stands. "Wearing a uniform in a basement doesn't make sense," she states.

"I second that," Katie shouts from her cubicle.

Oh, shit.

Kirk looks at me. I want to tell him I didn't do this. I'm turning over a new leaf. I need this job and I'm not interested in any more headaches. But that somehow seems like a betrayal to Wanda, Rodney and Katie. I bite my lip and wonder how much of a jerk I'd look like if I stepped in and tried to mediate. The fact is, they need this job as much as I do.

Rodney walks in, sans uniform. He's carrying a cup of coffee from the café across the street, looking smug. I would laugh if I didn't think it would come back to bite me. I take off my headset and stand up.

"We're writing a letter," I tell Kirk. "To Mr. Schmidt. About the uniform thing. And we thought we'd do a trial run. See how well it works out before we send it."

"So this was your idea?" Kirk doesn't seem surprised at all.

"Well. Yeah."

"Shut up, Stark," Katie snaps and strides over to Kirk menacingly. Kirk backs up. "We're protesting because it's stupid to wear those ugly uniforms in a basement. And before you say anything, this *is* a basement. There are no windows and we're about two floors underground. Everyone treats us like shit as it is. I'm tired of people making fun of my uniform in the cafeteria."

Kirk doesn't say anything for a long time, and Katie glares at him the entire time. She is officially insane in my book, but I think I like her.

"Katie, Wanda and Rodney," Kirk says calmly. "Please wait for me in the conference room while I pull your files."

Katie is a little surprised, but she obeys. Rodney and Wanda also leave.

"Kirk," I say. "Don't write them up, okay?"

Kirk ignores me.

"Kirk. Listen to me."

Still, he ignores me. He pulls all three files and stands. He looks at Trina curiously. "Do they really make fun of your uniforms in the cafeteria?" he asks.

From the other side of the room Trina squeaks, "Sometimes."

Wanda, Rodney and Katie are written up for insubordination. It's Wanda's second write-up. Three strikes and she's out, Kirk tells her when they return. I sit in the cafeteria without eating. Something about that incident really bothered me.

I call Sage at Front Desk. He's surprised to hear from me.

"I miss you," I say vulnerably. "I have no one to turn to when I'm having a bad day at work."

After nearly a minute of uncomfortable silence—made more uncomfortable by the fact that I've never felt this jilted by anyone before—I tell him I have to go.

"Give me five minutes," he says.

He picks up two black coffees the second he walks into the cafeteria and carries them over. He sits across from me, looks sorry for me. I hate that look. I can't stand that it's on his face.

"You're not sleeping well," he says, pushing over a coffee. It's painful that he knows me without trying.

"Not last night."

"And now you're having a bad day, and you don't have anyone to turn to."

I ignore the sarcasm and tell him about what just happened in the office. He manages to laugh at how ridiculous Kirk is, and tells me it's not my fault.

"Even I heard about the shit Kirk gave you about your friend," Sage says. "He's getting tons of crap for it from people."

"Really?"

"They think it's romantic," Sage admits. "They didn't have to drag him up to his room that night."

"Thank you for doing that," I say.

"How is he?"

"I don't know."

"He checked out."

"Yes."

We don't say anything for a while. And then I ask him about Paula.

"We're fighting," he admits, and I'm surprised by his candor.

"I'm sorry."

He meets my eyes. Now the sadness there isn't directed at me. "I can't go through it again. We won't make it."

"Oh, Sage."

"The thing is," he continues, "how do you marry someone you aren't sure you'd be friends with? I mean, she calls me here and I start thinking, why is her voice so high? Can I really spend the rest of my life with a woman whose voice is so high?"

"That's a tough one," I say.

"When we fight, I feel like I need to hear a friendly voice. So I immediately think about calling you. But she's there, so I can't call you. And it makes me feel like something's wrong if I can't call a friend in front of her."

"So let's be friends again," I tell him. "Just friends."

He shakes his head. "I can't."

"Why not?"

He stares at me for a long time. "Because."

I reach out for his hand, and then I stop myself. Something in his face tells me it would be wrong to touch him.

"Because I want you," he says. "That isn't fair to her, is it? What's the point of even trying if I keep seeing you?"

I lower my eyes, feel sad. "And you're still angry with me."

"I want you. That's all."

The cafeteria phone rings and Sage knows it's for him. He stands.

"If I was fighting with my boyfriend," I say, "I would want to call you, too."

He wipes something off my face, then answers the phone and tells whoever it is that he'll be right there.

"Why don't we see how it goes?" he says, hanging up. He avoids looking me in the eye when he kisses me good-bye.

I go after him. Sensing me, he turns around, and we em-
brace. We hold tight, not wanting to let go. Being like this feels
right, but it also feels like the very last time.

My doorbell rings a few minutes after I walk into the apartment. The male half of the twentysomething couple on three is
standing in the hall, looking slightly embarrassed.

"Uh, hey," he says. "Betty can't find her keys."

The twentysomething couple on three hasn't been speaking
to me lately. I don't feel the need to be kind to him. "I haven't
seen them," I say coldly.

"She wants to know if she can climb through your window
so she can use the fire escape."

I stare at him, incredulous. "She asked you to ask me that?"

He shifts his weight. I realize he's still dressed in his work
clothes. Something about this really irritates me.

I take off my coat and shake my head. "I just walked in. . . ."

"She can't get into her apartment," he says testily.

"That's not my problem."

"Okay," he says. "But you realize the time we've just spent
arguing over this could have been used to let her climb
through your window."

"So you're going to argue *for* her?"

He sighs. "She needs to use your window."

"Tough shit," I snap, angry that a once-friendly neighbor is
giving me shit on behalf of Betty.

"Fine." He backs up and I close the door.

Less than a minute later, there's another knock on my door.
I consider ignoring it, but I'm all worked up now. A rush of
adrenaline propels me back to the door.

"Yes?"

"It's Betty. Can you open the door?"

"What do you want?"

"It's an emergency," she shouts.

I open the door a crack. Betty pushes it open with a force that almost knocks me over.

"Hey," I shout as she storms past me, into my bedroom. I rush after her. She walks across my bed in her shoes, leaving a trail of sidewalk soot on my comforter, and starts to open my window.

I'm floored.

"Get the fuck out of my apartment," I scream.

"Do you know who I am?" she thunders as she struggles with the heavy window. "I'm the PRESIDENT! I own you."

There are so many reasons why this moment is *wrong*. I haven't felt this enraged in years. Actually, I'm not sure I've ever felt this enraged. I take a deep breath and exhale slowly. It doesn't help. My heart is racing with indignation. I'm going to hurt her.

"You need to get out before I drag you out," I threaten darkly.

She hears the rage and she turns to look at me. "And if you lay a hand on me I will sue you."

"*Get out.*" Fists clench. I'm not to be messed with.

"Tough shit," she says, turning back to the window. "Tough shit for me *and* you."

I'm surprised for a second. My own words are being thrown at me. That's also wrong.

"You tried to kill my cat," she says as the window gives. "Everyone knows you're a killer. The girls told us."

"You're going to believe a little girl over me?"

"You're nothing," she spits as she lifts the screen.

Against my better judgment, I grab her hair and tug. She

shrieks. Her hands shoot back to grasp mine. She's strong. Stronger than I am. She pushes me away, turns around and raises her hand to slap me. I don't flinch, and she stops.

"Hit me," I say. "I dare you."

She may be able to kick my ass, but I am not afraid of her.

"I've been trying to avoid this." She points her finger in my face. She's breathing hard. Her eyes are flashing dangerously. "As the president of the co-op board I have the right to throw you out. You are not co-op material."

"Does anyone want to *be* co-op material?" I say, and she looks a bit surprised. "Is that something people aspire to?"

She huffs, and then she turns around, opens the window screen again and steps out onto the fire escape. I let her go without another word. Because I'm too upset to continue this. I'm tired. I'm confused. I'm stuck. And her sense of superiority both frustrates and enrages me.

I ask myself why I care. I ask myself why I'm letting her reach me. I take a few deep breaths. She's not worth anger. She's not worth tears. I scream "bitch" a couple of times at the ceiling, but it doesn't help. I strip the dirty comforter off my bed and lie down to listen to the intentional stomping, dragging and pounding in misery.

After a while, the *doomp*ing and *thunk*ing become a cacophonous lullaby my body responds to with spasms. The next thing I know I'm waking up from a fitful sleep to the sound of my doorbell. I lie in the dark, feel the rage mount again. I'm disturbed by its speed.

I get out of bed, propelled by this rage, and wrench my front door open aggressively. And the relief I feel at the sight of Jack standing in my doorway is overwhelming. So overwhelming I start to weep.

Startled, Jack grabs me and enfolds me in his arms. He hushes me, closing the door and locking it while ushering me back into the apartment. I hold on to him, feeling embarrassingly vulnerable. But I don't let go because I'm desperate for contact that isn't hostile or angry. I tell him about work and Sage and my vicious fight with Betty. I'm not sure how much he understands because I'm telling it all into his coat.

He walks me to my bedroom. I point to my comforter in a pile on the floor. He looks baffled, so I describe how Betty stormed into my room and walked across my bed with her shoes on.

"I own that," I tell him. "And she treated it like it was nothing."

Jack inspects the comforter and shakes his head in disgust.

"She called me nothing," I say quietly.

He looks at me fiercely. "You're not nothing. This can be cleaned."

"I can't afford to have it cleaned."

"Why don't you move out?"

"I'm stuck," I say before collapsing on my bed and burying my face in my pillow.

"Why are you stuck? You have nowhere else to go?"

It all rushes at me now. The reasons why I'm stuck. My credit card bills. My loneliness. My job. My new neighbors. My inability to get anything right. I cry as it all comes down on me, choking me. And this feeling of despair is so new and so strange. I hate it.

"Don't cry." Jack sounds tortured. "I can't stand it."

I take a deep breath. I don't move for a minute. And then I say, "No one has ever shown such total disregard for my stuff. For me."

I feel Jack sit on the bed next to me. He rubs my back, touches my face, wipes away my tears.

"Why are people so cruel?"

"Because someone like you—" He stops for a second. "Because you know what we are and we don't want witnesses."

I look up to see his face. He wipes more tears away. It seems right that Jack is the one to see me like this. Weak. Emotional. Reduced to nothing. UnKendall. He's not judging me and I need that now.

I need not to be judged.

"She's not worth all this," he says softly.

I shake my head. "Not just her. She triggered it. I've . . . I've been thinking for a long time that I've made all the wrong decisions so far."

"Join the club."

"You've made all the right decisions."

He caresses my face. "No one makes all the right decisions."

"Life doesn't give a person a lot of time to make up for mistakes," I say.

"No. But it's never too late to fix things."

His hand rests on my face and I lean into the touch. I tell him how, every day, it seems harder to find a purpose. I go to work and suffer through it. I come home and suffer through it. It's like I exist without a purpose. I try to make it matter. All of it. I do. But it doesn't work. And he lies beside me and listens to it all. He strokes my hair. He doesn't call me crazy. He doesn't tell me I'm too strong or too old to be carrying on like this. He just lets me vent. He just lets me cry. He just lets me be a girl. He just listens until I fall asleep.

In the morning, Jack is up earlier than me. When I come out of the bedroom he holds up two cups of coffee, the coffee single tabs hanging over the cups' rims. I beam at him.

"Thanks."

"You slept like a baby," he tells me.

"Well, that's the one thing I could be truly excellent at," I say. "I could be an excellent sleeper."

"Stop talking about yourself like you're worthless," he says fiercely, and it surprises both of us. For a moment, we're silent, realizing even the slightest things give feelings away.

"Okay," I say and go to the bathroom to brush my teeth. The apartment, I realize, is strangely quiet. The usual *doomp*ing that serves as my early morning wake-up call didn't wake me up today. And my upstairs neighbors, who are usually storming out of the apartment this very minute, seem to have left early and quietly.

When I come out of the bathroom, Jack is sipping his coffee.

"Like it?" I ask, grinning.

He nods and holds the cup up. "Yum."

"Did you work some kind of voodoo on me last night?"

"No."

"Are you sure? No black magic to make sure I slept through everything?"

"No. You just slept."

I look at the clock on the VCR. "I never sleep until nine."

"Nothing mystical," he says. "I promise."

"Well, thank you."

"Payback for the other night," he says. And then he tilts his head, looks serious. "Why can't you move? You shouldn't be here."

"I'd have to move back in with my parents," I tell him. "But, you know, adult now."

"Plenty of adults move in with their parents when they need to," he says. "All that matters is being surrounded by people who love you."

I nod. "It's nice to be surrounded by love. Sometimes you need to go home and reestablish ties with your childhood. Whenever I go home I realize I kind of wish I was in high school again. I liked high school. I had hope."

"Yeah," he agrees.

"But I can't go back to my parents. You might as well stamp a big L on my forehead."

"Ken, I don't agree. You can't be tortured where you live. Give yourself a break. No one's judging you."

"We slept in our clothes," I change the subject.

He nods.

"You must be uncomfortable. I'm sorry. You probably need things."

He shakes his head. "There was an unopened toothbrush in the medicine cabinet. I used it."

He leaves the kitchen and leans against a wall near one of the windows in the living room. He pushes the curtain aside, looks out. And suddenly I remember last night. He came here uninvited. Unexpected.

"What did you want last night?" I ask. "Why did you come here?"

He lets the curtain go, then takes off his glasses and rubs his eyes. When he puts them back on, he focuses on me.

"I'm not sure. I was walking around the neighborhood and I found myself here."

"Well. Thank you," I say. "For coming. For being with me when I really needed . . . someone."

He nods. And then he says, "Gary and Nick are going to spend Christmas in Maine."

"Oh."

"They said they'd ask you, but since I'm here—"

"I don't know if I have Christmas off," I say.

He nods. He runs a finger across the curtains idly, then adjusts his glasses again.

"And Christmas is double time, so—"

"I can't marry her," he says abruptly.

"What?"

"You know I don't lie to myself. Rae has always been a lie. We don't fit. She knows it. I know it."

I start to panic like a guy. "Look, don't let this be about me. If you have things settled, don't go messing them up because I . . ."

He's silent, waiting for me to finish.

"You shouldn't make it about me."

His eyes don't move from my face.

"Really, Jack."

"It's not completely about you."

"It can't be about me at all."

He smiles, but it's a sad smile. His eyes are tired and cranky. "This is familiar. You let me in. Completely. And then you turn away from me like you used to—"

"I used to turn away because—"

He shakes his head. He doesn't want to hear it.

"No," I say. "Listen to me. I turned away because . . . I needed not to feel about you the way I felt about you."

"What does that mean?"

"It means. Very simply. And not so simply. That. I didn't want to love you. But I did. Love you. So much. And I need not to feel that way again. Because it hurts, and I made myself a promise that I would never let myself hurt again." I take a deep breath. "And you have Rae."

His cell phone rings.

Perfect.

I want to grab it out of his hand and throw it out of the window. He answers the call. He doesn't say much. Just one-word answers like yes and no and soon. He watches me watch him. After a minute he asks if he can take the call in Gary's room. While he does, I take a shower.

It's not terribly surprising that he's gone when I come out.

On my way to work I slip going up a flight of stairs, hitting my shin. Several people walk past me, including a cop. I use the banister to help myself up, and a man behind me sucks his teeth because I'm in his way.

Kirk asks if I'm okay when I enter the office. I'm limping. We look down and notice I'm not wearing my uniform. He doesn't comment.

"I'm okay. Thanks."

I drop into my seat and stare at the memos on my desk. I'm still preoccupied by my emotional breakdown last night. As I dressed for work, the blur that was my evening with Jack morphed into a crystal-clear memory, and I was horrified. What was I thinking? Since when do I sob and confess my true feelings and fears to ex-boyfriends?

Before I left the apartment, I realized my comforter was missing.

"Did you look at the memos?" Rodney asks.

"Not yet."

"Look at them."

One is an internal memo from Sales announcing the arrival of a princess and her brother from Bahrain. I skim the five pages of instructions, searching for the telephone operator section. There isn't one. The other isn't a memo at all but a letter addressed to Mr. Schmidt requesting he take another look at the uniform policy for telephone operators.

The letter is brief, and it's signed by Wanda, Katie, Rodney and two evening operators.

"You wrote this?" I ask Rodney. He's wearing the requisite black pants and a sweater.

"Wanda wrote it. You like it?"

"Yeah," I say enthusiastically.

"You're going to sign it?"

"Immediately." He holds out his pen and I take it, sign my name at the bottom of the list.

"We almost have Trina," he whispers as I hand the letter and pen back to him. "I'm going to accost her when she goes on her break."

I give him a thumbs-up, and he winks.

"Kendall," Trina calls out, "I'm passing a call to you."

"What did you say to her?" Gary asks the second I take the call.

"Who?"

"The Evil One upstairs."

"Betty?"

"You haven't checked our messages?"

"I just got here."

"Joe called," he says. Joe is our landlord. "I called him back."

"What did he say?" I ask.

"What did she say?" Nick asks in the background.

"What did you say?" Gary asks me.

"It's not so much what I said," I tell him hesitantly. "I pulled her hair."

"You did do it," Gary says.

"Get out." I hear Nick laugh. "She did?"

"What did Joe say?" I feel my heart speed up.

"Maybe you should sit for this."

"No. I mean, I am sitting."

Gary takes a deep breath. "She's trying to have us evicted."

"*What?*"

"Apparently we're not co-op material."

"Oh, Jesus."

"She said you called her a bitch," Gary adds.

"I didn't."

"And she said you threatened to kick her ass if she ever tried to speak to you again."

"Another lie," I say.

"Well," Gary says.

"What does Joe want us to do?"

Gary doesn't say anything for a minute. Then, "Nothing. Not really. He just wanted to find out if any of it was true. He also wanted to prepare us because he thinks she's really going to try to do this. Evict us. Evictions take months, but she's some kind of real estate lawyer."

"Shit," I say. "Really?"

"Are you going to be home later?"

"Around seven."

"We'll talk then," Gary says. "I'm late for work."

We disconnect just in time. Kirk walks into the office and hands out another memo. The holiday schedule. I've forgotten what month it is.

Way back in July I requested to work all the major holidays. I need the money. But according to Kirk's new holiday schedule, I'll only be working Thanksgiving Day and New Year's Eve. New Year's Eve is the absolute worst holiday to work because, technically, it isn't a holiday. No holiday pay for your troubles.

Rodney says, "I'll be in Chicago that week."

Kirk doesn't look up from his desk. "What week?"

"The week of Christmas," Rodney says. "I requested the entire week off."

"No, you didn't."

"Yes, I did," Rodney argues. "Over two months ago. And we had that talk. I'm Macbeth."

I look at Rodney questioningly. "You're Macbeth? In what?"

"A play," Rodney says brusquely, standing up to get a better look at Kirk. "Can't just not turn up to my theater company's run of a play in which I'm the lead."

I look at Kirk. He's shuffling through a pile of papers on his desk. "When is this again?"

"Opening night is Christmas Eve."

"You're in a theater company?" I ask.

Rodney nods, eyes intent on Kirk. Trina leaves her cubicle and moves over to Kirk's desk. She waits patiently while Kirk continues to look through his papers.

"What theater company?" I ask.

"Okay," Kirk says, holding up a piece of paper and waving it at Rodney. "I had that with the vacation requests and didn't take it into account when I did the holiday schedule. I did give you that week off."

Rodney looks relieved and sits down again.

Trina tells Kirk she has a family and can't work Christmas Eve. Kirk stares at her for a minute, and then he asks if she thinks no one else in the office has a family.

"Amen," Rodney mumbles from his cubicle.

"Why would I want New Year's Eve off?" Trina asks. "I have kids. I want Thanksgiving and Christmas off."

I'm about to offer to work Trina's days when she looks at me. "Haven't I been here longer than Kendall? Why does she get Thanksgiving and Christmas off?"

I open my mouth to defend myself, and Kirks says "Zip it" before I can retort. Then he tells Trina I am working Thanksgiving and no, she hasn't been here longer than me.

"People," Kirk says loudly. "The hotel is a twenty-four-hour business. Major holidays are no exception. We all knew this when we were hired. Come on. Work with me here."

I lean into Rodney's cubicle. "I'm sorry, I had no idea you're an actor."

Rodney shrugs. "I would have told you, but I didn't think Shakespeare's your thing, you know?"

"I can do Shakespeare."

He shrugs again. "You don't seem all that interested in . . . us."

"I'm interested." I sound offended.

"And Wanda has what?" Kirk asks no one in particular.

"Fencing," Rodney reminds him.

"Fencing?" I blurt. "Wanda fences?"

"Right," Kirk says distractedly. "But what about the fencing?"

"She's doing the tournament in Vancouver the day after Christmas, but she's leaving on the twenty-third."

Kirk shakes his head as he tries to work on the increasingly difficult schedule.

I try to remember a time when I asked my coworkers about their lives outside the hotel. I don't think I ever have. And I start to wonder if I'm one of those people who just assumes this is all we can do. I look at Rodney, busily answering calls in the no-nonsense way we all answer calls. I imagine him as Macbeth with a gut, and I smile. I would love to see him be Macbeth. He's so right for it. Why have I never thought of it before?

"I'm sorry," I repeat regretfully, and Rodney frowns.

"It's okay, girl," he says. "Relax. I'm not losing any sleep over it."

*   *   *

When I walk into my building, every child in Brooklyn is running and screaming through the halls. I stop in my tracks and listen for a minute. What the hell?

On the third floor, over the sound of the children's gleeful screams, I hear cheering.

"You can do it, Hercules! Yeah, boy! You can do it!"

I stop again.

"There you go! You can do it, boy!"

On the fourth floor, right outside my door, a group of women are on their knees in a circle. In the middle of the circle is a cat. Betty's cat. Hercules. And the poor thing is wearing a cast on his hind leg, and he has this enormous plastic ring around his neck so he looks like a clown. He's limping along, trying to make his way to Betty's open arms.

I feel like I've just stepped into a bad episode of *Twilight Zone.*

Only two of the women besides Betty are familiar: Lisa and the female half of the twentysomething couple on three. The other three women look up at me stiffly. I think they live on the block. Lisa crawls away from my front door so I can put my key in the lock. When I open the door, one of them hisses.

I stop, look at them

"Did someone just hiss?" I ask.

No one looks at me. They all look at Betty, who in turn looks back at them. I shake my head, almost laugh before I close the door.

"We were just about to order Thai," Nick informs me from Gary's bedroom doorway.

I start, surprised to see him here. I point to the door. "Did you witness that?"

"The cat physical therapy?" Nick nods. "It was very moving, but a little weird."

"What do you want from the Thai place?" Gary calls out.

Nick moves out of the doorway so I can walk inside.

"I'll just pick on your leftovers," I tell him.

"Your comforter came," Nick says. "We put it on your bed. I didn't know you use the guy near me. He's good. Expensive, but good."

I'm about to tell him I don't use the guy near him when I remember the missing comforter from this morning.

"Sometimes," I say.

Gary hangs up the phone and sits up on his bed. "So. This thing with Betty," he says.

"Did Joe change his mind?" I ask.

Gary shakes his head. "He doesn't want us to go. That's the final word from him."

"Good."

Gary and Nick share a look.

"But it's not the final word from you," I say.

"Well," Gary begins slowly, as though what he's about to say is really tough. I'm sure it will be. "Nick asked me to move in with him."

My heart sinks, but I smile. I want to be happy for him. "Great," I say, glancing at Nick. "It's about time you two get hitched."

"It wouldn't be immediate," Gary says. "I mean, not before the new year."

"Some time after you get back from Maine," I say.

The two share another look.

"Jack told me," I explain.

"When?" Nick asks.

"This morning," I admit. "We ran into each other . . ."

Nick nods, preoccupied. "I just ask because he went back to

Maine this afternoon, and I wondered where he was this morning."

"He went back to Maine already?"

"Yeah. Business."

Nick and Gary are watching me now. I try not to have a reaction to the news that Jack is gone, but not having a reaction is pretty much like having one. I stare at the floor.

"We were going to tell you about Maine today," Gary says, "and then this happened and we forgot."

"The guestroom is yours," Nick offers generously. "For a few months. If you need that."

My first instinct is to jump on it. But something about the way Nick and Gary are trying hard to remain expressionless makes me decline.

"You won't leave before January," I say, and Gary nods.

There's a long, awkward silence. Nick clears his throat and says he needs to use the bathroom. Gary watches him leave.

"This is home," I say quietly.

"Do you really think of it that way?" Gary asks honestly.

"Not as often as I'd like. But." I shrug.

Gary kneads his duvet. "We don't have to go," he says after a while.

I shake my head. "You have to go. If this is what you want. If you're ready."

He smiles. "I think I'm ready."

"Then you have to go," I insist. "Don't worry about me."

"You're sure?"

"You bet," I say.

The buzzer rings, and Nick comes out of the bathroom to let the delivery guy in.

"Aren't you eating?" Gary asks when I head for my room.

"In a minute," I tell him and close my door behind me.

In my room, I listen to our front door open, allowing the sounds of wild children and their wild mothers into the apartment. Nick laughs at something the delivery guy says. Gary takes plates from the cabinet in the kitchen, and they prepare to eat.

"Is Kendall coming?" Nick asks.

"In a minute," Gary says, and then I can hear them whispering.

I lie on my bed next to my newly dry-cleaned comforter. The ticket reads SULLIVAN, JACK. RUSH. DELIVERY BY 7 PM. Heroically, I fight off the urge to cry myself to sleep.

Thanksgiving is uneventful.

It isn't the worst holiday to work, just boring. Maria, Victoria, Rodney, Trina and I work the day shift. Maria and Trina stay on the phone all day, and Victoria doesn't speak to any of us. Rodney and I eat cookies, read the *National Enquirer,* and giggle at all the stories we know are true.

No one calls.

Nick and Gary are having Thanksgiving dinner with a few of Nick's coworkers in Long Island. They rented a car and headed out there last night. Amy's having Thanksgiving dinner with her family. My own parents are in Connecticut, celebrating the holiday with friends. And Jack is in Maine with his fiancée.

In the cafeteria they've put out the usual Thanksgiving gibberish: tacky decorations of smiling turkeys and Pilgrims and Indians. Last year Sage drew knives sticking out of the Indians' backs and was written up because someone tattled on him. This year I assume he's home with Paula and her son.

For lunch I eat a slice of dry turkey with gelled cranberry sauce. I eat slowly, smiling at the other pathetic employees whose bosses spent an entire week reminding them that a hotel is a twenty-four-hour business and we're all required to work major holidays no matter how long we've been here.

A guy from Valet goes up for seconds, and one of the cafeteria workers tells him he can't have more turkey. The guy starts to flip out, saying it's Thanksgiving and we should be able to eat as much turkey as we want. I push my lousy lunch away. It certainly isn't worth fighting over.

When I come back from lunch, a celebrity singer has checked in with her husband and band. They've blocked fifteen rooms on the forty-seventh, forty-eighth and forty-ninth floors. The last time she stayed here, we tagged her with the flattering alias Diva.

"Why is she checking in on Thanksgiving?" Victoria inquires. "Doesn't she have a family?"

"She isn't American, honey," Rodney explains. "And she's doing Madison Square Garden tomorrow night."

Front Desk calls Victoria with phone instructions for Diva and her entourage. Apparently, Diva is ill. Her husband has requested all calls go to room 4903. Diva is resting in room 4902.

Victoria blocks room 4902 immediately, then rushes to the dry-erase board and scribbles the following: ROOM 4902 IS BLOCKED. ALL CALLS FOR GUEST IN ROOM 4902 MUST BE DIRECTED TO ROOM 4903. PLEASE! ABSOLUTELY NO CALLS TO ROOM 4902. GUEST IS ILL.

Ten minutes later, Front Desk calls Victoria again. Diva has moved to room 4903 to rest. Her husband is requesting all calls go to room 4902. Victoria curses at her switchboard, unblocks room 4902 and blocks room 4903 instead. Trina rushes to the board and corrects the instructions.

Now the board says: ROOM 4903 IS BLOCKED. ALL CALLS FOR GUEST IN ROOM 4903 MUST BE DIRECTED TO ROOM 4902. PLEASE! ABSOLUTELY NO CALLS TO ROOM 4903. GUEST IS ILL.

"Damn, I hate that bitch," Rodney mumbles.

The office is quiet for a while. Rodney starts to rehearse some lines with me. I'm Lady Macbeth. He says I'm perfect for the role because I'd make a great crone. I give him the finger.

An outside call comes in on Rodney's switchboard. It's for Diva's husband. Rodney checks the board carefully, repeats the instructions out loud to confirm them. Only after everyone in the office agrees the instructions are correct does Rodney send the call to room 4902.

Less than a minute later Diva's name flashes on my switchboard from room 4902. An ominous feeling rips through my body, and I pass the call.

"Kendall, did you just pass this damn call to me?" Trina asks.

"No," I lie.

"Hotel operator Trina," I hear Trina say. "No, sir. Um. It was my understanding that all calls were to go to room 4902."

Rodney and I share a look.

"Um," Trina continues. "Well. I believe you made the switch with Front Desk . . . no, sir. This is not Front Desk. *Hello?*"

"What happened?" Victoria asks, leaving her cubicle to look over Trina's shoulder.

"Some guests peg you as the enemy the moment they hear your voice," Trina comments bitterly. "I'll never buy one of her albums again."

"Yeah," Rodney says. "Too bad they don't realize we're part of the album-buying public."

"What did he say?" I ask.

Room 4902 flashes on my switchboard. Damn.

"Hotel operator Kendall," I say.

"You fucking imbeciles," the man spits.

"Excuse me?" I say.

"There's a very sick person in this room." It's Diva's husband. I can tell by his thick French accent. "Are you fucking stupid?"

"I don't think I am, sir," I say. "No."

"Didn't you understand when I told you we don't want any fucking calls to come to this room, you fucking idiot person?"

I love when guests think everyone they speak to in a hotel with fifty-two floors is the same person.

"I believe you made that request with someone at Front Desk," I say calmly. "You requested the telephone in room 4902 be blocked."

"Correct," he snaps.

"And then you informed someone at Front Desk that you moved to room 4903 and wanted room 4903 blocked instead."

Silence. And then he says huffily, "But we moved back to room 4902."

"Okay." I really hate stupidity. "Did you inform anyone that you were moving back to room 4902?"

More silence.

I continue, "Since you didn't inform anyone of the third room change, we continued to honor your request to have all calls directed to room 4902."

"*No, no, no,*" he shouts. "You got it fucking wrong you fucking stupid, moron people."

"Would you like Front Desk?" I ask impatiently.

"*You're a fucking moron,*" he screams.

"Certainly, sir," I say and transfer him to Front Desk. I switch my headset to mute.

When Front Desk Assistant Manager Janice picks up, Diva's husband demands to know the name of the person he was just speaking to.

Janice is baffled. "I'm not sure, sir. I assume you were speaking to a hotel operator. May I be of assistance?"

Diva's husband explains his predicament, conveniently leaving out the very important fact that Diva has switched rooms three times and he forgot to tell Front Desk about the third room switch. Janice doesn't seem to be familiar with the situation at all. She clucks appropriately and apologizes profusely.

"Our telephone operators are *soooo* stupid," she says. "I will certainly look into this unfortunate incident and make a complaint for you. Allow me to send up a complimentary fruit basket and a bottle of Dom Perignon, sir."

I disconnect the call. I'm so incensed that I don't think twice before telling the room what happened. We're a sensitive lot, telephone operators. Even though Kirk has difficulty believing the hotel world looks down on us, he once sent out a memo to other departments after Victoria and Maria complained about the lack of respect we receive. "PBX is an integral part of the hotel," the memo said. "Our operators are the first people potential guests meet. Please be kind to them."

We're a laughingstock.

Right now, everyone in the room gets stuck on the "telephone operators are *soooo* stupid" bit. Before I can stop her, Victoria dials Kirk's voice mail in a rage and tells him about Janice. I motion to her frantically, but she ignores me. She ends her message with an indignant "I'm tired of the way we're treated. You better do something about this."

I roll my eyes. When she's finished, I say, "I have a question."

Victoria doesn't say anything for a few minutes.

I wait.

She says, "What?"

"How are you going to explain to Kirk the way I overheard Janice call us stupid?"

Rodney sucks his teeth. "Shit."

"Exactly," I say.

Victoria is quiet for a long time.

"I'll take care of it," she says. "Don't worry."

She doesn't sound terribly confident.

The train is empty. I take a window seat and put my foot up on the chair in front of me. The idea of actually going home to my empty apartment fills me with dread. I think of the kid running across the floor above me. The *doomp*ing and *gork*ing and *thunk*ing is not how I'd like to end my Thanksgiving.

I get off the train at York Street. I splurge on a four-dollar hot chocolate from Jacques Torres and feel both surprised and pleased he's open on Thanksgiving. The young woman who makes my hot chocolate smiles at me and wishes me a Happy Day. He remains open for people like me, I decide. People with no place to go on Thanksgiving.

I walk to Brooklyn Heights. Some part of me is also pleased that shops are still open. It's dark, chilly, Thanksgiving. But people are strolling in and out of the shops that have decided to capitalize on holiday cheer.

I sit on the Promenade to finish my hot chocolate.

In a record shop on Montague Street, I find the latest John Tesh CD and bring it to the register. I recognize the cashier. His name is Billy. We dated over a year ago. We keep in touch irregularly. He sends me stupid group e-mails I delete without ever opening.

He's reading a magazine. He doesn't look up when I put the CD on the counter. I hand him my credit card and he stares at the name. When he looks up he's grinning.

"Stark," he says.

We grin at each other.

"What the hell is this?" He holds up the CD.

"A compact disc," I say.

"Oh no, Stark," he groans. "You're way too young to go down this road."

"I like John," I say.

He shakes his head and tosses the CD in a box behind him. "I can't let you do it." He voids the sale, hops over the counter and gives me a hug.

"How's it going?" he asks.

"Fabulous," I say.

"Me, too," he says. "As you can see, I'm in sales and loving every minute of it."

I laugh.

"What brings you to Brooklyn?" he asks.

"Live here," I say. "Always have."

"Good. Good for you."

I nod, can't help grinning. "When do you get off?"

"Funny you should ask." He glances at his watch. "In five minutes. You want to come back to my place? I live, like, twenty minutes away. We can eat something. You celebrate Thanksgiving yet?"

"Actually, no."

"Cool," he says.

I start to back out of whatever he thinks we're going to do now, but I think of the kid. She's probably skipping rope above my living room. They probably have guests. *Doomp . . . doomp . . . doomp.* A dull thud, like a headache.

I wait for him outside.

He turns on the television before I even figure out how to lock the door.

"Don't worry," he calls out. "The building's safe. Want something to drink? There's a Star Trek marathon on FX."

Then he's in the kitchen searching frantically for something to quench my thirst. He looks at me and smiles awkwardly. I've always liked the way he smiles. I try to work with that.

"I don't have turkey or anything holiday-ish," he says.

"Water's fine," I say. "I'm not hungry."

"You sure? I have orange juice and Pepsi and . . . milk."

"Water."

He reaches up to get a cup and then stops midreach and comes over and kisses me. He's still clumsy, thinking a kiss should automatically lead to a taking-the-clothes-off moment. I let him fumble with my shirt and I pretend it's erotic and romantic and just what the doctor ordered on a lonely Thanksgiving evening.

Sex with an almost-stranger.

But I liken his penis to a metal rod jabbing me over and over. I shut my eyes and say to myself, "Kendall Stark. Attention!" When it's over, I can't get the sensation out of my mind.

Billy climbs out of bed. A few minutes later he covers me with a warm blanket that smells like Downy fabric softener. He gets back into bed and wraps his arm around me.

"It's good to see you again," he says.

Moments later, he's snoring lightly. I slip out of bed, get dressed and leave the apartment. As I walk home at dusk, I realize my moment with Billy—as brief as it was—is the loneliest moment I've had in a long time.

On Friday the office is ominously silent. Two women from Reservations are helping Maria answer phones. And Maria isn't even answering phones. She's slouched in her seat, arms folded across her chest. Her headset is on her desk.

I sit down, look around for some sign of anything, then put my headset on. And then Kirk walks in with Cheryl. He says,

"Kendall, would you turn your switchboard off and come with me to the conference room? Bring your headset with you."

Trina plops into her chair and drops her head in her hands. Maria gets up to comfort her.

In the conference room, Kirk doesn't look at me, which means he isn't in the mood for my shit. Most of the time I think we have a little rapport going on. I say what I feel and he gets pissed off about it. It's like coffee. We have to get our jabs in before we can start our day.

Today, he isn't having it. He looks like he'll blow any minute.

I put my headset on the table, and he reaches for it. He puts a finger on the button that clicks from Sound to Mute.

"Ever do this?" he asks, pushing the button to Mute.

I stare at his finger there. I have no idea where to begin. And he waits.

"You can't even make something up," he says.

"What are you asking me?" I say. "Have I ever hit Mute by accident?"

"By accident, on purpose—"

"No," I say.

Kirk watches my face. "I hate to think my operators are spying on guests."

His operators.

"I've fired Wanda and Trina."

"*What?*" I say. "Why?"

He leans forward. "Had a message on my voice mail last night."

"You check your voice mail from home? On a holiday?" I ask, appalled. Then I sit back, realize I have to concentrate on the disaster at hand.

"When I came in this morning I had a talk with Janice," he

says. "Someone overheard her conversation with a guest. She called our department stupid?"

My mouth is dry. "Well. That wasn't very nice of her."

"She denied it. She did say there was an incident with a VIP guest yesterday. She was on a call with him and believes she may have said something about the department that was misconstrued. She wondered how that conversation could have been overheard by one of us."

I nod, eyebrows raised as though I'm just as curious. "Someone told someone else? . . ."

"Every console has been checked," he continues. "Every console has evidence that calls are holding long after they should have been released. Since no operator has an assigned console, I don't know which one of you is eavesdropping on calls. It could be all of you. I don't know."

I think of the times he caught me switching seats, listening to the Texan. I've always had a lame excuse. Wanda always backed me up. And this thing, today, is my fault. And Victoria's.

"I have to let two people go. Any two. My choice. Unless someone steps forward and admits it."

"Did Wanda admit something?"

"No."

"Then why her?"

"Because," he says bitchily. "I've written her up two times. She was on the verge."

"And Trina?"

"She doesn't want to work any holidays. Ever. Now she has them off."

"Just let me go," I say boldly.

"Why? Are you admitting to this?" He can't hide his smile.

"I'm not admitting anything. Just. Trina has kids. Wanda fences. You have to fire people? Don't fire them."

"When you're sitting in my position, you can make my choices," he tells me, then motions that I'm free to go.

I sit for a second longer, confused.

Kirk says, "We like to think there are heroes in this world. There aren't any in our office. No one has admitted to listening to calls, even though an admission would clear Wanda and Trina. No one has defended them. Everyone breathes a collective sigh of relief when they find out their job is secure."

I push my chair back.

"Except you," he says.

When I look at him again his face is expressionless. I'm not sure if he's accusing me of being the culprit or the hero. He holds my gaze for a second, and then he lowers his eyes. I consider telling him I'm a culprit, not a hero, but something stops me.

He glances at me again, and I see fear flash across his face. He assumes I'm really mad at him about this. Part of me is. It's true Wanda was a friend, even though we never bothered to exchange numbers. And even though I don't give a damn about Trina, I don't want to see a single mother with kids lose her job. But I have to admit most of my anger has nothing to do with the firings. Listening to the guests' phone calls was my only salvation. Now I've lost that.

I'm going to be so fucking bored.

"By the way," Kirk says, eyes still lowered. "I've had a response from Mr. Schmidt concerning the uniforms."

I nod, wait. Kirk riffles through the pile of papers in front of him. Then he finds the one he's looking for, skims the letter and looks at me again.

"Uniforms are a necessary part of hotel life," Kirk tells me.

"You are required to wear them. So why don't you put yours on before you start your shift? I'll tell Rodney and Katie to do the same when they come in."

And then he smiles, like he really has me.

He doesn't.

Because I quit.

that rare good moment

I wake up very slowly. Casually. On my own time, not anyone else's. Voices drift up to my room, seep under the crack of my door. They're soft. Serene. Nothing here is loud or intrusive. I stretch, brush my teeth, stare out of the window and watch the rain fall for a while.

We arrived last night after a ten-hour drive from Brooklyn.

We left New York in a heavy rainstorm, took I-95 all the way to Portland, and then switched to Route 1. Amy wanted to stop in Freeport to shop at the L.L. Bean outlet store, and Gary wanted to stop in Camden for fish chowder he'd read about in a magazine from a famous restaurant called Cappy's. Nick said we didn't have time for shopping. He wanted to reach Bar Harbor by seven. And Cappy's was closed. It's off season in Maine, Nick explained, so many popular, touristy spots close early.

We didn't stop for dinner at all.

In Ellsworth, Nick called Jack to say we were only thirty minutes away. Jack was on a business call and told him that he'd leave the door unlocked and we should come in through the mudroom.

"A mudroom," Nick repeated excitedly.

The town of Bar Harbor is nearly deserted this time of year, and Nick drove slowly down picturesque Main Street, pointing out shops he'd visited when he was here a few years ago. The popular restaurants and local bars are still open, but everything else is closed and seemingly abandoned until some time in May or June.

Amy spotted a sign for Sullivan Brew in the window of a bar.

His house is handsome. The path leading here is narrow, winding behind inns and a bank, which all appear as deserted as the town. The house sits on four acres of land along the Shore Path. It's enormous and wealthy and somewhat intimidating. We all sat in the car and stared at it for a minute. Nick whistled low. So uncharacteristic of him.

As promised, the door to the mudroom was open. Two maple benches, built into the walls of a room the size of my bedroom, welcomed us to sit and take off our shoes before we entered the house. Hooks shaped like trout were anchored above the benches, calling for our coats to be hung on them. Skis and snowboards littered the room haphazardly, as though they aren't expensive and precious, just an annoyance. As we took off our shoes, Amy investigated the walk-in closet where extra mittens, hats and scarves lined the shelves.

"All this from beer?" she said.

"Some of it was Sully's money," Gary told her officiously, though I'm sure he doesn't know that for certain.

Jack was in the kitchen, leaning against a shallow fireplace, cordless phone stuck to his ear. He looked young, tough, and unapproachable. The way he used to look in college. His face lit up when he saw us come in, and it reminded me of the way he used to perk up when I arrived someplace. He would straighten and smile, anxious to wrap his arms around me and let everyone know I was with him.

He didn't wrap his arms around me last night. I hadn't expected him to. I had expected a nod or a smile, though. Some acknowledgment. But he barely looked at me.

I haven't spoken to Jack since that morning he woke up in my apartment. I called him once. To thank him for having my comforter cleaned. Got the number from Gary, who got the number from Nick's phone book while Nick was in the shower. I don't know why we treated it like some covert operation. Gary never asked why I needed the number, and I never told him. We just assumed it was something we didn't want to share with Nick. I left a message on Jack's answering machine. He never called back.

About a week ago, Nick and Gary told me Jack's engagement to Rae was broken, and it seemed Rae was permanently out of the picture. They didn't say how long they'd known about the breakup. I didn't ask. And it didn't matter. By then I'd decided I was going to accompany them to Maine, whether Jack had followed through with his decision to leave Rae or not. I wanted to see him again. Almost desperately.

So, we were seeing each other for the first time in nearly a month, and he wasn't looking at me. He motioned for us to follow him into the living room, and then he indicated we go upstairs and get settled. Briefly, he interrupted his call to tell us he'd be finished in five minutes.

There are four guest bedrooms on the third floor of the house. The master bedroom is on the second floor. We couldn't stop ourselves from taking a quick peek inside the sparse room. Nick whistled again when Amy pointed out the French doors and the porch they opened up to. Gary asked him to "stop doing that."

The color scheme switched completely once we reached the third floor. I shook my head, annoyed with myself for even noticing something like a color scheme in the first place. But it was so extreme—from rugged browns and masculine beiges to cool blues and greens—that it was hard not to notice. Amy and I chose not to share a room, even though two of the guest bedrooms have lovely twin beds. Amy can't sleep in a twin bed, so she chose one of the guest bedrooms with a double. Gary and Nick took the other room with a double bed.

We ate warm spinach salad with grilled salmon in the dining room quietly, and Jack promised to give us a full tour of the house the next day. And he ignored me through dinner. Made me feel invisible. In response, I couldn't take my eyes off him. All I wanted him to do was look at me. It seemed like only yesterday the tables were turned.

Gary and Amy told him about our trip, leaving out the bits about our arguments and binging on crap food and crankiness. Jack handed out glasses of brandy and suggested we drive to Castine tomorrow, a coastal village at the tip of the Blue Hill peninsula, while he was at work.

"Home of the Maine Maritime Academy," he said.

"Boys!" Amy shrieked.

"Sailors!" Gary shrieked immediately after her.

I laughed, and for the first time since we arrived Jack looked at me. He used to say he liked to see me laughing. I thought I noticed a hintp of something in the expression on his face. He knows I'm here after all. I imagined I saw desire in that expression. A plea for me to meet him somewhere once the others went off to bed.

I was wrong.

After he finished stacking the dishes in the dishwasher—with help from Amy—he said he needed to get some sleep after a long day. He insisted the rest of us stay up and finish the second bottle of wine he opened and the brandy. And then he told us to treat his home like our own home, and he went up to bed.

This morning I'm surprised it's only Nick and Amy in the kitchen, a kitchen that overlooks Frenchman's Bay and the Porcupine Islands. Amy's sitting on a barstool at the counter in the middle of the room, staring out of the French doors that lead to a deck.

Nick's brewing coffee. He's also mesmerized by the view.

"I'm going to marry Jack," Amy tells me the minute I walk in.

"Good luck," I say, grabbing an orange and sitting in the breakfast nook. The breakfast nook disturbs me a little. People I know don't have mudrooms and breakfast nooks framed by bay windows with views like this one. "Where is he?"

"Work," Nick tells me. "He says he'll be in late so he can take the next couple of days off. He thinks we should do Castine today, but I'm tired. I think we'll stay close to home."

Amy says, "I know why he'll never leave here. Everything about this place is peaceful and beautiful."

I nod, agreeing.

"I am not going back to Brooklyn," she says. "Really. I'm going to call my mother tonight and tell her I'm not leaving this house. I could just stay in this house and never leave it."

Nick grins and looks genuinely happy. The structure of this house—a combination of wood, glass and concrete—is what Nick calls "elegant." And I've yet to detect a hint of jealousy, which pleases me. Not once last night did he try to compete with Jack.

I watch him prepare a cup of coffee for Gary, who is still in bed. He blows on it, tastes it, adds a little more milk. He tastes it again, and then he shakes his head to indicate that it's perfect. I stop eating my orange and stare.

He loves him. Nick loves Gary.

Since they started dating I've searched and searched for signs of it. His love. Because there are always the little things that make me doubt it. The way Gary comes home unexpectedly and stares at the television screen until the phone rings. The way the phone rings after midnight and they talk in harsh whispers deep into the night until I drift off to sleep. The way Nick makes us feel like we aren't good enough sometimes. The way I always feel like Nick is using Gary until something better comes along.

And then there's this. And it's so subtle, but very true. And I feel a surge of happiness for Gary for having this. I think maybe he's in good hands after all.

I stand up and kiss Nick on the cheek when he comes back into the kitchen. He thinks I'm going to whisper something in his ear and he waits for it. The kiss takes him by surprise, and his eyes try to hide confusion and some pleasure.

"Thank you for loving Gary," I say happily.

Nick shakes his head, smiles a little.

"You are such a girl, Kendall," he says. "It always manages to shock me."

Tonight Jack returns to four giddy adults who have yet to leave his house. He stares at us, crammed lazily in his breakfast nook, unbelieving when we admit we haven't even been to Acadia National Park yet. Only seven minutes away.

"We have ten days," Gary reminds him.

"And you have enough food to feed an army in that refrigerator," Amy says.

Nick points at it. "You have a Sub-Zero refrigerator."

Jack looks at me, expecting me to add something. I don't.

"We like it here," Amy pipes up, and Jack turns from me to her again. "Right here. In your kitchen."

Jack raises an eyebrow and Amy nods.

She continues, "We're easily pleased, you see."

Jack moves to the French doors and stares out at Frenchman's Bay. He's preoccupied.

"No one even went for a walk along the path?" he asks.

"I did," Gary says. "Nice."

Jack shakes his head. He's baffled by us.

"Can we have lobster?" Amy asks.

Jack looks away from the window at us.

"I brought lobster for dinner," he says softly.

After dinner I go outside to have a cigarette. But I know I really go outside to get away from them. Him. Jack.

If only he weren't so different from what he was, then I might not feel this way. If only he weren't so much the same. I might not feel like this. Like I'd never fallen out of love with him in the first place. I've spent the evening looking for him, waiting for him, wanting to talk to him. I think he felt the same way. He wanted to talk to me, wanted to be the only person in the room with me. I could tell by how hard he tried not to look in my direction.

So, now I'm overwhelmed. Flushed. Asthmatic. The whole world is caving in on me because I know I'm still in love with him. I'm not sure if I've ever not been in love with him. A boy should not be able to do this to a girl. A woman. Not after so many years. It isn't fair.

Someone comes outside, and his presence is so familiar to me that I'm sure it's him before I even see him. I know it can't be anyone else. Still, when he says that soft "Hey" I used to be so used to, I jump. And then I step away from him, embarrassed like a little Catholic schoolgirl with a little Catholic school crush on a priest.

He apologizes profusely; so much I actually can't stand it.

"Lobster. Good," I say primitively. "Thank you. I'll cook tomorrow."

He smiles. "I'd like that."

"You have a gorgeous view," I say, pointing at the blackened water. A cruise ship is floating slowly by.

"Sometimes I sit out here and stare into the night," he says. "I get a lot of thinking done out here."

"I bet."

"I'm sorry I didn't call you back," he says.

"No problem."

"Ken, I was hurt."

I hear the sorrow in his voice. When I look at him, I see it in his eyes as well.

"You never promised to stay with me forever," he continues slowly. "And I realize we were young and I wasn't right for you. But I was madly in love with you. I couldn't imagine life without you. And I thought, while I was in New York, there were hints that you still had feelings for me. I just couldn't work out how to get you to admit them. You've always been stubborn."

I don't know what to say. That he's right? There were feelings. There *are* feelings.

"That morning at your place was all about trying to get you to admit how you really feel about me," he says. "When you told me not to make my decision to leave Rae about you, I was hurt. Tough way to get my answer, but you were never easy about stuff like that."

We hear Amy's high-pitched laugh, and I smile.

"You know," I say, "you remind me I'm a failure."

I can't make out the expression on his face, but I think it's a mixture of hurt, anger and understanding.

He says, "You know the thing you never got about me . . ."

"What?"

"I've never wanted you to be anything but Kendall. Kendall was never a failure. She was just Kendall. She was my girl-friend. She was my best friend."

"Yeah." I smirk, take a drag from the cigarette. "I like that answer, but I have nowhere to run with it."

"Is that why you're angry with me? Because I'm a re-minder?"

"I'm not angry with you," I say.

He stuffs his hands in his back pockets, looks like a young boy. "Then I'm not sure why we're all of a sudden not on speaking terms."

I almost laugh. He sounds so sweet, so insecure. "I'm not sure either."

We watch the cruise ship slip by; I think I can hear the guests on board laughing and clinking wineglasses together. What a silly moment to tell someone *I love you*.

"I wonder if working on a ship is like working in a hotel," I say. "Only worse because you don't get to go home at the end of your shift. I wonder if I'd be able to work in a hotel with normal people. People who aren't rich and famous."

"I heard you quit."

"Yeah." I nod.

"Where will you live in January?"

"I'll be between apartments. And jobs." I smirk at him. "How's the brewery?"

"Things are good."

"Do we get a tour?"

"If you want one."

"Yeah, I want one."

"Maybe the day after Christmas?"

I nod. "The day after Christmas it is."

"Gonna go now," he says.

I touch his arm as he moves toward the French doors. "This is nice," I say. "I don't want it to end yet."

He doesn't go. He frowns and dips his head.

"I miss you," he says. "Not just for the past nine years. I really missed you then. I miss you now. Even though you're standing right next to me."

"Oh, God," I say, trying to keep my tone light. "That's heavy."

"Yeah." He's watching me. "That's heavy."

We're quiet for a long time.

He opens the door. "Good night, Kendall."

"Good night, Jack."

The door to Jack's room is open a crack. I tap on it.

"Yeah." His voice is muted.

I venture inside. Near the bed is a Victorian desk cluttered with stationery and pens and books. There's also a plush love seat in the rugged brown so prevalent throughout the rest of the house. A chair in the corner of the room is off white and exquisite. Looks like it has never been used.

Jack comes out of the bathroom in jeans, a towel draped across his shoulders. A cloud of steam bursts out of the room after him. He doesn't look up.

"Do you think we'd still be together?" I ask.

He looks startled. And then, "What?"

"If I'd given us a chance. Do you think we'd still be together?"

"No," he says simply.

"Why not?"

"You think we'd still be together?"

I shrug. "I don't know."

He pulls the towel from his shoulders and tosses it into the bathroom, and then he closes the bathroom door. He sees his glasses on the bedside table and reaches for them. He still has washboard abs, though not as cut as they used to be. He's heavier, not as toned. But his body is still beautiful.

I swallow hard.

"Why do you ask?" he says as he adjusts his glasses and stares at me curiously.

"Because . . ."

He adjusts his glasses again. It's this gesture—the adjusting the glasses bit—that makes me decide I can't answer this question. It was a stupid question. Unanswerable. I thought I wanted to explore this with him now, but all I want is him. Right now. It's the only thing I'm thinking when I walk over to him. I'm not thinking about how it will make him feel, or how I'll feel afterward, or whether or not anyone will be hurt. I touch his face, reach up to kiss his nose and his cheeks and his lips.

There's some resistance at first; he pulls back. But it's so slight it doesn't deter me. We kiss for a long time—longer than that night at Nick's house—only pulling apart to catch our breath. Then he laughs, resting his forehead against mine.

When we start kissing again, his hands rest at my waist and he pulls my shirt out of my pants gently. He touches my skin; his fingers climb up my stomach, rest just below my breasts. For a split second, his lips come away from mine and our eyes meet. His hands come out from under my shirt.

"Jack," I say.

"Yeah?" His voice is gruff.

"I really want you to make love to me," I say softly.

"I—," he starts.

"You." I put my fingers over his lips. "Don't. Have. Rae. Anymore."

He smiles through my fingers. "Is this because you like my house?" he says.

"Go to hell," I say.

He drops his head so that his mouth is in the palm of my hand, kissing it. With his other hand, he caresses my cheek gently. "Right."

His voice tickles my skin.

And then we're on his bed. He slips off my shirt and my jeans. His hands are shaking a little. He's trembling. He's watching my face. When he stops, I raise my hips. I try to tell him what I want, but his mouth is suddenly on my mouth and my words only sound like moans against his lips. When he's inside me we stop kissing. He wants to see my face, wants to hold my gaze. This hasn't changed about him. It takes a while to establish a rhythm, and when we do we take our time. We go slow, watching each other intently as though we're afraid one of us could possibly get up and walk away. And then he asks if I'm ready, and I say yes. He was always good at telling.

He doesn't ease off of me afterward, and we kiss a little bit longer.

"You're okay?" he asks, wiping hair from my face tenderly.

"I'm good."

He grins. "You're good."

He captures my bottom lip between his teeth. And then he rolls off of me, lies beside me, stares at the ceiling.

I sit up. The desk lamp is still on, switched to low. I can tell he's checking out my body, curious to see what's changed since the last time we were like this. I've already noticed he has a tattoo on his hipbone.

He says, "Don't go, okay?"

*   *   *

I wake up in Jack's bed alone. I groan inwardly, hoping one of us doesn't think we've made a mistake. I sneak up to my room to shower and get dressed, some part of me disappointed we didn't wake up in each other's arms.

Gary and Nick are sitting in the breakfast nook eating bagels. Jack's sitting on the floor, drinking coffee and reading the paper. He looks up.

"Hey," he says with a sweet smile.

I stare at him on the floor, fascinated by this Jack in blue jeans and a sweatshirt.

So familiar.

"Hey," I say.

Gary and Nick are smiling at me. I frown. I wonder what Jack has told them. I wonder why they're staring at me so intently now. And most important, I wonder why I'm so happy to be here with all of them.

"You disappeared last night," Gary accuses.

"Coffee," I say, ignoring him.

"How do you take it?" Jack rises from the floor.

I stare at him a little too long. He stares back.

"Black."

"Me, too." Amy has dragged herself out of bed and is standing in the kitchen's entryway. She notices the buffet breakfast of bagels, lox, cream cheese and tomatoes laid out on the kitchen's island. She makes her way over to the food and starts to make herself a plate. Then she joins Gary and Nick at the breakfast nook. Nick slides over to make room for her.

"Thanks, Jack," she says, smiling.

He doesn't look up. "Your coffee's on the counter."

"Thanks," she says again, getting up to retrieve it.

I grab a slice of the perfectly thin lox and stick it in my

mouth. Then I join Jack near the sink to try my coffee. I smile my thanks, and he winks at me. Pleased, I link my pinky with his, and he lets me.

"You look cute when you wake up," he tells me. I look at him, surprised. Everyone else looks at him, too. There's an odd silence.

"Thanks," I say, uncertainly.

He nods.

The silence continues to blanket the kitchen. Jack moves his hand out of my reach and concentrates on the coffee in his cup. I grin, and I can tell he's looking at me from the corner of his eye, because he grins, too.

We're like new lovers, I decide. Not wanting to give this newness away just yet, and at the same time feeling this happy urge to tell them. I concentrate on trying to touch him again without anyone noticing. I touch his cup, rub my finger over the spot where his mouth was. I touch his fingers. I look at him, to see him smiling, almost shyly, at our hands.

And then he goes rigid, so I move away, stare at the floor, listen.

"You want to go, Kenny?" Amy asks.

I look up. They're staring at us. I flush. I have no idea what Amy's talking about.

"Yes," I say.

"The brewery," Jacks says under his breath.

I smile at him, nod. Even though I thought we'd planned on going the day after Christmas, I say, "Sounds great."

We visit Sullivan Brewery, which is located in a large warehouse in Ellsworth. The minute we walk in, Jack is inundated with phone calls. We have our tour with his head brewer, Jeff, who Amy thinks is sexy and attractive. I can tell by the way she tosses her hair when he looks in her direction.

I don't pay much attention to the tour. I'm fascinated by how big the space is. I'm fascinated by the woman who climbs out of the big steel tank, waves at us, and then climbs back in to finish cleaning it.

Part of the space is set up like a saloon, which is where we end up after Jeff finishes the tour. He pours half pints of all eight beers to keep us busy while Jack finishes "doing his thing" in the office. He shows Nick the proper way to fill a glass, and then he leaves us alone so he can get back to work.

Sullivan Brew tastes different from the tap. Better. And Nick gets up twice to refill our glasses.

"You like it here?" Jack asks me when he comes out of the office.

"Love it."

"Then stay," he says casually.

I look at the others. Amy is wandering, probably in search of Jeff. Nick is trying to convince Gary to give the Winter Solstice another try. I look at Jack again.

"Oh, right," I say. "I'll just stay in Maine for the rest of my life and be happy. Maybe I'll become a lobsterwoman."

"I don't want to regret you anymore," he says simply. "I want to get to know you again."

I swallow hard. "You're serious?"

He nods, his eyes remaining steadily on my face. "Completely."

That evening, I go to Geddy's, a bar five minutes from Jack's house. I drink a Sullivan Brew and watch television with some locals. And I think about iffy.

What if all of the wonderful things that belong to Jack begin to feel like they belong to me? What if, one day, we have that argument that makes Jack remind me who I really am? What if?

I remind him who he really is. I decide. You, of all people, Kendall Stark, know how to do that.

Twenty minutes later, Gary and Amy come in to join me. We watch television in silence, share a cigarette. Then Gary says, "If you fuck this one up, you deserve to be alone."

I say, "Yeah."

"You're happy. And you never got over him," Amy says.

"Yeah," I say.

"When shit like this happens," Gary adds, "you step up to the plate."

I look at Amy, and then I look at Gary. "I know," I say.

They realize I've already made my decision. We sit for a while. Silent. Gary orders another round of drinks.

"We were in no way trying to advise you," Amy says quietly.

I smile down at my drink and nod. "I know. I decided all on my own."

I look at them, and they're smiling. And I remember what it was like in college to know them. How new and important it was. How I didn't want to fuck it up because I really, *really* liked them and I didn't want to lose them. I think about what Kirk said a while ago. My world is small. And I think it doesn't matter what size my world is. What matters is the amount of love my world can fit. I know that sounds sappy and stupid, but it's true.

"I like you both so much," I say.

"We like you, too," they say in unison.

Some guy across the bar is watching us. When we all make eye contact, he says our next round is on him.

In the morning there's only Jack in the kitchen drinking coffee.

"Where's everyone?" I ask.

"They went to Blue Hill for breakfast," he says. "If you want to go, I can drive you."

"I want to stay," I say.

"Okay. We can make pancakes or eggs—"

"I want to stay," I repeat.

He puts his cup down, walks over to me. "Are you sure? You've thought it over?"

I nod.

"Because you can't decide something like this and take it back."

"Yeah, I know."

"I mean it, Ken," he says solemnly. "I won't let you take it back."

"I know."

We're quiet, letting it sink in.

"God, I've missed you," he whispers.

"I've missed you, too."

Jack and I spend every moment together and see amazing things. We climb Mount Battie. We go hiking in Acadia National Park. We walk along the Shore Path, drink coffee while we sit on the rocks and watch the sun rise. We see Galloway cows in Camden and buy Maine T-shirts at Big Al's in Wiscasset.

And one evening, after a tour of the Pemaquid Point Lighthouse, Jack decides we should have dinner at The Newcastle Inn and stay overnight. We drink a bottle of red wine, and our hostess sits with us and tells me a story about the first time she met Jack. And as she speaks, I watch Jack flush, and I decide I won't ever leave him again.

Our hostess touches my hand and tells me Jack is good; she likes him. And someone from the kitchen calls out for her and she cries, "Oh my, they need me," and she winks and says it's been a while since she's seen Jack this happy.

We're quiet after she says this, and before she leaves she tells us she has saved the biggest room in the inn for us. And Jack stares at me for a long time, and I think I know what he's going to say, but instead he doesn't say anything. I ask him if it will take too long to drive back home, and he smiles, a little relieved, I think. He says he thinks we should go home, too.